— In Winter —

Five books in THE GOD'S CYCLE

God's House:

Return to God's House
Within Without
In Winter

God's Wilderness:

Mystery Gottheim
Balder's Wilderness

Plus

Gott'im's Monster, 1808

GOD'S HOUSE

In Winter

S. Dorman

~ ~

S. Dorman
P.O. Box 172
Greenwood, ME 04255
USA

(Third book in *The God's Cycle*)

God's House In Winter
Copyright © 1994, 2014 by Susan C. Dorman.
ISBN: 978-0-578-07347-7

Cover illustrations by S. Dorman

Dedication

To John, who is loved

"Winter deepens behind us…. The heights away north are whiter than they were; snow is lying far down their shoulders. Tonight we shall be on our way high up towards the Redhorn Gate. We may well be seen by watchers on that narrow path, and waylaid by some evil; but the weather may prove a more deadly enemy than any. What do you think of your course now, Aragorn?"

—The Fellowship of the Ring

Contents

Layer of Life

On a slope above a white lake the pine stands among a tall grove of white pine. Resting lightly in winter, the pine reports once like a gunshot in the deep settled cold. Then, quiet is here, snow-filled silence. But next, from far upslope near the road, the distant *buzz* of the chipper drifts down through snowy woodland. Passing through trees comes the jingling of winch chains and great chain-dressed wheels, mixed with the gunning of a skidder. Jingling on this twitch trail cut by loggers late last week, the big skidder rumbles right down to the pine. Halting, wafting blue smoke and fumes, the skidder looses a logger.

Alvin and Ansell Robichaud have come to take pines. Their father, Robbie, has contracted with the developer to harvest these trees selectively. Wearing hard-hat and visor, chest and leg protection and steel-toed boots, Alvin steps up to this Eastern white pine and lightly lays his gloved hand on it. He looks up, admiring its straight length. His cascading breath becomes a last bit of carbon dioxide drifting upward to mingle among the needles above. *Good money tree*, thinks Alvin. But there is something more in his thought, an unconscious gratitude, reaching up to gather the pine's own clean-breathing patience.

He rips the starter cord and stoops to notch the trunk. The saw's speeding teeth deftly cuts a neat wedge. Alvin smells Christmas, fragrance released from resin. The pine shudders almost imperceptibly along its great length.

The great bole's bark is chunky, fissured, having guarded its inner bark and a fragile layer of hidden cells. The life of this white pine is in this slim satiny smooth layer. For all its mass girth height age, here only, and in this present moment, does this tree renew itself. The rest of the tree is its history. Outer and inner bark, sapwood, heart and pith: Each layer, itself once risen from *cambium*, lively, now serves but to support the pine and preserve its identity. *Cambium*, this fine cell layer, is present life, conveying vitality to the whole. It is life in very light wood, a soft wood. And its uses in these 1980s are many.

Spot clearing for the developer, these two loggers will not cut here many days. Mr. Fay will show up later when the mercury rises above zero; a blond bespeckled representative of investors. Fay likes the lay of this wooded slope. He will wade about through the snow, talking rapidly at Alvin and Ansell, pointing out trees already earmarked for cutting, wanting to make sure they don't take the wrong ones or too many. It's supposed to be a wooded subdivision with some views of the pond below. He'll think, *If only I can get the speechless loggers to take off some of this hemlock.*

The old pine groans. Alvin pulls the saw away. The tree shudders visibly, shifting on its fresh stump. It comes down with the swiftness of a shadow falling across its neighbors; cracking and thundering. The tree lies prone, covering more earth in this separation than in its hundred upright years. A hush lingers around the severed trunk but, heedless, Alvin jumps aboard, running along its length to the branches. Easily he limbs them with his *awwi*ng saw. Brother Ansell backs the skidder up to the massive butt and jumps down, exclaiming over its great size. Alvin must cut the trunk to length on the spot, making the climb to the yard easier for the old skidder. Sixteen-foot lengths is right for Bearce's sawmill. Father will have a time loading them onto his truck. The size of these will spark Robbie Robichaud's imagination. Such great old trees are rarer these days, seems, than blue tourmaline.

Alvin removes his hardhat and safety glasses, and the twin brothers stop for a smoke. Lighting up, Ansell looks around peaceably, saying, "Too bad we caunt just mow'em all down." The other takes a long drag, looks up, exhales, agrees.

The skidder is idling, the chainsaw sitting silent on the big white stump. From a distance comes a new noise. "What's that?" Their square dimpled faces turn, listening in the cold air.

Ansell reaches up, absently fingering a blunt spike on the chains of the skidder wheel. Got to find money to replace the chains. Lately they've been slipping on the steep icy grades. Staring through trees across and down the slope, he answers the joint query, "Sounds like a team'o new skiddas. Who'd have s'many in the woods?"

"S'go check it out," returns Alvin. Still clutching their half-smoked cigarettes, they wade down through snow toward the wide expanse of the pond.

On the opposite shore above the cove, the big red machine roars. It is new all right, a mechanical feller-buncher, rocking and roaring, three trees clenched tight in a hydraulic fist at the end of its steel arm. The whole machine pivots on its tracks, laying the trees off to the side. Incredulous, the two watch as the red machine snips more standing trees—like so much grass—laying them aside to turn and grasp more trees.

Ansell stares at the sea of debris forming around it. Two other machines work the cut as well, one to twitch them, another to top and delimb. Only three men to clear the entire stumpage, taking everything at the rate of two or three every five-ten seconds. Fascinated, the twins watch the tiny trio sweeping the forest away. At last Alvin nudges his brother. "Fatha's not gont like this. You know what it means."

"Means we out of work. Ah days is numbered. Caunt afford those machines. One of em's worth half of Gott'im."

"The half without Jaspa Mountain."

Ansell nods. "Father's gont be pissed. Thinks theya's nothing betta'n what we got."

"Ain't no betta, li'l brother," says Alvin, who is nine minutes older. "Woods all be down in no time. Bet theya won't be enough left t'cut till our kids' kids." He looks back at the tree eater. "Think of a logger throwin'way his chainsaw!"

"Must cut down on comp payments, though. Won't no one get hurt inside that thing."

"What'll we need comp for, when we out of work?"

"Speaking of which—"

The two men toss away their cigarette butts and trudge back up through the trees and snow. Alvin's back is suddenly weary and his legs leaden. What's the point—just one tree at a time? And now there'll be none for their sons. It will be a glum week working the shore selectively for the developer, no matter how good the trees, watching the activity on the ridge opposite. And who's gont tell Fatha?

"In't nothing new in this," declares Robbie Robichaud at supper.

"When I started in the early '40s, it took three t'do what one Alvin does today, using crosscut saws, axes'n peavys. You twitched'em with hosses, o'course. I heard those new fella-bunchas'll do the work of six, seven Alvins. Before you stotted, maybe a quarter of your class bought chainsaws and dropped out early. 'Memba that? But I made you stay in school—like I didn't. That machine'll drop a thousand trees a day, but we caunt afford it."

The men and children sit around the supper table, Alvin and Ansell's wives serving. The twins' mother, Esmeralda, stands at the steaming stove, dishing up. There are three dwellings sitting small below the steep ledge, which rises darkly over the property of these descendents of French-Canadians. Two are single-wide mobile homes, the other an old connected farmhouse. Sometimes the family comes together for the evening meal, filling Robbie and Esmeralda's house with the talk and tumble of but a part of their offspring and grandchildren. This jumble of relations, clatter of cookware and tussling of children pleases Robbie. He is one of sixteen siblings and the father of twelve. Ezzy gave birth to the last few in the hospital but raised all in this helter-skelter farmhouse.

"How many cords you cut today, Alvin," asks Father.

Alvin is patiently chewing a bite of cube steak. "Ten."

"And I'll be paying $260 for it, which you two split. Not bad money—if you was both in Enan Pale's mill over theya. (He'll nevah pay it.) But you'n I know you got equipment t'keep up, payments and such. And *I* pay good. May be because you're my sons. Someone else wouldn't be s'kind."

He winks at Emma, Alvin's auburn-haired wife, who just got her chance to sit down. She spent a half-day at the Headstart then shared the cooking with Ansell's wife Joanna and their mother-in-law. Joanna has her own half-day at the Headstart, sharing the job with Emma. That way there is always someone to watch the toddlers and babies not ready for school.

"Some o'that wood'll go to Bearce's. What I give you for a whole cord will be what Bearce gets fah one 16 ft. board of select wood." Seeing the shock on their faces, he chuckles. "Cuss, he's got overhead."

"You taking this a lot betta'n I thought," says Ansell, swallowing that last bite of meat. He has been hearing bitter complaint ever since he can remember. It once made him think of going into the mills. But Father's temper overflows like that. It doesn't always signify his heart or mind.

Robbie takes a heap of steaming potatoes, passing the bowl to his gray-eyed granddaughter. "Things's coming to a point, Ansell, a big change. Look at that budworm. Takes decades to come back up fom that. That, the big machine, clearcutting—woods'll be a different place in twenty years. But lookit Bearce. He's holding his high-grade in reserve because he knows that once the century turns, depletion will increase demand. We might be looking at the bottom of the barrel. George'n Jim's chances is slim," he says referring to his son's twins.

"Now, Bearce is a smot man. A bastid, but a smart one. What's worse though is the paper maker—cunning like the devil. Paper mill's run the same way the devil runs hell. Knows my cost t'the half cent, and sets his price to squeeze me. They know we won't organize. If one of us has t'dropout, theya's always someone to step in and take his turn getting squeezed." He shakes his head, jowls flushing. "And we think we work for ourselves! We're working fah them without benefits! Doing everything at their rates, n'the way they waunt! How much we make last year, Ezzy?" He stops chewing and turns to his man-dressed wife.

Esmeralda wears overalls and flannel shirts. She has short steel-gray hair and the fullest heart-shaped lips Robbie has ever seen. It was those lips made him fall for a Yankee like her. Ezzy keeps the books and handles the contracts for Robichaud Logging. "Twenty-five thousand," she duly answers. It's what they make as a team.

"If Ezzy'n I each had a job somewheres we'd make more, maybe. Let them take care o'the overhead." He stops to point his fork at his sons. "Prepare yourselves. 21st-century's the land of less wood."

Behind the house soars the steep tree-clotted ledge. Across the street sits one of the area's prosperous sawmills, a competitor of Lyman Bearce. At night the Robichauds sleep to the sound of the running sawmill: rumbling conveyors, humming blowers, whining chippers, the *yumm* of the saws. Some of Robbie's many relations work there. Mornings, on his way to the day's work site, he heads into Gottheim for a second cup of coffee and gossip, but not before first looking up along the ledge back of the house, sometimes in moonlight. Before climbing into his rig he checks up there for the flag. Everything on that high ledge looks tiny, tiny pines, tiny flag. Still, it is a surprisingly noticeable slip of flying white, precariously placed, heroically hard to reach. Who ever put it up there had to climb the ledge, then climb the tree clinging to the ledge, straddle a long bristling limb and hang on.

"That flag's a story," says Robbie if someone mentions it. But he never tells it. Robbie figures the flag tells its own story.

The ledge is named for early settlers, who came here from New Hampshire. They lived here awhile, worked every kind of job, did some farming. Then they packed up and went back to New Hampshire, leaving the mountain their name. It soars above the Robichaud House, above the mill yard of Bearce's competitor, Enan Pale. Before he enters the door next to the trimmer's table, Robbie's cousin can look out and see the tiny flag high on the somber hillside. Flags have appeared there over the decades since this extended family of French-speakers moved here from Québec. But, for all its small fragile and fluttering appearance high up there, the Robichaud flag is actually a sheet for a double bed. Every so often it gets swapped for a fresh one. The wind up there is fierce enough to rip it to ribbons within the year.

After the kids are put to bed, Emma and Joanna join Alvin and Ansell on the deck of Ansell's trailer, where the two are smoking sweetfern picked by Ansell last July. He hung the plants in the attic of the old house to dry in the dark. They still had the deep green color when he went up to roll them into crisp little cigarettes. Ansell was fed up from losing his license and getting sick on coffee brandies so, having heard from an old-timer that the leaves are relaxing, he decided to give them a try. Sweetfern grows in sandy soil in the half-shade between the roadside and woods. And its legal.

Tonight is cold and white, gleaming with the moon. The two couples stand in this silverness, taking hits off the shared herbal cigarettes. High on the ledge the flag is visible, riffling, visually echoing the white of snowy outcrops between the dark pines.

After the manner of identical twins, Alvin and Ansell are thinking alike, recollecting father's grievances of mill owners, and his fiery condemnation of environmentalists. "They hate loggers'n logging s'bad it'll injure or kill you. Inspect evah tree for signs of it. Say they love trees! Who'd spike a tree, leave it wounded, open to attack by bugs'n rot? If the paper maker's a devil, they're the devil's mother."

Alvin exhales slowly, looking up at the ledge. "Flag's in sad shape."

"Thing's in tatters," Joanna agrees.

Emma doesn't want to think about it. She shivers in her old parka. Sweetfern smoke dribbles through her chattering teeth. There must be some other subject to get on.

"It's your turn," says Ansell.

Alvin says nothing. He shakes his head and passes the joint to Joanna. He looks away from the ledge toward the sawmill across the road. The buzz of the headsaw floats over to them, punctuating the drone of the separators.

My turn. But Alvin is tired of negotiating that ledge, weary of climbing the tree that seems no bigger than when he was a kid. He remembers the feel of the branch lying beneath as he reaches, trembling, to knot the sheet tight. He would tell himself not to look down, that he should be less afraid than he was last time. Even now he can smell that old pine pitch sticking to his clothes, caught in his hair. After all the cutting he's done—he still can't get used to it.

"I d'know," he says at last. "I think that flag's good f'another six, eight months. August, maybe."

Or maybe we just won't change it. He does not say this aloud.

16

The wind is brutal. The hood of his insulated coveralls is up; Robbie sits hunched above the cab of his pulptruck. Off his shoulder overhead—outside the reach of the hydraulic loader—naked branches creak and crack. The loader *hums* and *haws* as he works it back-and-forth, lifting the logs his sons have cut and hauled to the landing.

A half hour ago he was warm in the cab, eating chicken sandwiches made by Ezzy early this morning; washing them down with lukewarm coffee from a thermos topped off at 4:30 a.m.. Then he glanced out at the thermometer by the sideview mirror, reading five below. But just now, in the seat above the cab with wind-chill added, it aches like -40. His coveralls feel like something Ezzy might wear to bed. Even with the hood up, the fine bones of his ears hurt.

But Robbie can finesse that loader. In wind that could peel his scalp he loads ten cords an hour. He might curse it when it breaks down, but after sixteen years this loader is still his prize. Broken, this rig has taught him how to fabricate almost any part he might need. Operating the levers has so honed his touch that he could pick up a soda in its great steel claw without breaking the bottle or spilling a drop.

He sits pushing pedals, shifting levers, swiveling in the seat, setting logs between the vertical steel bars of the truck bed. And he thinks of the old days when he had to load with hooks and rolls, his youthful strength muscling those great logs up that pile. Now he's grateful for every drop of compressed hydraulic fluid ramming the loader, lifting these logs. He recalls the day he started with Father, being the rhythm end of a two-man saw with brother Louis, cutting trees girthier than these today. Father twitched them to the river with Claude and Claudette, his sleek Belgian draft horses. Together they saw the last decades of the great drives on the Arossagunticook.

Don't make woodsman like that n'more. But his thought snags on the sight of his father lying in mud, his back broken by the butt of a Norway pine. He shies at it, shivering and setting a log on the stack building below.

Saddened, he takes his attention to the talk he had with his neighbor last night when they stood by the woodshed laughing over the idea of bringing a $400,000 machine into the woods. Seriously then to Albert he said, "But they'll save three, four dollars a cord, even time you reckon their interest'n payments, over expenses for hiring reg'lar cutters. Bogs my mind, Albert. Weah kissing the woods g'bye. Won't be enough for ah sons to finish with."

Albert Clough looked down on bits of bark at his feet, his laughter gone. A long sigh came soughing where they stood by the shed.

Now Robbie recalls that sigh. He can hear it, sense it... even with this wind piercing him. Piercing where he sits hunched, loading logs at the landing.

—

Bearces' Mills sprawl along Oak River valley where old Beatitude Bearce started his operation early in the century. Led by Lyman, his sons have souped-up the operation with the latest 1980s technology. In the sawlog mill they can turn James Fay's white pine into a stack of boards almost before you can think of it. Gottheimites count themselves lucky that this white pine isn't shipped to Europe or Japan or someplace, instead of being debarked sliced edged trimmed planed graded stacked and dried by their husbands wives fathers daughters or sons. Asa Bartlett, amateur historian and wood-turning worker at the local spool mill, was stunned when he heard that Oregon had begun sending unmilled logs across the Pacific.

Bearce Mill sawlog workers go at it nonstop, hustling the heavy sap-saturated boards. Five thousand boards a shift is a very sweet thing: this being the mid-1980s, they get a penny for every board over 4000. Yet, 3600 is the limit a trimmer is physically apt to turn in an eight hour shift. After that he's trimming into those last few years at the end of his life, the years he is turning and trimming these extra boards for in the first place: Bearces' retirement plan consists of arthritis and air.

The several lengths of James Fay's pine tree have been hauled to the mill by Robbie Robichaud after Ansell and Alvin are done with it. Here these lengths are scaled in the yard and piled, after the unusual girth is exclaimed over. Hoisted with difficulty to the debarker, they are then stripped with blades and conveyed, patchy and bare, to the carriage of the headsaw. Sitting in the climate controlled cab above, pushing buttons, Thankful Thurston will roll one denuded log off the conveyor with a mighty slam. The machine takes the log in its hydraulic embrace, steel "dogs" nipping it tight, a line of laser red falling along its mottled length. The great girth forces Thankful to depress a foot pedal, bringing down the hammerdog to hold it in place. The carriage hurries the great log into the headsaw, a bandsaw with 900+ teeth vanishing in the speed of its fury. The blade rips the pine's fibers end to end along the red line, spraying wood dust across the cab like snow. These first mottled slices are junk, falling to the conveyor beneath, sent to the chipper blades at the far end of the mill. All this junk wood will be minced and used in the new generating system. Some of the more poorly run, smaller, wood-turning mills in Gottheim survive by selling their waste to Adirondack Paper in Guildford downriver.

When Thankful gets done with this massive pine log, it will be a squared-off cant; its visual identity as white pine tree done. The history of this life, told over more than a hundred years span of chromosomal replication and cell differentiation, will be reshaped into something else. Wages will change hands, human life being nourished and supported, but the life of this tree has already fled. The saw buzzed but no words were said over it. Where did this life go, now that its history has come to the blades of the resaw?

The cold of winter on him, Lyman Bearce stands in the doorway near the circuit of the resaw, surveying his operation. Winter's breath gives way to a sticky-sweet smell of ripped pine. This is the day on which the great Eastern white pine, taken off the subdivision under James Fay's supervision, is in progress of being turned into lumber; lumber, building material for sideboards or sashes or paneling—anything for sheltering, comforting, making convenient, decorating the lives of humans.

They are instantly aware of him, those whose posts permit a peripheral view of outdoor light slashing through the dim recesses of the mill. The mill sounds roar, whine, vibrate into Lyman Bearce. He pulls his ear covers from where they are buried in his vastly bearded neck, clapping them in place. Bearce likes coming into his mill; feeling this ruckus, watching the men work, seeing the blocked cant go its rounds in the resaw circuit... each time a little slimmer as its boards flop off. He likes everything about the place, even the noise: The screaming headsaw makes talk nearly impossible, a boon to productivity. The saws also isolate, encouraging contemplation of improvements. He can design for economy in the men's movements, test the function of each machine—think it all through to determine the shape of the future.

The place is snowy with sawdust—sills, corners, floor, machinery. Old brown piles of it are everywhere heaped with fresher white—wood dust from whatever happens to be passing through on a given day. Today it is pine from a ski resort development, though Bearce is unaware of its origin. The creamy white cant going by is a monster, the girth of which he considers would have disallowed it in the days of the King George navy. It would've been branded with the broad arrow in token of this. Today it is Lyman Bearce's bole.

It almost makes him smile, this clear light-hued limb gliding past; knotless and straight, and slimmer than when he first step through the door. Lyman watches the steel hands of the cant turners heave it toward the sawyer as he depresses one of five petals beneath the conveyor. The turners cradle the cant, rocking it like a baby as the operator draws it into the screaming saw. Aware of Bearce's presence, he is more awake now than a moment before when daylight poured in. And his boss is aware of his refreshed wakefulness, another reason why it is useful to visit the sawlog mill.

His workers are the best, and best paid, within a 25-mile radius. Only Jasper Mountain Ski Resort and, lately, Theodora Prescott's Gottheim Chair, come anywhere near Lyman Bearce's great wage of nearly one third above minimum. His workers know they have the best jobs around and are properly loyal and grateful. Like Bob Hastings over there on the edger. Bob is one of the best, if not the best; has been faithful 40 years, seeing all kinds of innovation. His job—hell! All their jobs have gotten easier, safer, over the years. Look at Hastings' hands, those twisted fingers, where he grabs those heavy boards.

Pleased, Lyman Bearce watches the edger heave a 16-foot board onto the table, aligning it between laser lines, sending it through with his enlarged arthritic hands. Comes another board and another and another.... Won't stop for hours, not till quitting time or some unforeseen breakdown. Then, maybe even reluctantly, Bob will stop ramming those boards through to the trimmer. Lyman shakes his secretly sentimental head in admiration. The man has been with Bearces since Lyman himself was a teenager getting ready to go off to college. Bob knows how lucky he is, having a decent job at the same place all his life. These men would give their lives for anybody. They saved the mill from burning to the ground last year, really put their backs into snuffing that generator fire.

Why does Rhetta keep on at me, anyway? The old thing just doesn't seem to understand any more what Bearces have done for this town, keeping it afloat all these years. Her!—married for decades into the best, the helpingest business in town. And born into one of the first operations in the area, too! Old Swann, her own father, was one of the originators of wage security!

Yet she's on Lyman day and night to own up to his sins. Sins?! Hell. Without those so-called sins her position would be less lofty, and Gottheim would not have fared so well. That mutual agreement on wages, even the blackball arrangement—it's where employment stability came from. She ought to go down to the Arossagunticook River, smell that: She'd know what *sin* is. Besides, they discontinued those meetings ten years ago.

That widget head Theodora Prescott. Lyman Bearce is deeply offended. Peewee Prescott died and left Gottheim Chair in the hands of his idiot daughter. Now she's upsetting the balance of business in the whole town (hardly to mention what it's doing to life at home).

But.... Maybe it's not that bad, her setting wages up almost even with his. She'll go under any day now. Have to. Her ramshackle ways will bring down that ramshackle place. That disgrace of a mill should be pulled to the ground before it collapses under its weight and someone gets killed. Let its shoddy remains be plowed under to rise in some tolerable form. There's development potential—God no. He'd rather buy the place himself than let the stripping of Gottheim continue. The skiers are uglifying the town at a rate swift enough. *At least Rhetta and I agree on that.*

At waist level the sawmill really moves. Boards whiz by, a stream of white gleaming in channels between headsaw and trimmer. Bearce steps onto the catwalk bridging the chipper conveyor. Below waist level his sawlog mill has a different pace. The creeping lower regions—where gears turn, chains snake slowly and conveyors move byproducts—cannot compete with the speed of higher regions where screaming saws, fast handwork, and the rock-and-rolling of the upper body prevail. Crossing the catwalk, Bearce glances into the chipper conveyor as a matter of course. A metal detector under the walk is a last check for debris before waste wood leaves the mill for the knives of the chipper.

The trimmer's table stretches to the mill wall, just this side of a door leading out to the grader and the yard below. Approaching, Lyman Bearce senses refreshed alertness in the rhythms of Moses Merrill. Merrill's job is to increase the worth of a board by cutting it to length. A good trimmer can shove the price of a board two, three, even four grades higher, depending on how he trims it. Always looking for that select board, Moses is quick. He can spot the face of the next board while cutting the end off the one he is releasing, eliminating as much as four feet to bump that board up to clear select.

Bearce stands back of the stocky trimmer, eyeing the perfect lumber coming through, watching as Merrill turns and trims in a smooth repetitive motion. This wood! Even demanding Lyman Bearce is impressed. Board after board of flawless pine. So broad that other mills would not be able to process it. So broad that Moses can hardly turn it.

"Some wood!" Merrill tosses the observation over his shoulder loud enough to be heard above the whine of the 16-foot saw.

"Not a knot anawaya!" Seeing it, Bearce can hardly keep a smile off. Board after 16-foot board, select. The world can't be as bad as they say, not with this kind of wood still around. Almost he feels like clapping Merrill on the back. As though the boy had prayed and pronounced over it when a seedling, saying, *Thy wood shall be select*! It's the purity they have waited for. All that cutting, edging, trimming, and seldom seeing such wood. The sight of it coming should lift the boy's heart; *it does mine.*

But when Bearce turns away Moses grits his teeth, turning a heavy board, cursing under his breath. When the boss has gone he can coast. No use turning these boards. There ain't no knots in this wood. Won't slip my discs over the old man's lumber. And, at night, when Moses gets back to his house—cold as a back house in January—he'll recall before reaching the lane that Lydia is gone. That the kids live in Lewiston with another man, one with wealthy Bath Ironworks wages. Moses will feel like walking around the frozen woods with his head chopped off. Wondering what there is to live for but those fucking sombreros.

From the corner of his eye he catches Bearce leaning over the conveyor. Now the old man straightens, hurries back to flip a toggle switch on the wall behind the trimmer. At the conveyor again he climbs over the catwalk and comes up with a bit of something his hand. Moses keeps flipping boards, punching buttons. Turning again he sees the boss heading back toward the headsaw. Merrill stops flipping the killer boards.

Through a door near the headsaw Bearce enters the dingy dim maintenance shop. Elmer Robbins, mill manager, and Artemis Kimball a mechanic, are bent over the bench conferring on a piece of machinery. Halting, Bearce holds up a bolt, reflecting fluorescent light back at the pair. They look up from the helter-skelter of the workbench where vices, tools, solder, a welding mask, etc... are spread. The smell of hot metal and scorched bench are stronger than sawn pine.

"Found this in the chippa conveya." His tone is curt.

"Metal detector must be down," says Robbins.

"Guess maybe," Bearce barks.

"Right on it!" Elmer brushes past while Kimball drops the piece he is working on to grab his tool belt and ear protection.

Lyman Bearce leaves the shop speculating about the bolt in his calloused hand. Maybe it fell off the headsaw. He yanks open the door of the cab and steps up, closing it to shut out the noise. Thankful Thurston is pushing buttons, playing the pedal, slamming down on the last of James Fay's white pines.

In the relative quiet it is as if Thankful, sitting high and setting pace for the entire mill, is somehow removed, above it all. Momentarily mesmerized, Bearce stops as the last great log is gripped in the dogs; mesmerized, as though by the last virgin pine in the state. He cannot believe the immensity of this tree. His only wish is that it came off one of his lots. Should look into that. He thought he knew their 35,000 acres... but maybe not. He watches as Thankful draws off its patchy flanks, the last remnants of *cambium* with inner and outer bark; the life, that which formally nourished and protected this great tree. A blizzard of wood dust passes and Lyman sees the tree, naked and light, scarcely touched with a delicate reddish tinge. Now the great blocked cant goes its way to the resaw, on a path to becoming a stack of new boards.

Bearce understands. It has to go. It was perfect, not a speck of rot, but it has to go. It gives place to seedlings, to saplings, to the whole of its spawn—at first sheltering them but ultimately blocking the necessary light of life. The young trees beneath would otherwise stunt, die out, in its towering competition. Woodsmen understood this. He felt it well expressed in the poetry of one of Gottheim's daughters, the master smart child of the mill scion now dead. Rot would surely have come to this tree. No way to keep rot out of living things. No way at all. Better this wood should go now... into cabinets or paneling or planking. Like in the poem: medium and light construction. Useful.

Lyman Bearce's hand on Thankful's shoulder brings the carriage to a standstill.

This is the moment of Life, the present moment. The only moment currently available to Gottheimites. The next moment is but a suggestion, the last is already hardened in history. For all the mass girth weight of the town's unchangeable history, only now is it alive, renewable. In this moment can Gottheim take heed to what it is doing, think, as it proceeds to its finished destiny. Last day comes, everyone "gets done," each looking back through time to discern the rings; sap, hardwood, and pith, formed in these moments when *now* is what we have. When we get done, all *this* will be monumental. An identity, fully fashioned and formed.

These are the translated thoughts of Asa Bartlett, amateur village historian, things he thinks of while walking twice-weekly to wind the tower clock in Gottheim. But he does not consider this metaphor in *cambium*, the living cell layer: No, he thinks of present moments as a tick of the clock, a single stroke of time's hands. Even so, Asa knows wood. He works with it every day. Turning birch into dowel rods at the village wood-turning mill, he handles wood constantly. The blades of the machine hone each rod, cleanly, as Asa feeds them through. One rod at a time.

Daniel and Balder

Some days, getting up from the chair by his window after a night of non-sleep, Balder Simon gives thanks for Lyman Bearce. He gives thanks for the sawlog mills, the little wood-turning mills in all these communities around Gottheim. Some days he even considers making a gesture toward Jasper Mountain with its ski trails running down the north slopes like white wounds: the ownership is nominally local, at least as of this moment. Balder would rather the owners around here had names like Bearce, Carter, Kimball, Chase, Corriveau, Hebert, Ouellette, Clark. He needs Yankee and French names to make him feel stable and whole. You never know. Someday the tree farms might be called Mitsubishi, Yamamoto, Honda. Maybe they'd be clone farms, or deformed berry farms or sludge farms creeping with chemical and miasmic mists. Not that Japan, particularly, is going to take over the world. At this late date, the last fifth of the last century of the millennium, it looks to him like multinational corporations are moving to grasp that distinction. Maybe junk-bond speculators in the cocaine casinos of Wall Street will trigger the metastasizing of greed. He is convinced of the speed of its malignancy, that it will astound everyone in the year 2001. As if he were in heaven, looking down through the ozone hole, watching corporate gluttons gobble up companies and land, vacuuming their way across continents. One day, he says, international trade legislation will supersede local laws protecting the community and its surroundings. "One day," (he said last week to Daniel after a night helping to install computer regulation of pulp and paper production in the mill) "Big Brother will jump his Communist ship to take the helm of capitalism. Forget the lack of privacy in government, we'll be too busy trying to escape the corporations' KGB."

This morning, his mouth foaming as he rinses his toothbrush in the sink, he says, "Gott'im's the residue. The iron monster's gont stomp on us in its furious fulminations. Free market caunt take ana value into account not measured immediately in money."

Peeling paint hangs off the bathroom door. His teenage son Daniel hears him saying this as he comes down the hall in his underwear. Balder nearly knocks him over, clipping through the door on his way to the staircase.

"What's it mean?" Daniel asked this, rubbing his eyes against the glare of the bathroom light.

"What? Who?"

"That. About iron monsters'n money."

Balder raises his bearded chain, eyeing the questionable ceiling. "Well, take borrowing. If a company has to rebuy the equivalent of itself evah few years, they'll decrease worker's'n make'em work harder fah less." He looks down at Daniel. "And have t'use creation down to the nub. How do they know what to do with Gott'im if they don't live here and be fond of it? And, all that shipping stuff around—you can only take out the amount of oil God put in the ground to begin with. Unless theya's some way to siphon it out o'the sky where we been flinging it. Think we can do that anatime soon?"

"But—we don't really *need* to, do we?"

The inarticulate Balder taps Daniel's tangled head with his comb. "I'd advise you to stot separating yourself from your deplorable dependence on consumerism."

He stuffs the comb into his back pocket and heads down stairs. "Stot today!" He shouts, trouncing down the stair. "Start yestadee!"

"How much land we gut heah?" asks Balder.

"100 acres?"

They are painting drywall in the children's house, upstairs. Daniel knows the history. The children's house is an extension of the pioneer's dwelling, added in the prosperous 1880s. Beneath the protective north wall of Jasper Mountain, farming was life. Skiing was something you read about in books. Every scholar in the schoolhouse at the foot of the hill knew that you couldn't get around Norway or Switzerland unless you had skis. Daniel's father wants the whole house prepared in case he ever has a bride to bring to it. He must want a wife pretty bad.

And Daniel thinks he knows which one, too. She's a beautiful blonde with startling eyes and a jutting dimpled chin. Whenever he sees it, he thinks of a man's chin. But Gloria is sweet and nice. Fresh lightly powdered donuts come to mind when she strolls into The Village Voter, where he works setting type for Mr. Nutting after school. She comes in with items on conferences and meetings, things pertaining to town development. She works, somehow, with the resort, which wants to change the town around.

"Daow. Way way back, when Simons was settlers, they had a few lots, hundreds o'acres. Hevn't near that now, maybe near 25."

Dabbing with paintbrush, Daniel nods. He is edging around the window trim. Balder lays long even ivory strokes on the drywall, stooping once in awhile to load the roller. Even with the window cracked, the smell of fresh latex fills the room. "Know what we could do with it?"

Solemn, Daniel shakes his head, waiting for the answer. He knows better than to say develop it.

"Put it to wuk. Theya's the woodland... and we got the barn. We might hire us a bandsaw, stot harvesting bad trees."

"Market bad wood?"

"Good wood, but we take the worst trees. Cull the injured and diseased from the woods, leave a few of 'em for critters, woodpeckers, like that. Coons, bears'n such'll eat the bugs right out of trees. Wood ants taste like cranberries to'em. Decayed wood goes to make soil.... We mill some of the trees, making room for healthy ones t'come. But theya's more going on in the woods we could profit fom. Edible mushrooms, balsam'n spruce tips for making wreaths. We could make weather sticks to sell to tourists." He grins. "Got to get ah li'l piece of the tourists."

This is too much for Daniel. He has enough to do without playing medicine man: working at the The Voter, helping out here, and school on top of that. Mother's been prodding him to do maple syrup maybe next month. He can't stand the thought of all this *work*, but he says only, "Mother says roots'n stuff make good medicine."

"Theya y'go! S'pose she'll find all kinds o' stuff in that woods up theya on Blackwell. What we need, though, is markets for all this. Where'n how t'sell. Got do a li'l research, see. That's where you come in—with those budding reporter skills you been learning at The Voter. If we caunt sell stuff heah, we gut look elsewhere."

More work. *Wuk wuk wuk.* It's all that goes on here. Mother works two jobs and all she talks about is that farm up on Blackwell Mountain. He is supposed to help with that. There isn't even a house up there yet, just an old camper six sizes too small.

"Uh, Fatha?... does this have anything to do with what you was saying the other morning? Deplorable dependence'n all that?" And now he slips in the dig: "Cause I was wondering about that job you got in the paper mill." *Your thoughts are holy but what about your hands?* Look what Adirondack Paper is doing to the Arossagunticook River. The mill's a massive stinking inhaler of trees. The mill yard is a boneyard concentration camp for trees. You're always telling tales of how wasteful they are, how they make workers work unnatural hours, use evil chemicals, demonic machinery.

The man stops painting. "It looks hypocritical...." Slowly he begins laying a white swath with the roller. The grin he usually wears when caught in some ludicrous act is missing. Some act like that of the other day, when he overshot the bog trail in the Skidoo and landed in a beaver pool that wasn't quite frozen. They were up to their necks in ice water, and it took fifteen minutes to hike-jog out of there. And the snow machine is sitting there still, now probably locked in ice.

"But I'm thinking about that job all the time, thinking of ways to t'get loose. If I 'memba right, I took that job to have money to fix up this house. Guess I got kinda bogged down." Here he does grin. "But you're right, Daniel. It is hypocritical. I'm working on it, though. Anything else bothering you?"

"Well... what about Grandmother's animals? Waya'll she stash 'em if you use the barn fah farm animals?"

Balder half turns to the boy and Daniel sees speckles of ivory paint in Balder's short black beard. The speckles just about match his towhead. "Haven't got that fah in my calculations yet either. Interfering with her critters'd be a formidable exercise I don't doubt."

Balder grins and Daniel almost smiles. Elda was as small as an elf and a pushover in just about any area one might intrude on. Balder thinks how she gave up her habitual privacy without a peep when he was surprised by fatherhood and suggested she make room for three boys every other week. Now that Peter is in the area Nathan and Ben don't come as often, but, still, it's not easy for her. Even considering Elda's seemingly pliant nature, Balder is wary of testing her limits concerning the animals in the barn. He suspects an awful surprise.

"What else? Can I take these questions t'mean I'm out heah on a limb by myself? We might *could* act out a living in this place, if we don't get greedy. *Simons Ledge* might sustain itself again."

Daniel isn't about to bring it up, but the "what else" he is thinking of is Gloria Fay. Father is gooey over her. Daniel can't picture her cleaning house, let alone mucking out the barn. She might clean the toilet of her condo, but Daniel can't picture it. He stoops to pick up the paint can and take it to the next window. Time to change the subject.

"Evah see that white flag over theya, other side o'the valley? Across the road fom the big sawmill, Pale's Mill, I think it is. Flag flies on a pine, way up on the ledge?"

Rolling on the paint with vigor, Balder says, "Theya's nevah been a time I in't seen that flag up theya. Been flying over Robichaud's since I was a kid, maybe 'fore that, even."

"Why's it theya?"

Still laying the paint, Father says, "Thought you was the reporter. Find out, tell me'n we'll both know."

Turning eggs in the pan one morning, Balder says to Daniel, "What we need's a way to market what we'll have t'sell."

They are in the woodpaneled kitchen, fixing breakfast. Sunlight reflecting snow-light comes in through divided windows, whitening the wooden cupboards with rectangles. This is Sunday. They are up late with the sun.

Not this, thinks Daniel, dropping whole-wheat slices into the toaster. The slots insides begin to glow red. He smells the wheat toasting, thinking of an assignment Mr. Hebert has given the freshman English class. They are supposed to start keeping a journal. Daniel isn't sure he wants a record of his days. Writing about real-life sounds like a big thing, but he's tried it before and knows better. It's all little things. Lots of little things. Things you aren't even excited about doing, let alone writing about. Things like fixing and eating breakfast, making your bed, riding the noisy school bus, talking about little things with your friends. Or having to listen to your Father make boring plans for your future. Father seems hands off about after graduation, but Daniel is certain to have his life niggled away in the meantime. Mr. Hebert is usually in absolute brick—as they say in England. He makes English interesting. Like that reading he gave of Tolkien's "Leaf by Niggle." Hebert is an *Anglophile*. He gave that word to the class along with *Anglophobe*. Daniel relates to Niggle, a little man whose life is being niggled away by the claims of others.

Still he says nothing, getting the butter out of the refrigerator. The toast pops.

Balder does not seem to notice Daniel's lack of response. His rangy muscular frame leans happily to the task of shoveling up eggs, his talk continuing right along. From the way he moves about, flipping eggs onto plates, talking, Daniel could not know that he spent half the night reliving explosive and bloody scenes which took place on the other side of the planet well over a decade ago. He spent the other half scheming to break off daily association with deafening noise, toxic fumes, obscene and idiotic conversation, and a profound waste of trees. Here and there, tucked in at the edges of all these thoughts, came a healthy merry face, stunning blue eyes, gold hair, and a cleft chin just a bit too pronounced: It was the sun, peeping through chinks in his sometimes dim life.

That is all the sun will do: peep through chinks. Even so, Balder will not scheme to bring it live into his house.

"'N that's waya you come in," he says hopefully to his son. "You can research what markets we got."

Is that all? All I got to do is research markets, help you fix up this house, work at the newspaper, get straight A's, help Mutha collect sap, build her a house out of nothing, babysit my brothers, collect mushrooms in the woods, plant a garden in spring, saw trees, and write it all down in a journal? No sweat.

Daniel edges the plates with buttered toast and carries them to the table. "How do I find these markets?"

Hot dog! The boy has acknowledged his request. Balder pulls out his chair and sits, looking over at his serious son. The man grins. "I d'know. That's why I give the job t'you."

Daniel dips his toast in the gooey yolk, inwardly mouthing the words as Balder says them aloud: "You're the reporter."

The boy thinks, I liked you better that first time, when we went bass fishing. They were just getting started on the relationship.

Balder sat in that boat and worked harder at getting Daniel to like him than he had worked at anything since the Asian war. But Daniel knows little about the war, except that Balder got scarred by Agent Orange. Daniel once heard Balder say he was glad he got into that Agent Orange. Adults can be pretty mysterious, when they aren't being dull as dirt.

Daniel thinks Agent Orange sounds like a name for a rock group. There *should* be a rock group named Agent Orange. Maybe there is.

"Take black birch," Balder is saying.

It's as though his father has been reading his mind, because immediately Daniel thinks that Black Birch would be a good name for a band. He looks blindly at Balder's face, awaiting further information. But, seeing yellow goo rimming his father's mustache, he suppresses a smile. *Yellow Goo.* He can see its drummer wail.

Grinning, Balder takes a napkin to his mustache, to his beard. "Have ana idea how well sap flows outta black birch? Betta'n maple sap. 'N' you don't have t'gather it in the cold. We could extend the sapping that way. When maple gets done'n leaves start on black birches—there y'go, a premium syrup! What a market theya'd be fah that! Takes twice as much sap as with maple, though. And then there's black birch tea. You might be interested: Indians made it."

This was a reference to Daniel's heritage through his mother, who is part Native. Chrischana's own mother, Hattie Trueman, was descended from Abenaki Indians who frequented the Arossagunticook River. They belonged to the same clan as Jasper Mary, Native storyteller of history and legend, who lent her identity to Gottheim and surrounding towns. *Murdered by thieves out to steal my treasure, I crossed over the dark river in the late 1700s. It is believed that no one ever found my peculiar treasure—some think it may have been found by some ordinary pioneer seeking it diligently in the earth without telling a soul. But know, oh reader, my greatest treasure came out of the storehouse of stories I told.*

"Try that book I got out o'the library. The old one on the table in the front room. It says black birch tea was used to wash out sore mouths, and helps diarrhea and rheumatism."

Bound to be a market for that, thinks Daniel.

"It's loaded with vitamins A, B1, B2, C and E. They made wintergreen out of it in the old days."

Wow. But Daniel refrains from rolling his eyes, saying only, "Nevah saw black birch. Seen papah birch and yellow birch, though. And theya's one looks like papah but don't peel like it."

"Gray birch," says Balder nodding. "Don't know if we even have black birch around here anamore. Look at bark on black cherry saplings, it's easy to mistake, they looked s'much alike."

But Daniel is not interested in black birch tea. He mops up the yolk on his plate with a piece of limp toast, saying thoughtfully, "You're always looking to make a living off the land... why can't we look for gems? People say theya's gemstones'n minerals in the woods. That's what I'd like to look for."

Balder looks at him. Now they are back in the boat. He is teaching Daniel how to cast for bass. Daniel has asked him for something, something maybe worthwhile.

"We could. Evah since the Hamlin boys down to Mt. Mica found gem tourmaline tangled in the roots of a blowdown, folks have been poking around, digging out the woods'n blasting out the sides of mountains. The Simons nevah did." He grins. "Now might be the exception. If evah theya was anathin in these woods—still theya! We can take it long's we don't disturb things too much. Valuable things like ginseng'n certain mushrooms should be preserved unless weah sure something's down theya, okay?"

"How'll I recognize those things?"

"Books! We'll learn what t'look fah from them this winter—plants and minerals. Theya's clues, what they call indicators."

They have finished eating, but no one moves to clear. In pauses between conversation, Daniel can hear the dripping of the faucet, the ticking of the clock in the next room.

"I been out a few times with friends, looking for minerals," Balder continues. "'N' we find gemstones by minerals not so rare being nearby. When we get done heah we'll go out to the shed'n see some of the dusty samples up in the loft."

" 'Simons nevah did?' "

"Maybe black tourmaline, feldspar, not rare. Don't know how we come by it. Indicators, though. We got books in the front room. They might help."

Daniel stands, beginning to clear the table. Balder grabs dish liquid from under the sink, sets the plug, turns on the faucet. Sunday is going to be a day absorbed. Later they will be ice fishing on the pond. *My people are still hunting my treasure.*

Old Tires

Legends of Jasper Mary have always abounded in Gottheim and surrounding towns. A part of her story is set in one stretch of backwoods, in neighboring Quaker Plantation also known as Quakertown. This tale tells of her hunts for medicinal herbs in a place called Medicine Mile, and of how she marked the stretch with pouches of deerskin decorated in porcupine quills. Gemstones, it was said, could be found there in clay and rock not far under the surface of woodland earth. Why did she never unearth her trove or carry it away to make her rich? The tales do not explain, but for nearly two hundred years folks have searched the stretch deep into the woods. Pits were dug, trees chopped; and people farmed it, breaking the soil with harrows. Nevertheless, nothing shiny was ever discovered between root or rock. The treasure eludes, its secret keeps, and myth abounds; yet the uses of Medicine Mile have changed.

One old son of settlers, Ceylon Segar (pronounced Ceylon Cigar by townsfolk), has a business "storing" used tires. Set back from the old dirt road, millions of tires are piled in mammoth mountains behind a curtain of trees on Medicine Mile.

The trees where Jasper Mary once tied her medicine pouches are long gone and others have grown in their place. Through their branches one can hear the clanking of gears and rumbling of engines as truckloads come through each week... even as the fear of Quaker's scattered residents builds. What if one of those monstrous piles catches fire? They wonder it aloud among themselves and in desperate letters to the editor. They complain about "environmental terrorism," study the composition of tires, and wonder what kind of pitch, in what quantities would fill the sky around the communities of Gottheim if, say, a dry season with forest fire should set these dense lots ablaze.

One such writer of letters dreams of falling through clouds, bright and dark with flaming imagery. Through layers of expanding consciousness, she falls through the hellish halls. On other nights she dreams of little but trees, of white pine with arms outstretched, praising and resigned. They tower toward heaven, collecting birds, gathering songs from the sky; yielding up fragrance. They harbor weak bobbing heads and pointed gaping mouth. The dreamer's name? Eloise Patadoe. Of course. She is an artist. She keeps goats.

Having ascended on the Golding's private lift, Julius Golding looks out from the summit of snowy Jasper Mountain, a pair of black binoculars in his gloved hand. The round bulks of the Meguntics stretch away, mottled light and dark with conifer and snow. Southward the sun is far, white, diffuse. Beside him stands his niece Amanda, in ski mask and goggles, daughter of his late sister. The little girl stands patiently, strands of white hair escaping her patterned knit alpine cap. She is hooded and bundled in insulated jumpsuit, longing to ask for a turn with the binoculars. She hopes he will remember her standing by, and offer the glasses. The fierce breath of Jasper blows over them, fierce as the Arctic, quickly unbearable.

Below the summit sits the lift shack, a lonely little house at the end of the world. Skiers leap to its ramp under the bullwheel, before gliding away back down the mountain. Billy Glover sits in the insulated lift shack between the two lifts where a heater keeps him warm. He looks down the shining lines of cables and suspended seats, vigilant as skiers ascend. Sometimes they knock at his door and ask to ride to the summit. He just shakes his head, explaining that it's a private lift. Amanda knows Billy. Sometimes she visits him briefly at the shack on her way up or down. Her uncle only nods at him through the window, or raises his voice to ask how it's going when he opens the door for her. He doesn't let Amanda stay in there too long.

Billy operates both lifts from the shack. When any of the family ascend to the summit, he has to keep one eye up and the other down. It's really a job for a two-headed person, but Billy doesn't mind. Actually, he's kind of proud to be serving the Golding's like this. They are some of the most powerful people in the state. Harry Golding has brought celebrities to the summit. Billy has seen Stephen King up here with his own eyes, and the horror king is awesome all the way home. But Billy's wife thinks the writer should go back to the dry cleaners. That night he came up there was no end of glory for Billy and Rayona at the Muzzleloader. They needed a designated driver to get home. Since then he has read up and become an expert on King. "Did you know he once worked in a laundry? He could o'been a lift operator!"

Pierced through with Jasper's severe whole breath, Julius Golding stands looking out across the Meguntics. Shivering, stamping, Amanda slips her mittened hand in his gloved one, hoping to remind him of her presence. If she had been any other Golding offspring she would be jumping around, tugging at him, begging for the glasses. But she is only Amanda, she doesn't whine.

There are no trees here. Not as Amanda thinks of trees. There are some wizened crooked small bushes that Uncle Julie calls krumholz. She thinks them cute shrubbery, permanently bent as though kneeling. The wind seems to move them hardly at all and sometimes they are buried in snow. She has seen them in rime. They are little, but Uncle Julie says they are actually very old, much older than he is. Krumholz isn't handsome or vital-looking like the tall trees on the slopes below but she heard him say they survive here better than a great white pine could.

The wind is pointed, piercing through her coveralls like darts. Amanda is beginning to numb up and bend like krumholz. In a moment she will crumble. Trembling, her hand jerks in Uncle Julie's. Still he looks through the binoculars. At last she cries in her high-pitched voice. "What are you looking at?"

Golding looks down on her suddenly through his ski mask, surprised concern in his eyes. He stoops to hand her the glasses, saying close in her ear, "I wanted to see the tire piles in Quakertown. Sometimes heat from them prevent snow buildup, but it's too late. I think they're covered for the winter."

Below wooded Mount Marriott, 60 million tires are thought to be stored. The exact number is in question. Three years ago there were 20 million, documented. Current estimates set it much higher. Amanda pulls down her goggles and looks through binoculars in the direction he points, seeing only a patch of pure white snow. "Where there's no trees?" She yells, pointing.

"Exactly!"

Amanda is very concerned about the tires. Last autumn she heard Uncle Julie express anger over them and wondered aloud why he didn't call someone to take them away. He and Uncle Harry were always calling people to do important things. Her class studied about Jasper Mary and Medicine Mile on local history day. In science they learned about pollution and recycling and other ecological concerns. She was glad Uncle Julie was indignant, but, when she asked him to call to have the tires removed he smiled faintly and said, "It's not that easy."

"But it's not harder than building a condominium or a ski lift is it?" Moving tires must be easier than most things she saw happening at the resort where strong detailed structures were put together. But Uncle Julie said that things like rights and policies got in the way. He said someone must figure out how to use the tires. Then she came home from school one day to tell them the class had it all solved for him. The paper mill in Guildford was putting in a generator to burn things like tires and produce electricity at the same time. The high smokestack would burn them very clean. Now, if he called, the tires would have some place to go.

But he said the tires were not his, the land wasn't his, and he could not tell the paper company to come take the tires away. The Maine DEP said the tires had to stay, and that was that.

"What's the DEP?"

"The Department of Environmental Protection."

This was beyond Amanda's understanding.

The conversation about tires took place during the drought last fall, when Amanda was afraid the tires would catch fire. It was one of Julius Golding's big fears. There'd be no stopping a fire like that any time soon. He knew how a fine resort with a hoped-for international clientele would fare if shrouded in a volcanic and enduring cloud of soot. The prevailing winter wind would blow its desolate load upon them, the fair white slopes becoming a pall in rains of ash. And skiers would head for Goldings' competitors. The best he was able to do was get the governor to consider the problem of tire dumps statewide. Together they learned that Maine has more tires than Michigan, 60 times more, with a population statewide roughly equal that of Detroit.—One more ironic and idiosyncratic snafu of American life.

Here on the summit of Jasper, in polar wind fierce as an ancient deity, the Goldings lives are hazarded. Up here Julius sees how casually human control is negated. A man may take precautions, pay heed to safety but, ultimately, vicissitudes shall prevail. Below, when he is skiing on Jasper's pristine flanks, or driving along on the thread of highway and looking up at its massive bulks, its almost perfect rounded head, Golding forgets what he has learned up here about his own lack of power. Being on the summit can give you insight, even as you turn your back, fight for breath, feel your heat leave. Julius knows he should get Amanda down from here, shelter her away from these mighty elements but, if he waits maybe a moment more, something may come. One clear thought to guide. It sometimes happens.

But, waiting, no thought comes save the urgency for shelter. Shelter *now*. With his pole he urges her to the slope, gesturing that she precede him. The wind burning his face, he watches her red suit whittle away in the distance. Now he slips down after her, clipping through his turns. She waves to him from a clump of spruce opposite the bullwheel. He stops before her in a spray of white, crisply saying, "Good to get out of the wind. Ready for cocoa?"

She nods, a little red ridinghood in goggles, but Amanda does not turn immediately. "Uncle Julie? When I was up there I had a thought. Don't those little old trees look like little old men? One of them remind me of Mr. Cigar. In class, we saw his picture in *The Voter* when Mrs. Gravalos was getting us to think of him as our neighbor. She said he was—uh—a man making a living, so why couldn't we, you and me, write him a letter about the tires? Or call him on the phone? And talk nicely to him? Couldn't we, Uncle Julie?"

His hesitation is frowning and long. Julius does not want anything to do with talking to Ceylon Segar, nicely or otherwise. Ceylon Segar is thick-headed, vulgar, filthy. He generally sits in his trailer office and watches the trucks from all over the country pile in. Mr. Cigar feels himself a going concern. However, the problem for the little unincorporated township of Quaker is that the used tire business is sedentary. The tires sit there, going nowhere. At the moment this did not concern Mr. Segar. He had the famous land of his ancestors, and people from away were falling all over themselves, spewing money, to get their tires-by-the-ton moved onto his property in rural Maine. Truckloads came, sometimes almost hourly, and Ceylon, who once probably delighted to count them and the piles they made, most likely gave up keeping track long ago. He probably has no idea how many millions are piled on his property. He would know nothing about compromise, diplomacy, courtesy, or how to get along in any way shape or form. It's all there in *The Voter*. He is all ego, a prickly old fart. Julius once saw the old man drive past Janine's ski boutique, flipping it the bird. He probably couldn't read a contract if shown one. And Amanda wants to make friends! A picture of their meeting flashes on him: self crisply attired, smelling of aftershave, cuff links glinting; Segar smelly in grubby hunting jacket, hands and fingernails lined and caked in dirt. Not in a decade of diplomatic negotiation would it work.

"Well," he says to the little red-framed face. "It can't do me any harm to think about it. But I've got to warn you not to get your hopes up. I don't think it'll work." He gestures, saying, "Let's go get that cocoa."

Amanda starts down and is soon a red dot amidst the swirling throng of color. Julius Golding follows. He follows Amanda down.

She is on her way to sign up for a course in carpentry at the Adult Education office, when a rear tire on her 14-year-old Bonneville blows. Chrischana Twitchell is due at Farmingham Royal Tavern to wash luncheon dishes before the hour is out. Now she will have to change the tire and come back another time to apply for a course she hopes will help her in building a house on Blackwell Mountain... someday. It is first lunch period as she limps into the parking lot of Hazel Newell high school/middle school. Spitting snow at 20° and the wind blows, making it feel more like 0. Chrischana sighs, shoves open the door.

Won't be easy, the shape this car's in. She looks from the flat tire to the distant row of cafeteria windows. Sure hope Daniel's not in lunch, or Benaiah. This could be embarrassing for them.

The wind riffles her secondhand parka, bought at a hospital sale in Guildford a month ago—her first real winter coat since living with father as a teenager here in Maine. Until last spring she was living in the metropolitan desert southwest, ever since Daniel's birth out of wedlock almost for fifteen years ago. Now she is back, struggling on her own to make a life for herself and her sons.

Standing at the trunk she looks bleakly at the clothesline holding one end of the bumper to the frame of her car. It will have to come off if she wants to get at the spare in the trunk. Fingers rapidly numbing, she begins working the knot. Swearing but once under her breath, she loosens it and begins unwinding the rope. With a *clunk*, that end of the bumper hits the icy pavement. Chrischana looks over her shoulder at the row of windows. A few kids look out at her through descending snow. *Maybe it's not them. Can't tell.*

She opens wide the lid, heaves out the spare. It's a rummage through the gaping trunk full of junk: tattered sleeping bags, a broken toaster, kids' holey sneakers, newspapers, the livetrap Benaiah got for Christmas, some scattered tools. She can see ice on the pavement through a hole near the wheel well. Where is the jack?

She finds it shoved toward the back under their tangled tent, pulls out its pieces and tosses them onto the gritty ice beside the spare. Where's the hammer? Might take a pounding to get that wheel off.

More rummaging. Doaw. No hammer.

Chrischana stands back, searching for a place beneath the rust-eaten car to set up the jack. The body around the wheelwells is disintegrating. Rust holes lace the old fenders of the dull gold frame. If she sets the jack beneath the door and it breaks through the chrome they won't be able to close the door.

It's all standard procedure. This is how you live.

She could be under Peter's wing, maybe get a good used-car on the wealthy wages he now earns from Adirondack Paper. The pattern of violence seems to be broken, or maybe just abated. She isn't ready—*they* aren't ready. *Got to give it more time to make sure he won't be drinking, won't be hurting me again.*

When she and the kids ran away and came back here to what she knew growing up, Peter sobered up and came looking for them. He got counseling and seems to be recovering. And ever, except for that awful example of intermittent drunken brutality, he has been a pretty good father. She will admit that. Now he wants to be a good husband and she can't deny that he is working at it. But she's been working too. A lot of effort has gone into living without him, into ridding herself of the pain caused by their common-law marriage. Instead of giving the relationship a chance she's out here by herself, working at being independent. Being alone.

Snow thickens the air. The air is white, her clothes are whitening, the spare lying on the ground is already coated in white. She gets down on her knees, looks under the car. There's the axle, use that.

Daniel is calling her. She turns her head, sees him coming through the flying snow. He wears his leather jacket, the one Peter gave him Christmas before last. He has outgrown it and his wrists showing a good three inches of shirt sleeve. No one is thinking to get him a coat. Not Petey, not his biological father, not Chrischana herself.

She stands, rubbing her palms, trying to get rid of the grit. "Sorry fah embarrassing you."

"No problem. But, if you do this in front of English class—with no way fah me to escape?—" (He smacks his knuckles into his palm).

It's a joke but he does not grin like his father Balder would. His face is grave with Native American features, features like Chrischana's own, and that of her deceased mother.

Watching out the window with other kids in his freshman class, he realized that being out here helping was preferable to listening to them mock-direct the operation. Most were unaware that it was Daniel's mother out here. He might have slipped into the hall, escaping without notice. But it doesn't really matter much to him. Breakdowns happen. Embarrassment will come later, when some cop pulls them over for that bumper. Tying up bumpers with clothesline *has* to be illegal. The whole car is illegal. No way it will ever pass inspection. She's been putting off Maine registration for that reason.

Mother is always complaining about overregulation. According to her it should be legal to drive down the road in whatever you can afford. "But no!" She goes on: "Theya's got be expensive restrictions only yuppies can afford. Got be x amount o'sound metal in relation to rust—and now they want t'make it impossible t'drive without insurance! They want all the bumps smoothed out. Think theya entitled to risk-free life! Don't even *see* the rest of us down heah, struggling just to stay operable on theya rules. Imagine working in a place like rural Maine'n not being able t'drive? Caunt they see if you caunt get to work the next stop's welfare? And what would ah forefathers say bout these regulations taking away ah freedom? *They* took food'n shelter, medicine fom the woods. The settlers'd roll in theya graves." Mother's ancestors on her father's side were Yankees, the first to settle Gottheim she sometimes reminds Daniel.

After a teenage requisite roll of the eyeballs, Daniel can see her point. Rich people with computer jobs and skis will be coming in, forcing land up, then wanting to write codes to protect property values and make the place look less junky. Even Balder saves useless everything, saying it saves on parts. But, so what if codes make things more difficult? Both Dad and Father have good paying jobs. Mother complains but won't accept help from anyone. It's like she enjoys hardship. She just likes to pick the system apart.

Saying little, Daniel blinks snow out of his eyes and stoops to pick up two pieces of the jack. "Won't work," he says, trying to fit them together. "You've got parts of two different jacks."

"Figures." She goes to the trunk, rummages, comes back with a different stand. "Try this."

They squat beside the flat and he puts the jack together. Chrischana sets it behind the wheel under the axle, some precarious, but at least the handle reaches. Pumping, she begins jacking up the car.

"Hold it!" warns Daniel. "Car's rolling!"

She lets it down as he runs to the trunk to grab a piece of leftover firewood. He moves quickly to shove it under the front tire. "Try now!"

As she pumps the car holds. Cranking with the lug wrench, she begins loosening the lug nuts and handing them to him one at a time.

If he puts them on the ground they will be lost in gathering snow, but they are too cold to hold so he lays them flat on the snowy car roof.

Chrischana is pulling on the tire, jerking hard, but it won't budge.

"I'll get a hammer." He says this heading for the trunk.

"We don't have one!"

Mother is getting pissed. Daniel turns and runs toward the back of the school calling something over his shoulder.

He is gone in the obliterating snow, taking his explanation with him. Chrischana yanks viciously on the tire. Having been checked by her son's appearance, her anger now flows in his absence. She grinds her teeth, barking out a curse while tugging on the wheel. Standing she barks three quick curses in succession and kicks the tire after each.

How the fallen are mighty, she thinks ruefully, recalling her gentleness of last spring when she was escaping, hurting and vulnerable. Oh well. Best to get it out before he returns. Can't have him thinking it's okay to go profane ballistic. He saw enough of that elsewhere.

The tire and its corroded bolts have fused together. She sinks to the snowy pavement, weary, letting January ice seep into her bones. If she sits long enough her own joints will fuse and then she can stop worrying. She will become sculpture, a work of art: "Woman in Winter, with Flat."

Why is it we're better when things are tragic, and worse when circumstances merely irritate?

Appropriate that my destiny is one with this piece of junk. They found the car in Phoenix, cheap. For $250 the Chrischana Twitchell/Peter Prince alliance gained an ancient luxury sedan that had ferried drivers from Chicago to the desert Southwest, a shuttle. "Those winter city streets." The salesman had exclaimed: "All that sand and salt and weather. But how else could you get something for so little?" Seeing its spottty fenders made her nostalgic for Maine. And Peter was always there to keep it running. But this winter... this first Maine winter—without him.... clothesline kept it together. Chicago, the desert, and Maine have combined to corrode this car to lacework. Untrusty, rusty metal, held together with very iffy attractions. The car is ready to drop. The Bonneville will shred its own weight back into the earth. If she plants it in the woods below the farm on Blackwell Mountain she will see trees nourishing themselves from it within a year.

Daniel is back, thrusting a sledgehammer in her glazed face. "From shop class." She does not respond. Her joints have fused. Chrischana raises her gaze to him. "Maybe y'betta." She says it slowly. Stiffly she stands to move out of the way.

She heads for the trunk and hoists the spare off the ground, resting a moment with it wedged between her parka and the lip of the trunk. Now, for the first time, she notices bits of wire protruding from bald spots in the tire. Disgusted, defeated, she heaves the tire into the open maw. Rust particles sift to the ground on impact. Rust from the holes around the wheelwells is printing the icy pavement. Ahead, Daniel beats on the tire, shaking the car.

"Stop!!" She screams it, fearful less the car fall on him. "Shitting thing's not coming! Tighten the lugs'n let it down!"

But Daniel merely moves out a bit, beginning to beat it all over with the sledgehammer.

A red Chevette rolls by through pouring snow. The pimply driver leans out, saying something obscure. Grinning he rolls past and keeps going. Chrischana grins back. She yanks happily on the fallen bumper, manic and trying to wrest it free. Nights with father, lit by kerosene in the crumbling farmhouse, come back to her: hand pumping water into the kitchen sink, hacking deer meat from the frozen carcass hanging in the shed, chopping wood in the dooryard. Laughing, she runs around to Daniel. "I'll get that tire off!" She grabs the hammer out of his hand and throws it at the jack. The car falls in a shower of tinkling rust. The lug nuts fly off the roof, but the tire holds.

"It's my life." She throws up her hands. Snow pours down the cuffs of her parka, melting on her wrists. "It's Maine. Why else would anyone live like this?" She scrabbles about, picking up the scattered lug nuts, maniacally twirling them back into place.

Daniel stands watching and distressed. It troubles him to see any of his adults acting antsy. Chrischana reaches under the car for the wrench. "Can I tighten them up for you?" He steps close.

But now she is stripping the nuts off again. "Not necessary. I'll just drive around the parking lot till it falls off."

Daniel takes hold of her arm and she stops to look at him, still smiling.

"Mother, you gont embarrass me in front o'the whole school?"

The smile fades. Empty, she looks at him, arms drooping in defeat. She mumbles something, resisting the urge to reach out and brush the layer of snow off her son. It makes her ache to see him standing there, his cuffs hanging out.

She must look pretty dejected herself, because Daniel smiles. A smile from him is rare enough to bring back her characteristic half-smile in return. The false grin is gone and he finds himself comforted: the half-smile is what he knows. She hands him the lug wrench.

He squats to load the nuts and begins tightening them. Standing he offers, "Want me t'call Balder or Dad? They both at work now?"

She has retrieved the jack parts. Together they move toward the trunk and she tosses them in. "Help me tie up this bumpa?" She lowers the lid. "I'm late fah the tavern. It'll be okay till Petey gets off." She says this to give the impression that she plans to call him. Maybe she will. Maybe not. He would be glad if she does, but the feeling is not hers to reciprocate. Her numb fingers fumble with this rope, with this knot being tied with difficulty. She feels sick in her soul, very low. Chrischana always feel so after behaving badly. Briefly, for the first time, she wonders if Peter ever felt this—truly—after his raging. If he did, he didn't admit it, just played his self-deceiving sorry little role. Chrischana is depleted and sick. He must have been too. Beating up on his own soul while he beat up on her.

Mother and son stand together. He points to the flat. "You sure about driving on that?"

"Gont work, Daniel. But... thanks...." She wants to lean toward him, kiss him, but refrains. "Need a note fah class?"

Still looking at the flat and worried, he shakes his head. He watches her climb into the cavernous car and start the rough engine. The exhaust will go next, he supposes; the muffler.

She pulls slowly from the lot, hazard flashers winking red through falling snow. He watches until they disappear over the rise. How long will she be able to drive that car? Gottheim will never register it. And someday, soon, insurance will be required. He has heard her exclaim over this time and again. Shivering he turns, heads toward the cafeteria door. His feet feel like needles and pins. Heat has seeped out his legs right through his jeans. Daniel is snow all over.

Thumping down the highway at nine miles an hour, Chrischana smells rubber burning. Must be the flapping of my tire, tearing apart. Obscuring snow worries her as she tenses for some hit from behind. Awful smell! It reminds her of those rusting industrial cities they passed through on their way here. What was that stinky place where tires were made? They stopped for dinner and learned that two out of three rubber mills had closed. But you smell them like they were twenty.

The Bonneville 500 limps on, and the white buildings of Gottheim village materialize through the snow. Chrischana glances over at the white envelope on the dashboard. Its return addresses the town office. She picked it up this morning at the post office after breakfast dishes at the tavern. The car clock is broken; no watch to check the time. Late for work.

It will be evening before she gets around to reading the letter, a notice that their camper on the mountain is off code for a dwelling. She will look at Daniel and exclaim, "Our ancestors helped found this place. They laid out lots, surveyed the whole town. Their first cabins had no windows. People pooped in a hole in the ground!"

Daniel will recall that those same pioneer ancestors usurped the land from Abenaki natives... from whom they are also descended. But he won't remind her that land changes hands, that the yuppies are bound to succeed them. Instead he will just roll his eyes.

Known variously as Quakertown, Quakerton, Quaker Plantation, population 600, the entity has a problem it is not equipped to deal with. When Dr. Goodrich opened his plucky little rubber works for other purposes and products, in 19th-century Akron Ohio, it was primed to originate the vast work of filling the nation with tires. The great heroes and builders of a burgeoning industrial economy believed in latex, and iron, and coal. One thing led to another, and they came to believe in rubber tires and steel automobiles. Akron became the unofficial capital of West Virginia when young people from the mountain state filed north to fill the rubber shops of the formerly sleepy canal town. The place boomed with the clank screech roar stench of tire production. Goodrich, Siberling, Firestone and others had adapted the refinement of latex, using a process that combined sulfur, heat and pressure, to produce a substance durable enough to package compressed air. It made for a fast smooth ride when combined with the urgency of an internal combustion engine. The nation was on the move.

Where was it headed? Doesn't the word *progress* suggest some sort of destination? Living in a little handbuilt homestead with goats, acrylics and gouaches, Eloise Patadoe think she knows the answer to that. She thinks it whenever she walks past the dippy road leading to Jasper Mary's Medicine Mile. *We the people want to move. We want to keep going, don't want to stop. We need the illusion of movement in order to avoid recognizing self at a standoff.*

Ooo, I'm into it now.

She is pulling Hetty's milk down, steaming, into the galvanized bucket between her feet. The goaty smell of the Toggenburg nanny pervades her nostrils here in the small house cum barn, but Eloise scarcely notices. She is used to the variegated odor of goats, manure, mash, hay. Lately, her thoughts during such moments of domestic communion have been occupied with the process and marketing of goats' milk, but tonight she's thinking of tires. Having researched rubber and petroleum based tire-making, she is trying to come to terms with the mountainous pile of Ceylon Segar's lot. She keeps her eye on that once tiny patch, spreading now like cancer over terrain once devoted to medicine, cropland, and trees. She keeps her eye on the truckloads that lumber and growl past the corner pasture.

Movement progress industry revolt. It all stems from the desire to maintain comfort, security. Self cannot trust anything else with that job. "See, Hetty," she lectures, "It's because... when we're moving around in cars and dependent on the revolt of the Industrial Revolution for jobs, food, products—that's it! we're codependent!—we can forget that we're going nowhere but smack into the ground. People just don't believe we can grow vegetables! There is no faith in seeds unless they're produced and put to use in factories. Industry is big-busy-noisy-urgent-smelly and important. Something with that kind of heft, movement, and production convinces us that someone is watching out for us. Any big systematic monster— Adirondack Paper! with its network of trucking and trains booming along corpuscles of concrete and steel—any big system is worthy of faith by virtue of movement. *Yahoo!!*" Eloise tilts back to let the word fly.

Free of her load, Hetty skitters to one side, knocking the bucket, but Eloise grabs it before it can spill. The goat turns back her silly ear-winged face, saying, "Na-na na-a-a!"

"You sound like my sister!" It spooks Eloise, hearing Lisa's voice coming from the goat. She shakes her ponytail, smiles her horsey smile, laughing with a noise not unlike the goat's.

The goat barn, which keeps her tiny herd sheltered, is the shell of an old house that once sat a hundred yards up the road. Eloise had it moved when she was building her place in this sloping valley. "Goats live in houses," Eloise likes to say. Her herd numbers eight, with three in gestation. Come spring there'll be kids hopping and bounding. Eloise will laugh continually, watching them bounce. Kids are hilarious: They spring! (And that's why it's called spring).

The Toggenburg goats are rare because they aren't a product of commercial manipulation. We thrive without artificial hormones, vaccines, or extra amino acids to boost protein production. Eloise tells anyone who will listen. Helping to maintain genetic diversity interests her. "I'm one of those sickos who obsess on insignificant concerns like, Are we going to be able to eat in the next century?" (Forgetting her argument against security of a minute ago.)

Her bag painfully full, Marsha sidles up to Eloise who begins pulling milk down into the bucket. When it is full, she sets it on the sideboard where the kitchen used to be. She climbs upstairs in her insulated barn boots to a former bedroom, throws down two bales, clomps down, clasps her hands with finality and says, "That oughta hold ya!"

She turns, opens the door, picks up the milk buckets, steps into the rigid January night: cold with stars, cold with the unknowable vastness of deep heaven. She sets down the bucket and closes the door. "Inhospitable!" She calls to it, looking up. Searching the clarity of the cold multitudes, her eyes widened. Eloise is always surprised by them. "You outnumber the tires!"

She crunches toward the house, a moving shadow on the star-reflecting white; crushing the snow beneath her boots, shivering for lack of her goats' warmth. With her breath frosting her face she wonders about the virtually everlasting fire of stars. "If only we could get Ceylon Segar's tires to you! To the sun! 'Our God is an everlasting fire!' Away with you to a black hole. Turn those smelly black molecules inside-out. Vaporize 'em! Compact 'em to infinity!"

If that patch of Quaker were to come in contact with God.... The only thing to emerge would be Ceylon Segar, maybe unconsumed, but greatly altered. She loves Ceylon Segar—from a distance. She likes to see him gimping along, an animated set of grime with bits of clothes and boots holding it altogether. In small doses she can even take him in proximity: hear him talk, see his malicious yellow holey grin; hear him snicker, snarl and bark. In small doses only. If she had to live with someone like him or read an entire book about him... she would hitchhike to Cuba first. He's got buddies in high places, has ol'Ceylon. They wear suits and live in large gleaming houses and take fact-finding trips at taxpayer expense. They get invited to doings in Washington and eat under crystal chandeliers. And there are *no* tire dumps in their neighborhoods. They have assured the residents of Quaker that their department will make Ceylon told the line. "Our granting him a license will make it easier to control what goes on at the tire dump."

Eloise laughs like Hetty *bah-bah*ing. "Heck, you couldn't even get him to take a bath!"

Eloise admires Ceylon for having his own junkyard dogs in high places. They think they got him on a leash. But Eloise thinks, as does all Quaker and Ceylon himself, that it's the other way around.

Julius Golding was mad as hell. Yet the hell of his imagination is not a fiery place but ice cold. So cold its captive souls can scarcely move. Inert they sit, frozen mad at absolute zero. Not a molecule moving anywhere. Even the atoms stop their dance. Then slowly, ever so slowly, they begin to move again. A... Something, from Somewhere, reaches down. Down to absolute zero. Some... form of warmth, sent by the Absolute in infinite understanding of zero. It penetrates Julius Golding, and he begins to move again. Lately the hand of this warmth has been that of his niece. Amanda's touch has found a crevice somewhere for the sheltering of her warmth to get him moving again. Today he is less mad than yesterday but mad enough, still, at finding himself seated in Wilbur's Bar and Grille, in smelly Guildford, waiting on smelly Ceylon Segar.

This is not Julius Golding's way. His way is to delegate the disagreeable. He considers briefly that the hand of this new warmth, while enlivening him from his standstill, is the same hand that triggered his cold fury in the first place—by asking him to do something that he does not want to do.

Little golden Amanda kneels beside him in the booth, sipping a tall cherry Coke through twin straws. After the initial distaste of their entrance into Wilbur's—greasy smells and armpit odors mingling with those of stale pulp—Julius has been surprised to discover that fountain cherry Cokes still exist. Kids in a mill town in the 1980s can still get soda and syrup from a fountain. She is eating fishwich and fries. Her presence in the place is all that keeps him in the booth, stiff inside but for the presence of Amanda.

He considered his options before agreeing to this. 1. Invite Segar to Jasper Mountain or some other upscale setting in the village. 2. Invite himself to Segar's trailer office at the tire dump. 3. Meet him here—a good twenty-five miles from the resort. No one he knew would frequent this grille. But it is noon; Wilbur's is packed with mill workers—not Golding's favorite crowd. And Segar is keeping him waiting.

Julius has to admit he's not used to it. He has to give the old fart credit for pulling this. Sipping his coffee (the only thing he can bring himself to order), he thinks about that obnoxious term, old fart. Julius has always held it in contempt as undignified and insulting to anyone no matter the circumstance. Yet, it *is* the definitive description of Ceylon Segar. He can summon no other, and now must remind himself to use *mister Cigar* before Amanda. The offending term slipped out once during one of their conversations about the tire dump owner. He has prepared his niece for her first sight of the old man. Or, *is* he old? How does one tell? His eyes have that rheumy look; he's not young by any means, but his age is anyone's guess. Some of the townspeople could tell him but, now that he has surrogates to act for him, Julius no longer has many dealings with them.

Amanda stops sucking her cherry Coke in order to turn toward the back door of Wilbur's. Her gaze points down the hall past the phone. Uncle Julie's eyes have been on the front door but now, her eyes big, his niece whispers, "I think Mr. Cigar's here." He turns to see the old so-and-so coming.

Grinning. A disheveled colorless bundle, lightly iced in snow, its bewhiskered face framed with scraggly colorless hair sticking out beneath a grimy hunting cap. The grin is darkened by deep scary holes. Julius is seeing him with Amanda's dainty sensibilities. The sight of Segar must awe her small experience. Repulse it. She will probably dream about it all night.

He can guess by the man's grizzled grin that he is enjoying himself. He's hit the big time. Doing a power lunch with Julius Golding, an owner of Jasper Mountain Resort. The event will rumor around Gottheim when Ceylon Segar gets through hitting the big time.

Ceylon Segar comes out of the passage, gimping, threading his unsavory way through Wilbur's noon traffic: waitresses with trayloads, people entering or just sliding out of the plastic booths. He looks to either side before focusing on.... *Theya's Mr. Big, fom away, all shiny'n clean. Thinks*

46

he's gont make an impression. Thinks he owns Gott'im now. Hell, he don't even own Jaspa Mountain, thinks he does! Ceylon squints, thinking, what's that he got with 'em? Li'l gul! Jezuz, she's pretty. Like a flower, a buddacup. I get sit across fom her?!

He slides in uninvited across from Amanda, grinning at her, tossing a nod in Golding's direction. The thaw is on: Segar is so ripe that he has changed the temperature around him. Julius Golding smells old tires, old body bacteria.

"This is my niece, Amanda. Amanda, Mr. Segar."

Ceylon guffaws at Golding's glacial decorum, his use of the term Mr. "Just call me Uncle Ceylon, li'l gully!" He lisps slightly. "Amanda? That's a pert name. You put your Uncle Golding up to this, did choo?"

Amanda nods, her eyes like secret pools veiled in ferns and light. Until now Segar has scarcely thought of the niece mentioned over the phone. His thoughts were fused on this good-time opportunity, with a better time to come on its heels. A chance to roll a Golding over the edge has kept him in spirits since the call came. Anticipation kept him awake nights... but now that Amanda is here... things are different.

He looks a question at her. "You that li'l gul walked off Mount Will after that plane crash, year o'two back?"

Again she nods, her eyes silent, round.

"Said an angel walked y'down?"

A nod.

"Whad it look like?"

"Mr. Segar," warns Golding, frowning.

But she replies in a soft voice. "I don't remember." At the time she was concussed, bruised, picking her way down mountain in the aftermath: her mother dead in the crash. There was the light of a lone house near the bottom. It wasn't that far from Medicine Mile and the tire dump. "My sister says I told her it was an Indian."

A skinny redhead comes up for his order. Segar asks for the Hamburg plate and coffee, scarcely noticing the waitress where once he would have chewed her ears off with his pathetic jokes. She walks away scribbling on the pad, wondering whether to be miffed or relieved.

Segar says to Amanda, "If you don't 'member an angel, how do you say theya was one?"

For the first time Amanda moves her gaze off him. Taking her lips from the straw, she rolls her eyes sideways. "Well, you see... first I told my sister on the phone and *then* I forgot."

"She'd hit her head," said Julius.

The waitress is back with hot coffee. Amanda munches her fries, looks at Mr. Segar. She is thinking about the term "old fart." Every part of Mr. Segar looks brown. Even his teeth. "Where do you get your tires?"

Slurping, he smiles at her over the rim of his cup. He likes that piping voice. He has not been this close to a little girl, to talk to, since he was a young man too busy and smart to bother with little girls. He has been a hunter, fisherman , farmhand, woodcutter, mill hand, and treasure hunter. Then his old man left him this land. This time spent with a little girl is like a treasure, a sight from another world. A world where buttercups peek through in January.

"Tires just come. Someone stopped in once, says have a go." He lisps. "Now they don't stop coming. They call me fom all over. Or just show up—with money." He grins slyly at Golding.

Julius feels it time to facilitate the conversation. He has been more than courteous, observing the custom of small talk, avoiding the direct approach. Segar might have closed the conversation on that technicality alone, disappointing his niece. "Amanda is interested in seeing what can be done about the amount of tires on your property, Mr. Seger."

"Zat so?" He is asking Amanda. "How'd you get interested in my tires?"

"Well, we been studying pollution at school. We talk about recycling, paper mill rivers, sludge... stuff like that."

"They talk bout me in school?"

Happy as a child, thinks Golding with disgust. Pleased with the idea of such attention!

"Yes. We saw your picture in the paper. How many tires to you have?"

"Couple billion." He flicked gaze at Golding.

Uncle Julie looked incredulous then incensed.

"Whad they say bout me in class?"

"We wanted to know why you keep tires since it's bad for the earth."

"Whad teacher say?"

"That you did it to make a living."

"Guess maybe!" He cackles, smacking the tabletop with his palm. "Some of us knows how t'make money off land round heah." Again he shoots the look at Golding.

The muscles tighten along the other's jawline. He quells a sudden urge to take Amanda and leave.

From the corner of his eye Segar sees the twitch while his gaze remains on the girl. He cackles more. "Some of us can understand that— having the chance t'make money."

Julius is ready to leave but Amanda is piping, "Uncle Julie'n Uncle Harry understand. They own the ski resort'n make money, haw, Uncle Julie." She turns to him. "That's how you and Uncle Harry do it?"

Julius looks levelly at Ceylon Segar. "That's right, Amanda. We do."

Segar's grin grows. He lisps. "We're businessmen."

It is pointed, perfectly true: They each own land and use it to make money. I've let a trusting little girl lead me into this, with all its potential for humiliation; sitting in a bar and grille in Guildford Maine, the butt of an old fart's fun. Aloud he says, "There's a difference in the service we provide the community." His chin is up, he looks dryly away. He wouldn't have bothered to comment but Amanda has to see the truth.

Segar snorts. "The community? Skiers, fom away—same's my tires. Gott'im gets your taxes, 'sall. State gets mine."

He shouldn't answer, he shouldn't. "We hire hundreds of people from towns around here." Warmth seeps into him. Anger can warm him after all. He looks to see the waitress coming with Segar's hamburger plate, takes a sip of coffee, looks at his watch.

Segar notes these cues without taking his eyes off Amanda. When the woman sets the order down he stabs three french fries sopping them with gravy. He is now ready to tweak Golding with those notorious seasonal service wages... but refrains, recollecting what he pays his own part-time assistant. He has been bitter his lifelong over the low wages he got for mill work, farm work, logging. With this chance to make money on that cutover parcel of his family's he has found it easier to forgive and understand the tightfisted ways of others. He swallows, grinning his dirty yellow grin at Amanda, saying, "Goldings is good bosses."

The jawline of the man sitting across from him rolls again. *I need this old fart's pat on the back, his singing my praise to Amanda.*

The tire dump man continues. "Goldings fit in, if they do be from away. Us businessmen stick together, Mandy. Understand one another, we do. We can talk'n I'd be glad t'heah what pointers your uncle has fah me— t'get my tires unda control. Try's I might, caunt find no markets. Even with that monsta mill sitting out theya." He gestures with his fork toward the window although the paper mill is cut off from view by Guildford's brick blocks. "Theya online t'stot suckin' in tires for that fancy generator... like they suck in the woods to make papah." Ceylon is sore. He has called and visited in an attempt to get them interested, but not a tire dump in the state can sell to Adirondack. Instead, clean chipped tires will come from out-of-state by the trainload. "Think they do business with a 'memba the local community—help us out? They won't even talk't me. Mandy, I got tires enough to keep that generator going donkey's days."

"They're not *part* of the community." Golding says it quickly before Amanda can chirp in with some unthinkable collaboration. "Their headquarters are somewhere in the Carolinas now. They don't care about the quality of life here. Only one mill in the state is even locally owned anymore. If you went to Adirondack corporate headquarters you would see lush landscaping and open, glass interiors. The community there is proud to have the company among them."

A flicker goes through Ceylon's rheumy eyes, as he shifts his gaze from the girl to Golding and back again. He was humbled himself in asking Julius Golding for help and is accorded this compliment of a respectful response. God knows he needs help. He has tried getting a shredder to transform those tires into something marketable but no bank around Gottheim will lend money for fear of liability. What good's a shredder without markets anyway? Ceylon knows next to nothing about researching markets for used tires. He heard there was a market in Saudi Arabia or Africa. Did you just get on the phone to information Jerusalem? Ceylon Segar squirts ketchup over the remains of his gravy slathered plate.

Julius Golding winces but Amanda is delighted. She wipes her mouth on a crumpled napkin, then dusts french fry salt and grease from her small fingers. In silence Golding curses the DEP for licensing someone so ignorant of business, for sanctioning his storage operation before marketing mechanisms were established. Golding takes out a gold filled pen from an inner breast pocket and begins writing on one of Wilbur's napkins. He slides it toward Ceylon's plate but, on an intake of regret, he recollects that Segar might not be able to read. —Yet, the man must be adept at covering it if he can't. He will say something about leaving his reading glasses at home. "Here are the names of two local parties who might be able to steer you in the direction of specific markets. One is a fledgling consultant; the other a group of retired business leaders at the county seat. They volunteer expertise in such matters."

"Gloria Fay," reads Ceylon Segar. "The pipsqueak's family?"

A smile twitches at the corners of Golding's mouth. "She is the developer's sister."

"Gloria is nice," pipes Amanda. "She helped me wrap my Christmas presents."

"Zat so?" Ceylon is mopping the plate with his last fry. He wants to prolong the conversation, sit a while with Amanda but.... They aren't going to speak anymore, pressure him about the tires. They're going to say goodbye nicely and leave him here in Wilbur's without a fight. How does

Golding get anything done this way? Pure money, that's how, but you'd expect more arrogance, impatience, a sense of command.

"Tell you what, Mandy. You'n Uncle Julie come out'n see my ol'tires anytime. Give y'my personal tour. Like that?"

Amanda nods. She looks up at her uncle. "Could we?"

Julius looks down on her open expression. There is ketchup on both corners of her mouth. He takes his napkin and wipes it away. "Maybe when the snow melts in spring." He will regret this when the time comes. Neither Amanda nor Segar is likely to forget. But this meeting has been a way of trying.... Those tires are a menace. God help the old fart.

Time on Jasper Mountain

"How's it going?"

Billy was watching along the line of chairs coming up through shadow cast by Jasper Mountain now that the sun was slipping below the mountain's blue white crown. Billy thought he heard a voice, coming from outside the lift shack and reached over to turn the radio down. He spit a mouthful of tobacco juice into a Coke can, expecting one of the Goldings to pop his head in. Maybe Amanda was here for a chat. But the door opened and there stood a kid he had never seen before. The cold came in with the adolescent—maybe 14 years old, and a blue cinch-waist parka, his ski mask and goggles pushed up under his hood; eyes curiously searching the shack. He shut the door. Billy saw that his skin was clear and crisp, red from the mountain's breath. He looked like a kid newly minted. Like he had never seen a day of trouble, never a night of worry. That his father didn't scramble for a living. His car never broke down at midnight and 30 below.

"How much to ride to the top?" He was sleek and sure as a 40-year-old in a suit.

"Sorry, it's a private lift. Owners don't waunt no one up theya." His cheek was loading with juice again. He reached for the handle to open the door again, but the kid was quick to block it a bit and Billy stepped back. Had to respect the customers. The artist Prince was on the radio, moaning about his pocketful of horses. Billy's lip was full. He reached for the Coke can. Then switching his wad to the opposite cheek said, "What can I do f'you?"

The kid fumbled for the wallet inside his parka. "I want a ride to the top. Doesn't matter what it costs."

"Sorry," said Billy, all patience. His ponytail swished below his ball cap as he shook his head. "Can't."

"Just want to see what's up there." He was thumbing through the wallet, muttering, "Cut through this.... Here." He showed Billy what looked like a new hundred dollar bill. Billy couldn't tell for sure. He had never seen one before.

"Sure," he said pityingly. "Your father must have his own Xerox machine."

"Never mind," said the kid sticking the bill back, thumbing some more. His cheeks had already faded. The shack is the coziest place on earth—phone, heater, radio, insulation, paneling. A view across the Meguntics that won't quit. Billy swore once he saw God's backside up here. His wife Rayona accuses him of imagination. He reads too many books on the supernatural, spends too much time sitting up here chewing on Kodiak. He can get pretty meditative over that grotty Coke can.

The kid was fanning out five worn twenties. "These look real enough, don't they?"

Now he had the man's attention though Billy did figure himself a good and loyal employee. He stuck to the rules of the smooth running resort, but he had other obligations as well. Got to be a good loyal husband and father. In that hand is shoes for the whole family! Shoes and socks for everyone. What about that bill for Sam'n Kelly's mumps? Pay the health clinic, there'd be enough left for a night at the Muzzleloader. *Magnum PI* and the *A-team* were good shows, but he needed more sometimes. *Rayona needs more.*

Billy said, "Once is all y'get." He stuffed the twenties into his jeans pocket, picked up the binoculars to check the lift below. The long blue shadow of Jasper was deepening as the sun sunk rapidly behind. But the seats of the lift continued carrying skiers, emptying one after the other outside under the bullwheel. No sign of ski patrol anywhere. He opened the door for the kid, watched through the window as the boy seated himself on the upper lift.

Aren't the Goldings in Vermont now anyway? It was all hush-hush, rumors always are. He would read about it in *The Voter* any day. Sometime soon he'd transfer out of Gottheim—if he could. Rayona would kick his butt good—too much family here—but Billy liked to daydream of other places, other mountain tops.

Jason ascends Jasper Mountain on the private lift, feeling himself the last man on earth. Looking back at surrounding hills he feels they are his own. He looks down. Any tracks on that snow? None that he could see.

Having a bank account is good for something! Changes have come, I've made changes too. With money you can control destiny. You look into your future and see it all going exactly as you planned. I'm not going anywhere without my bills again. Dad is so guilty he'll see to it. God, guilt is good! All my life it's been used against me. Now I can use it myself. Divorce has its advantages. It's not *all* pain and confusion. Let Mom get hold of this for her support group: Pain is a paying industry.

He is suspended above it all, ascending the bald white head of the best Mountain in the East. *Gnarly!* Imagine owning your own ski resort, your own private lift. The summit is yours any day of the week, the tracks you make might always be *first* tracks. Ascending, the chairlift takes him out of the shadow and now he sees the sun as though rising. He glances back to watch the dark ants sliding down slope in cold blue shadow. The sun has gone down on the other skiers as Jason prepares to take to the summit. With this deepening bright breath of Jasper in his nostrils, he adjusts his goggles and mask. The cable above is silver in sunlight, the ramp comes up, he's off!

He plans to allow himself plenty of time for experiencing the summit before heading back... when it's about dark. That should give Brandon and Mom something to think about. He skates long strokes into the wind, pushing; poking at snowy stiff krumholz where exposed with his skis and poles; looking off across the expanse of surrounding summits. The wind here is unreal! Like knives. Feels like I'm wearing nothing! Is that Mount Washington out there? This summer Dad will have to take me hiking in the White Mountains. Jason had read that there was a network of trails with huts running along those summits out there. This is what divorce is good for: Dad now puts me right into his schedule. We are going to do all the things we couldn't when Dad was too busy. *The office, airports, hotel rooms have seen more of him than I have.*

And it's so good jerking loose Brandon. Can you imagine a grown man named Brandon? Jason had lost his mother's boyfriend on Blissful when he hid in the woods below that second knoll: The man, intent on keeping up, was unaware that the boy had snapped him loose. It was like cracking the whip, sliding into the woods on that curve. Slipping onto the utility trail, one quick stop and Brandon was history. Can she really think I'm going to be buddies with dad's replacement? Work this out in support group, Mom. Be your own woman, just don't expect me to adjust. I don't fit into your meaningless little recreation of a family. You like Brandon so much, *you* babysit him. Total stranger! Total fucking *stranger!*

Jason turns to be pushed back along the pate of the mountain by the wind. Relieved somewhat of its brutality he glides south toward the sun. He has always wanted to see the wild side of Jasper, the mysterious slopes covered in trees, not cut with wide white trails. The trails on the North Side were awesome, but he knows them all now. The great round solitary head has fascinated him from the moment he saw it, riding with Mom and Dad as a little kid. Solid, white, almost perfectly round, rearing above the lesser summits. All the others are low and dark with timber, but Jasper is aloof, ascendant, bright. Like a mountain from ancient history. And I'm here! Right on the lid of the fucking world!

Even so, he is intimidated by the unexpected force and fierceness, the freezing of summit's wind. It is a presence, pushing him, prevailing on him to leave. Up here is no shelter, no place to hide. God he has to get down! He looks at his watch—hard to believe! He's been here only four minutes!

It feels like five too many, but I just can't join that little party Mom has cooked up for me. I'm here to ski, goddamn it! Not bond with some banana. Going to ski all night if I have to. The hills on the south slope.... They're crisscrossed with logging roads, aren't they? Plenty of light once the moon's up, right? Gottheim is just down there back of some ridges. Logging roads lead to the highway. No restaurant is going to have a problem with that hundred. Enough for a room for the night even. He thinks about Billy in the lift shack. Yokel blue-collar was actually chewing tobacco!

Jason stands poised above the steep slope, pierced by the wind, digging in with his poles. The sun sinks toward the hills as he seeks out a likely route down the steep smooth bald slope. *Got to get into some trees fast.* But before he can scope it out the wind sweeps the boy off the summit. Speeding, struggling for control, he goes down, feeling the mass looming over him; rising monolithically as he shifts through his turns over the clean ungroomed powder. The great head gleams on his periphery, golden, now quickly fading to rosy cold. The swift hand of the summit wind has sent him packing without a map.

Jason is glad to be going, going through freshness and the joy of these wading turns. He speeds, blindly now, into the steep intrigue of the mountain's unfamiliar backside, knowing nothing of its territory. This is the adventure of his young life. That bribe of limp twenties has assured him of this absolutely. Here Jason will work through the turmoil and anger of bewildered relation his parents have called down on him. He did not let them tell him go here or there; that he had to accept this or that person in response to their desires. Her only reason is, "This is what I want." Well, Mom, likewise. I will not adjust to him! He will not have to adjust to me.

No way those owners can keep the summit, and the slopes, to themselves, once I tell everyone about this awesome adventure. No way. The clientele demands the whole experience. Southern slopes will provide the next thrill for skiers at this resort.

Down through trackless snow hurtles the boy with these thoughts—but now! There are no turns! It's a straight descent.

—

But in the beginning God spoke. There shall be Time, said God. Time and becoming. After and before. Pastpresentfuture, my riddle being Time. I will clothe Time with things—with particles, elements, creatures, events. Thought and emotion shall fill Time. In Time living things germinate, differentiate, grow. Time will expand and contract according to the movement, size, placement of its bodies and to the measure or interests of its occupying activities.

In Time things will fall and rise; minerals salts gases moisture; species and intelligence, dominions. All things cycle, cycling upward, drifting, falling. But light shall flow straight; yet here and there under certain conditions Time will see light bend. See it sneak around corners, shiver to colors, fall slightly through cracks. Memory and light shall salt the darkness of Time, overtake Time, turning backward and forward. But light shall see Time bend: as great celestial bodies turn, gravity will work out the course of Time. In earth time will be humbled. Forced to creep, weigh and sigh, shudder and weep. But it will pursue with implacable persistence.

In Me Time shall stop altogether.

I let my spheres loose in Time to keep and change its measures. Let gravity layer these spheres; and in some come a layer of life. Earth has magnetosphere, our radiant veil of star-particles; a veil of gas beneath for the protection of Life. Within, we set the veil of our breath. All exchange breath with me in the veil.

But Earth's pith is molten, full of the great power of melting... sulfurous, fulminating, inflamed. The great mantle above moves the crust about, thrusting up from below with tension and verve. Making mountains. Mantle crushes and cramps the earth, forcing edges under again, humbling, fusing and refusing the crust we call earth. Grinding, shaking with terrible violence, the continents heave and slide. Molten heads rise. Rounded, ballooning upward, these Plutons warp and compress the crust.

The energy of the command rises, shaking foundations. At our Word arise the plutons, ascending through layers and bearing unspeakable treasure. Monstrous with bending and folding, burning and pressure, the plutons form forth an array of gemstones, minerals, a catalog of Crystal: Chalcedony Jasper Agate and Beryl; tourmaline amethyst topaz and manifold quartz: there are myriad minerals here.

This! Say the Plutons, *This our treasure and glory! This, our implacable power!*

But these giants lay hidden inside the mountains, in warped, tilted or downturned layers of metamorphism and sediment; guarded and shielded in rock. And Jasper was one of these, a hidden giant, secure. Jasper Mountain patient in waiting.

But without... without move fast climatic currents. In the veil of Breath float a tumult, extremes of hot and cold; down falling, uprising vapors of moisture and air. Cyclic, these powers, whirling and twisting. Hot and cold blowing, drying and drenching, freezing and thawing; great Powers play over crustal surfaces, shaking these faces with Weathers.

Composing tiny crystals, water condensed around specks in the veil. Floating and falling they fill the bright veil; ecstatic innumerable; falling in lightness and blizzard. The Earth darkened, snow fell. Snow fell. Snow fell. Snowfall arched over mountains, sinking them under the burden of white. Ice and earth overlaid what was hidden but the grinding of glaciers wore their covering away.

Time wore, uncovering the hidden. Naked, the Meguntic Mountains emerged. Naked stood Jasper, crystalline and exposed. Bald in his beauty, he was polished and running with rain.

In his cracks seeds gathered, the gymnosperms dying then sprouting, stitching themselves together. Dark evergreen, their lacework gathered on the mighty flanks. They sifted their load of hard seeds. In Time came other plants, less hardy yet enduring on lower slopes, those whose seeds were wrapped in soft fruity ovaries. For the veil moderated to yield a Southern influence. Jasper's great features were fringed and garlanded, softened and green. Leaves sprouted, swaying, glimmering.

From south and westward came many manner of animals insects worms spiders; birds, the fingers of which are filled with feathers. People came, having faces, arms and legs, torsos and hands and imaginings. They gathered hereabouts clustering, clinging together; or sprinkled themselves sparsely. The People lived beneath Jasper. In winter they hunted, sheltering families. In summer they climbed and ate Jasper's blueberries. The People encouraged the berry's seed for its sweet ripe blue fruit, burning patches to renew springing growth. Later came people of another kind to Jasper Mountain, climbing Jasper's knees to set permanent dwellings. They falled his trees, building cabins. They gathered his rocks and turned earth that had collected in the feet of the gymnosperms. These people toiled and stored. Following a period of mutual stress, the two peoples dwelt together; but the first people were thrust to its margins. Yet, in Time, some of each came to share a common descent.

Above them all stood great Jasper Mountain, quiet for the most part, but not ever so. He might gather water from the veil in abundance, flooding them. He might bring snow. He brought aweful wind. Jasper collects storm. The Weather and Mountain colluded, holding their counsel in common. Sometimes they kept the water away.

Even so, over and around People of this great creation was the blessing of God in time. For God said, *Let there be Time!*

And the People answered, "Ever so! (Will it be ever so?)"

There are people who wonder if the trees on the mountain are as glorious as the catalog of its minerals. Beech, popple, hackmatack, four kinds of birch, many of maples; oaks, ash, spruces, four kinds of pine, Eastern white cedar. Robbie Robichaud has purchased stumpage above Gottheim Village on the southerly slope. Alvin and Ansell are up cutting wood, twitching it to the landing. Robbie's gone off down mountain with a truckload of pulpwood, heading toward Guildford. Slowly the landing begins filling with wood again. It is late afternoon. The sun is off behind a ridge, but, in woods above, Alvin thinks he can take a tree or two before Ansell gets back with the skidder.

They'll twitch these back to the yard, jump in the pickup and head down to supper. A long cold day, the woods full of snow, and he can taste Emma's pork chops and mashed potatoes already. Or will they be eating at mother's? He rubs a sore shoulder inside his flannel lined jacket then stoops to pick up the saw, yanks on the starter. Bawling, the blade sprays sawdust as it bites into the base of the tree.

Alvin is just laying out a tall spruce, cracking and thudding, when Ansell arrives with the skidder. They stop for a smoke in the dimming light. Dangling his legs from the cab of the skidder, Ansell gestures. "Who's that coming?" Alvin turns to look up the icy track, still glimmering in the dusk.

Keeping to the crusty side of the track, a dark shape descends, led by a stick. It nears and they make out an old woman in hunting clothes, boots, hat. The pack on her back jostles as though alive.

Alvin says, "Balda's mutha, in't it? She prowls the slopes. Probably got an animal in that pack."

"What she doing with that stick?" Ansell hops down from the cab, calling out, "Gettin'dock ain't it, Miz Simon!"

While still above in the woods coming down, Elda Simon heard the hawing of the saw, the cracking of trees, the rumble of the skidder. She cants her head toward Ansell's call, lets the stick lie still at her side. "Gettin'that wood out'susual, boys?"

"Gut keep up with demand," says Ansell, his square dimpled face breaking into a smile. The ash on the end of his cigarette glows as he drags on it.

"I'd say light's about gone," she says. "Best get on home. Caunt do n'more today, guess."

"I'd say."

The twins agree as one and Elda grins shyly, turning away. The union of their voices has told her exactly who they are.

The brothers watch her disappear into the dusk. "What you suppose she's doing with that stick? It's too long for hiking."

"Looks like she's feeling hah way with it, but it ain't that dock."

"Nevah saw anaone s'wussy'n strong."

Ansell agreed. He knew what was meant. He thought the same of himself sometimes.

They finish their smokes, snap the glowing ends into the snow. Ansell goes to snub up the butt of the spruce with the winch chains. Alvin climbs aboard the burbling skidder, and when his twin returns to the cab it's a tight fit but they ride down together.

Elda stands by the track, careful to give the heavy trailing spruce berth as they pass. Enduring the roar and jingling of chains she feels the length slide by. The sound of the diesel recedes in the distance and she is left alone. Elda Simon depends on her ears more and more. One morning, she woke up to realize that the dark spot in the exact center of her vision was not going away. But, if you have to get by on peripheral vision.... You do, that's all. It wasn't that hard to hide the fear, to panic and mourn secretly in the barn with her wounded and ailing wild animals. She can cry all she wants in the now-not-so-familiar woods. You get used to doing everything patiently and subtly, with secret care. Can't have just everyone knowing that she is legally blind. In fact, she'd like to avoid admitting it to herself so there's no sense bothering anyone else with it. They might try to—Balder has enough to do learning to be a father, trying to get the house shaped up. Caunt stand to have that kind of attention anyway, don't want'em looking at me, thinking about me, wondering what in the world he will do with a blind mother. Maybe I can even continue getting by with driving in daylight if I need to.

She wishes now that she had paid better attention to that reading she did last summer on diseases of the eye. Or remember it better. Did it say that macular degeneration took the whole of sight eventually? Maybe she can use a magnifying glass to help her in reviewing the material?

Geez Louise! Being able to pick up a book and just read! She mourns that loss terribly. Try as she might—how precious that fine, precise, detailed concentrated sight! It was hers all her life... till now. She failed to recognize how sublime good vision is. Not until it fled back to heaven, leaving her dimmer. God gave it for a span of time, taking it back before her own span is done. Light and time—not given for ever.

Elda feels her way down with the stick. She guesses, if time and vision don't coincide... you just do what you can. Gory! *It's dark.*

Many lights glitter on Jasper's northern knees, like tiny gold stars fallen in darkness. Condominiums cluster below his strong glimmering flanks, their lights a'shimmer, twinkling here and there among black boughs as though some of his glory has been unearthed. Within the scattered glow, many lives advance through time.

In one of the tasteful townhouses, a pretty white and auburn woman makes up her face while, remotely, on the other side of the mountain, a teenager is lost on its subarctic margins. But Time is not ripe yet for his mother's concern. She thinks that Jason is due in with Brandon after hitting the slopes this afternoon. The slopes, she notes, are expensive this year. With painstaking care she studies her face in the dressing room mirror lined with special lights. With a flick of the switch its lighting can be changed depending on what type she plans to be seen in, whether daylight, office, or evening. It's early still, but evening is preparing. The romance of candleglow waits. The cheekbones can use a touch more blusher. She picks up the brush.

Is that the tinkling of a key in the lock downstairs? They must be returning now. Jason will be more than happy to stay here and watch TV, maybe order pizza, ask a friend. He won't want to go to the Gemstone Restaurant with them. Adult conversation in candlelight bores him. Everything bores him now... so silent lately, sullen. Brandon certainly doesn't please him. Must face it, deal with it. Give it the attention it deserves.

...Maybe the afternoon on the slopes did something?

Brandon calls from the living room. She'll find out now. Her fingers crossed, Jason's mother stands up, surveying herself in the brown satin slip. She dips a bit to check that the highlights are just about right.

Gottheim Village has gathered close about the mountain's feet, so close that Jasper's cold bald head is cut off from its view. Slopes of conifer-covered rock rise darkly in mystery above the little New England village. The eyes of the village glow in its houses gathered below. Lights in the schoolhouse are lit for night classes. They glow also in the back room of the fire station where Boy Scouts are scheduled to meet, and in the hall of the Knights of Pythias, and inside village churches where prayer meetings and Bible studies take place. The village points heavenward its steeples, glows with street lamps, treads carefully where its sidewalks glare ice.

Here tonight Chrischana Twitchell will reaffirm her particular faith—which a more secular tongue might call life-style. She slinks into a back pew of the bare little church, just as the last bong of the tower clock sounds overstreet at the Congregational Church. Seven o'clock, and this little mongrel denominational service promptly begins.

Will you turn in your hymnals, asks the gangly young pastor of her scattered congregation. Holding the book in her confident right hand, she lifts her left and begins waving out three-quarter time. Her body is angular, long, moving unevenly. Pastor's energetic face makes up for the awkwardness of her form. Chrischana takes this in as she watches her from the back pew, singing. She feels for this lost soul, valiantly waving on the plain wooden dais beside the lectern.

What prompted her to attend service tonight? Rising from the supper table, in a moment she decided. "Anaone fah prayer meeting—get ready."

"I'm going to Boy Scouts," proclaimed Benaiah.

"I got rehearsal tonight!" chimed Nathan.

"Mr. Nutting's gut proofreading on the Linotype for me," Daniel reminds her.

"Well, let's get these dishes done." It's a command. "We can all meet at The Voter when we get done—if you think you'll be more'n an hour o'two, Daniel." That said, they got to work in their little apartment on the second floor of a large subdivided Victorian Gothic not far from the village center.

Chrischana has not been to church since the funeral of her mother, Hattie Trueman Twitchell, an Abenaki Native who died in the early 1960s when Chrischana was an adolescent. Prior to that they would bump down the mountain together, leaving father to his westerns and police shows. Reception up there was the best in town, and father had his own battery-operated television which he kept in juice by driving around with the 12-volt in his pickup. Besides the gossip and occasional bickering, the only complaint mother had about church was that the ministers from seminary were continually reassigned. New ministers of the Gospel were rotated fresh out of school, enthusiastic, but lacking a long intimacy and deep commitment to a single parish. Thus there was no possibility of a long-term emotional investment in Gottheim. They came, ministered, and left the community just as parishioners were beginning to feel a bond, exhibit budding trust. The loss was painful and somewhat humiliating. Mother said people couldn't shake the sense that they were being practiced on; that they were just a link in the chain of advancing careers.

The hymn ends and pastor is saying, *Please turn with me to Mark 14:3*, where she begins reading and interpreting in strong contralto: A woman comes in where Jesus is eating to break an alabaster box of spikenard over his desert-dry head. She proceeds to work it into his scalp with her fingertips. Why was this waste of such substance made!? It could have been sold for 300 denarii to support the poor!... But.... *She has come beforehand to anoint my body for the burying.* He says she will be remembered for this.

Sitting on a hard pew in the bare, plainest of the little churches beneath Jasper Mountain, Chrischana thinks, *That is so.* I have remembered her story ever since hearing it as a child.

After the woman wastes her precious ointment on Jesus, the one who objected went out to sell his betrayal. Well, what do you think of this story, this record of Christian experience?

Somewhere a telephone is ringing...in the pastor's office A woman sitting by the doorway slips out.

No one seems to know what to make of the story. Most of the members of the sparse congregation look not at one another nor even into their own minds for the answer. They look at the young Rev., waiting for what she will say about this expense. Why would he want his body anointed while it was still vital, alive? Death's maybe around the corner but it's not here yet. Maybe, says pastor,—did it really have anything to do with a concern for what would happen to his flesh in death? Remember what he had said about the body, the temple.... So, maybe it had more to do with the woman herself. Remember she was distressed.

Chrischana admits to herself it seems likely. She smiles: It certainly wasn't to make herself famous. The ointment stands for everything costly. She might have had a healing massage for herself with it... or used it a little at a time on her lover, or waited for a child to become ill. Maybe she could have sold it to buy a house! Chrischana has been thinking about building her own on the mountain, Blackwell Mountain, considering practical designs, economy of building materials. Something she might build with her two hands.

Jesus was concerned for the woman's well-being, says pastor. Her eternal well-being.

A woman approaches the dais from the doorway, a scrap of white paper in her hand. Pastor walks slowly to one side, takes the note. She looks at it, tucks it into her pocket saying, The woman believed Jesus when he said I won't be here much longer. I may be gone in a few days, Peter.

But the disciples didn't take this seriously. They just didn't get it. *I won't be here*. Anything you do for me is a waste. I'm going to die—Andrew, James, Thomas.

Pastor walks back toward the lectern. Even way back of the hall Chrischana hears her heels clicking on the wooden floor. But now pastor moves beyond the lectern to the opposite side of the dais.

Oh no, Lord. It won't happen. You're not going to die. (Not us either, Lord; we're not going to die.) There's time yet. We don't need to pour ourselves out. We've got important things to do, a kingdom to establish. You can't waste your existence, squander yourself as though time were ending. It's all coming together, they threw down their palms and their cloaks and you're going to rule. See how they adore you? It's your kingdom! Isn't that what you've been telling us?

In the excitement of the disciples' vision, pastor's voice rises. She's been walking back and forth, building to her punchline. Now she stops in her perambulations of the dais, silences the light sound of her heels. Her face glows with the glory of the story she's telling. The thought of it makes her happier than she's been all week. Her angular, animated body, with its ungainly spidery gestures, has focused the little congregation.

Her voice falls.

(Almost whispering.) *No*. Peter, you missed it entirely.

She turns and walks back to the lectern, grips it square in her hands saying, *This woman with her spikenard was just like Jesus*: squandering what was costly, healthful, fragrant. *On someone who is going to die.*

Pastor stops again. She looks at them, quietly. *Who* is going to die?

She steps quietly back, letting the question resonate.

Now she says, "I have just been handed a note, requesting prayer, from the mother of one of the ski patrol. A storm is on its way, and they are out on the mountain after a lost child. People let us pray."

There is always something to learn or rediscover. Tonight some will risk injury, exhaustion, exposure or death in an effort to discover what has been lost.

Away from the village, and along the stretch of back roads silvered in ice and snow, an old meetinghouse is one quarter full of society members meeting to rediscover a piece of the history of Gottheim. They meet once a month to hear lectures, see presentations, and discuss the esoteric and local past. Of course, members are always glad for the attention of people from away provided the setting is formalized and removed from the threat of encroachment. What after all can a stranger do to influence history? Yes, you can bring on the bulldozer and topple a sagging hundred-year-old spool mill, but what can you do to Uncle Ned Robertson's account of the night Amos Twombly burned his ferry on the 'Rossy River? We have memory, written in documents, photographs and mulled in conversation. Remembered. Asa Bartlett thinks of these things when he extends invitations to interested outsiders.

Asa is town historian, one of many. Everyone in Gottheim holds at least a little town history, unconsciously or not, guarding it with sharp eyes and devastating tongues. "What's gossip, anaway, but history?" He said this to Gloria Fay with a straight face when she inquired about the Society.

The young woman has been a Gott'im wannabe most of her life. She's from away, and what you'd call monied. Along with her parents, who are Evangelical Baptist Christians, and brothers and sisters, she has been coming here to ski since before they bought one of the first condominium townhouses on Jasper Mountain. He's in insurance or investments or pawn shops or something, down there somewheres about Boston; the mother, they say, is a study group facilitator for women interested in applying Bible principles to their lives and marriages. Asa's wife, Olive, tells him that she assumed this career once her five children were well on the road to worldly success. Gloria is the baby, and, when she buckled down to the business of living, she began doing very well. However, Olive will soon be avid to report, this new life of Gloria's may not be exactly what her parents would have desired.

Gloria acknowledges to herself and to anyone interested that she is no longer a believing Baptist. The new sources of her power are a little more obscure. The range of her ideas is inspired now by the invigorating belief that she can be or do anything her imagination conceives. There's no stopping this one. Like any missionary, she's determined to inspire her newfound neighbors with the vision. These Gott'imites are in need of her youthful can-do spirit. With her education, talent for organization, and interpersonal skills, Gloria and Gottheim are going places together. She tells herself this in the morning when she looks in the mirror, toothbrush in hand. She nods confidently, grins. And just being with her, seeing her beauty bright, listening to that melodious conversation, you begin to share in her confidence. This go-getter is not going to leave you behind. Even the ghastly grotty Ceylon Segar, with whom she has plans for consultation next week, will benefit from this talent... if she can get Daddy's help. Networking is at its best when it's all in the family.

Seated in their midst and interested, Gloria's presence gratifies the local historians. She is eager to hang onto these words of what happened to who, and when. She is also delighted to be networking with them: just what is needed to cement the influence of her committee for the renewal of

Gottheim. (Once known as the committee for Gottheim's alternative to IICE. The international Institute of Coordinated Experiments was poised to withdraw its regional headquarters last year, but has since been persuaded to remain in Gottheim. Town leaders are, ambivalent but for the most part, relieved.)

Another reason to be here tonight is that suggestion made by the best person in her life, Balder Simon. Long ago, last summer in fact, he suggested she talk to Asa Bartlett about the origin of the town's name.

Asa is now seated behind a table before the little group in the wainscotted meetinghouse, clearing his throat. His crewcut brick red hair glistens in the soft overhead light of electrified wrought iron candelabras. "Now that the business end of the meeting's over, it's time to welcome Gloria Fay. Please stay fah refreshments'n sociability after the meeting, Miss Fay." He looks her in the eye, gesturing toward the refreshment table.

"Tonight we gont hear fom Olive Bahtlett on some local'n Maine history of dowsing; and she's got stories of her own t'tell. Some o'you might know she's got considerable experience with the craft we know as water witching."

Asa and the secretary, Elsie Roberts, stand and move into the audience. His wife, a large woman, sways toward the table with a sheet of yellow legal paper clutched in her red-painted fingertips. She sets the paper on the table beside her, positions it nervously and with care, then with a hesitant smile launches into her talk.

"Some o'you know that I help people find water. I show'em waya to dig that well they might be wanting when they go t'build. 'S'really simple t'do. And how I got stotted was watching someone else—about thirty years o'go—when my brother built his house. Didn't really believe in it at the time. Tried it out as kind of a joke. Fact is, I must o'done it twenty times fah I even stotted t'believe it. After, that well, I recognized I could feel it working. I could find water evah time, and that's why I stotted t'believe."

Hesitating still, she glances down on her paper, straightening it with her polished fingertips. Now Gloria notices the y-shaped stick lying on the table beside Olive.

"People waunt know what I mean when I say—that I recognized the feel of it. Well, I could just feel it—pull. You take a forked stick—like this yellow birch." She picks up the stick, gripping it palm upward, by the forks, in either hand. "You just go along like this till you feel it pull." Olive walks toward the door, holding the stick up, an inverted y. She turns back, walking toward the window. The point of the y starts turning downward. She stops. "When you're just learning, go slow—because you don't know what you're looking fah. After while y'get to recognizing this pull. The closer you get to the vein, the more it pulls down. Theya's a vein right heah. Unda the floor."

She relaxes the stick and sways back to the table where she deposits it in order to resume her talk. Looking at it, Gloria is mystified. Just an ordinary twig?

"People ask what causes it. Nobody knows. It's not the stick itself— cause you can use anything. A coat hanger, two metal rods, a plummet, most any kind o'twig. I think it's in a person's body t'begin with. Not Evahbody can do it. Maybe it's like ESP—only some have more, some less."

Gloria is leaning forward, listening intently to this large plain speaking motherly woman. She imagines her with a houseful of grandchildren, the aroma of cookies wafting through quaint rooms.

Olive continues. "Onct give me the spooks—a couple years ago when I was at a friend's house (this was Brunhild Kenniston on Grover's Pond). She mislaid her wedding rings. I, joking, says, 'want me find them?' And she says,'witch fah my rings?' 'Cuss,' says I (but joking like). Well we went through the house'n long the dooryard with my forked stick—out on the sand by the brook, me thinking about the rings, the stick pulling. When it pointed straight down, she dug that sand away with hah fingers and theya was the rings right in that sand." Olive's smilelines deepen. "She looks at me s'funny. Just stared, putting on those rings. She said, 'You're a witch!' Jezuz, was I spooked! We both were."

Gloria is fascinated, but now sighing and leaning back against her chair. Olive continues, telling about old-time dowsers in Gottheim, and finishes with novelist Kenneth Roberts' curmudgeonly defense of the art.

Olive takes her seat and Asa returns to the table saying, "Anaone waunts see a demonstration of Olive finding water, sign up afterwards'n we'll call you come spring, next time someone wants a well done. If theya's n'questions, we'll have refreshments tonight from Sarah Harrington and Lorna Thibodeau."

Eagerly Gloria waves her hand. "Ms. Bartlett, would you equate this unique talent with the intuitive arts such as musical composition, dramatic arts, painting and so forth? Don't you think they are all somehow related?"

"No, I don't."

The young woman slumps a bit, deflated. Asa looks around for more questions and, seeing none, indicates the refreshments. Conversation begins slowly, as members stretch and stand. Two woman begin uncovering refreshments, Gloria rushes over to Olive, complimenting her talk and promising to signup for a demonstration. She peppers the older woman with questions about the sensation of dowsing and then gets down to what's on her mind. "Have you gone on to widen the variety of things you search out with your stick? Have others come seeking guidance on lost people or things?"

"Oh no. That's not something I'd be interested in. I just look fah water. Theya's nothing betta'n water t'find. That's enough."

"How much do you charge for your service?"

Olive laughs. "Don't. Oh, I get my gas money if it's much out o'town. People just give me whatever they feel. Sometimes I get deer meat, a bag o'something fom the garden, maybe a meal. Occasionally I get maple syrup."

"But you must *do* something with this. You could develop it to benefit all kinds of searches. Think of the pain you could ease. Could you find lost pets, do you think?"

"Gory, no. They'd have t'be dead, wouldn't they?"

"—Mrs. Bartlett, I could put you in touch with a group of women who are interested in developing these kinds of psychic pursuits. They've been sort of feeling their way toward a new worship of —a new kind of worship that's really old. There are ancient rites and the creation of sacred space, and the... invocation of the old goddesses.... I know these women would welcome you and be very supportive in helping you develop—"

But Olive's expression has changed from motherly humor to open horror. "Oh no." She shakes her head emphatically, but then remembering her manners says thank you very stiffly. She turns away, moving quickly toward the coffee urn and doughnuts. Gloria watches her go with regret. *That's pretty clear*! She sighs over the waste of talent. The sting of rebuff evaporates as she considers alternative ways of approaching Olive. At last she discards these, believing that Olive is too old and set in her ways to except new practices.

Spying Asa, she recalls the question of Gottheim's naming. The older bespeckled man is pouring himself a cup of coffee as Gloria approaches. She picks up a styrofoam cup. "Will you leave the spigot open for me, Mr. Bartlett?"

"Cuss!" His eyes are merry behind his horned rims. Olive has hissed Gloria's strange proposal to him just moments ago as they met beside the home-fried doughnuts. He was shocked of course, in a small way, but Asa finds Gloria refreshing. He enjoys the engaging minor false moves she commits from time to time. If she were 55 or 60 and tried these things he would be sour and mocking, telling details all over town. But Gloria is simply glorious; and he loves these morsels to chew on with Melviny or somebody in front of the post office. Gloria dated Balder Simon a while back but nothing came of it. That was interesting because Balder is such a smart boy, good with his hands and a Vietnam vet. Used to be a mechanic at the chair factory and she is this upscale beauty from away, hooked up snug with IICE and the Jasper Mountain resort. "Ain't that odd!" people said. And Asa was curious as hell about that relationship. He could almost feel his ears twitch forward now as she sips at the coffee he has poured for her.

She says brightly, "Balder Simon said *you* were the one to ask: Just *how* did Gottheim get its name? Apparently he thinks you can tell it better than he can. Guess that's why you're the historian!"

Asa's gaze just glows on her. Oh those blue eyes. Lashes all black against good skin. Ain't it a wonder—how her skin stays golden all winter? Interested in local history too!

"Doaw," he says modestly. "But Balda Simon probably don't know it well enough to speak."

"It was Farmingham Royal to begin with, I know that much. What happened?"

They step away from the urn to let others near, Asa finishing his doughnuts, Gloria sipping her coffee. When the meeting first started the room was still a bit stale and cold. Now it is warm and filled with the comforting aroma of coffee and sweets as Asa begins.

"Farmingham Royal came from the French and Indian wars—as the town was granted to descendents o'the veterans o'the battle of Port Royal Canady. The young men out of Farmingham, Mass'chussets took ship'n sailed to Nova Scotia, once called Acadia, which was held by the French at the time. Sacked the place. A few generations later—after badgering the legislature'n still hadn't got paid fah the job—theya descendents finally won a grant o'land in the wilderness of the District of Maine (being a province of Mass.). They called it Farmingham Royal in honor o'that battle'n the place they hailed fom. Gott'im wasn't decided on till come time t'incorporate. That's when they wanted something gut a li'l more sound to it, high sound."

"God's House! Guess that's high enough. But why the German? Why not Hebraic or Hellenic or something? Weren't the Classics big back then?"

"This was more of a popularity contest between two Gott'im fathers. One thought the biblical Luz was the ticket, tother wanted Gott'im in honor of his ancestors' origin. He was town clerk'n his name won out. He turned out to be a rascal. Even five years after, when he done his dirty deed, they'd got so used t'the name, they'd f'got it was him chose it... till the man whose name lost out reminded 'em."

Chuckling, Asa picks up his second doughnut, waiting for her to prompt him. He loves a show of genuine interest.

Her eyes widened over the rim of her cup. "Was he an adulterer, an arsonist? A horse thief—maybe a lunatic!?"

"Worse. He absconded with evah nickel o'tax money."

"God!" She is gratifyingly astonished. "How'd it happen? Did anyone see it coming?"

Asa shakes his head. "Apparently even his wife knew nothing about it. She nevah left, due to straightened circumstances. She did have the fine house, fust house in town t'have real glass panes, but she had t'take in boarders, husband gone t'New Orleans."

"Wow. How'd they find that out?"

"He died aboard ship heading north after three years. Some thought he was on his way home to repent. Others said he was gont New York to hide theya."

"*What* a story!" She crows as if the theft of funds from poor settlers were some sort of entertainment now that it's old stuff. She's visualizing a four seasons resort brochure with blurb of this history in pictorial detail. What luck to be able to add a touch of the rascal and the risqué—New Orleans?—to the otherwise puritanical atmosphere of this New England village. "Mr. Bartlett, you have made my day! I suppose the clerk's house is gone now?"

Highly gratified, Asa nods. "Lost in a fire. Oh we're full o'good stories. Come back'n heah s'more!"

The high beams of Balder's pickup light the icy highway on his way from work to the little village huddled at the snowy feet of Jasper Mountain. A trucker's lights shine impatiently in his rearview. Balder eases up a bit on the gas just to give the trucker something to think about before returning to his bemused thoughts on the divided heart of Gloria. In her ritual of distraction will she be seeing someone new tonight? Her dreary serial sensualism is chilling to him. Will she ever open to the possibilities of the vast mysterious continent of love? He believes in a territory yet to be explored... to which we have no access nor any knowledge of except through the care of children. There is treasure here: the treasure of sexual ecstasy and its offspring. It is what he desires of their union, nothing more nor less.

The glare of his rearview recedes to a glow. Balder pours on a little more gas. Now, into the last curve lights of the Village begin to show.

But he thinks of the nearer problem, of an older lonely woman, bereft of her husband and apparently now losing also her sight. Although...

he's sure she still has sight. He is more worried about Elda than he ever worried about anything except his own sanity. And she thinks she's putting one over on him.... And that Daniel doesn't know, either. She's wrong both places. They've each seen her stumble enough to know the lights are going out. Mother evades their hints like some little old fox but—till now—has not been pressed on the point. She'll do damage in the barn one day, or fall down a cellar hole in the woods, anything. But Balder has a surprise for her after supper. Tonight he's going to take her in hand, literally.

Grabbing hold of her arm he announces it, suddenly, after the meal. "Let's go fah a li'l ride, Mutha!"

Elda was shuffling toward the kitchen with empty plates in her hands, careful as anything. The clock on the mantelpiece chimed 7:30. They've been eating in front of the television, watching the NewsHour. Surprised by his unexpected touch, she veers. "Got dishes," but she's unable to pull away.

"I'll do 'em when we get back." He takes the plates from her hands, goes to the sink to get them soaking.

"Gut check the animals." She heads for the coat rack.

"Hold on theya sweet woman!" He lets loose the dish liquid, stepping to block the door. Light gleams off the darkened pine cupboards. Once this kitchen bustled with the controlled chaos of family interaction in the calling of one another's bluff. On hearing these words, Mother stops dead. She has not heard anyone say *Hold it theya sweet woman*, since Everett used it on her. Try as she might with various subtleties he was not one to be gotten around when confrontation was due. You had to face up to him and make your case. Surprised—hearing these words out of his son. He sounds like Everett! Everett Simon was a man quiet around strangers, a farmer among other things, adapted to the silences of woodland and field. Following the death of his own father it was that full-bodied silence which brought the quiet sense of his sovereignty into the household. Elda never allowed herself to resent it. One body can't be ruled with two heads. She reasoned thus with her own urge to rebel. And in those days the culture agreed with her. Or, maybe, she agreed with it. Consciously seeking not to challenge its assumptions. Either way, their household enjoyed unity and peace in consequence. After a straightening period of adjustment Elda enjoyed this unity herself. She came to enjoy Everett like she enjoyed the use of her own fingers. He was a part of her as though of her own body. The ache of phantom pain, brought on by his loss, has never left her.

Balder's *Hold on theya, sweet woman*, brings it all back. For an instant she looks hard at him but finds only that annoying dark spot where his face should be. Her glance slides away. Elda says, "Well, if you want it that bad...."

She hesitates, off balance and unsure. Is he going to tear into her about this? But suddenly... she is quietly taken with the thought of spending time alone with Balder on the dark road. Having some of his attention without his usual preoccupation. A ride folded in darkness with him might even be nice. Turning her head slightly, she grabs for her coat. The heavy rough feel of it comforts her touch.

Again the unexpected. Balder takes hold of the coat and helps her into it. Now she understands. Balder knows. But then again maybe she's wrong here, too. —Wrong about so many things. Always has been and only lately understanding it.

"Well... okay, Sarge." She grins mischievously, letting herself be handed out the door. He was a Sergeant—impossibly young Sergeant—in Vietnam; leading men to safety, leading men to death.

But Balder gives no sign that he has received this as a thrust. She does such things unconsciously, only recognizing the implication once the damage is done. She makes her criticisms inadvertently. But surely just the same.

The front end of the pickup is heavy with the plow he packs in winter. Balder picks up extra money plowing out driveways. At night the lights can trouble and confuse her, yet she keeps her gaze ahead, sensing Balder is looking her way. As the truck turns out from the Village onto the highway, he exclaims: "Look't that! Lights on Jaspa Mountain!"

"What, where?!" She turns toward the dark giant, dark as usual but with glimmerings faint and high above.

"Those lights up theya y'nevah see lights on Jasper—less someone's lost.—Oops, gone now." (The lights.)

"So cold out! Imagine being up theya on a night like t'night. suppose'd storm, too. No night t'be up theya."

"Deadly night." He shifts into third, shifting conversational course as well. "Mutha."

"Yuht."

He hesitates, uncharacteristically. He will seldom hesitate in speech once he has made up his mind to speak of something. He states all, plain and directly as possible. Now he starts again and goes right to it. "Mutha, I'm taking you to the health clinic. You ah going blind—stumbling and looking at things cockeyed. I don't think you should be driving, d'you?— and I'm not letting you go on like this. I got an appointment fah you."

The Gottheim health clinic is open some evenings to allow appointments for those who can't get off work other times. They also have sliding fees based on income. There are meetings for substance and domestic abuse, a room with therapeutic equipment, even a babysitter for the children of patients. Two doctors, physician's assistant, nurses and a counselor provide professional services. But Elda has always resisted setting foot over that threshold.

The pickup is silent except for the steady sound of its engine, the whispering growl of tires switching from pavement to icy patch and back again. Balder begins thinking maybe he's got her now. That just maybe she will submit. He has made his point and stance impossible to resist.

Comes a small voice from the huddled bundle in a corner of the cab. "I'm not going," it says.

"Yes you ah."

"No."

"You ah! We'll be in the pocking lot."

"No." The voice has retained its small steadiness.

"Why not?"

"It won't do no good."

Balder is tired. He was in the bleachery today. Head to foot in protective plastic, soaked in sweat—January. Four hours he was there, working on valves in that suit.

His lapse allows her to continue, slowly. "I read about this disease. Theya in't no rebuilding those cones at the back o'my retinas, Balda. Theya's a hole in the middle of my sight'n no amount o'knitting's going to put them back together. I can see t'get around a'foot, but I'll give up driving... if you say."

Balder is considering. "You sure about this—caunt be treated?"

"Certain. 'N I already faced it. You can too. Just caunt see cranking all that machinery they got in them offices today. I can see—it's called legal blindness. The worst is over now, I'm used to it." This is not quite true, but it is true enough. It will have to do. She will let him ask around if he wants—find out for sure for himself that the damage is limited to direct sight... and then she'll know it too. But she will be no invalid, not occupied by this ailment any more than she must be. Its gods twilight—like in the stories. She will find life, now, in the moving mist. She will live this tale.

Balder has been driving around, wanting to break the bad news to her with his talk before going straight to the clinic. Now they keep on though the road is icy and dark and steep walled with towering pines. The cold of January seeps in more than the heater can handle. The cracking cold of winter dark is with them in the Western Maine mountains. The man's thoughts are now on those searchers, roaming the awful heights with powerful beams of light. Someone is lost. No one would be up there if it weren't so. No one brings light where it's not needed. Light goes where it will help.

The boy made his blind leap into the screaming breath: airborne in sudden terror of the white wall beneath, a headwall already dimming in earth's shadow beneath his flying skis. The awful height of this headwall in taking off its pluming brow—surprised him. The approaching slope was no mere slope but the great white wall of a cirque carved in the wasting of the last glacier. Yet Jason had no thought for the formation of mountains. The cirque was an almost vertical drop, taken with reckless but wrenching skill. Afloat in taking it, *Jason The Defiant* found himself schussing the headwall, streaking the holy white veil a gash from top to bottom. He screamed. And the breath of Jasper screamed back: Like an aggrieved old woman, or squaw (he thought), burning through the ski mask and swallowing his own scream out of his face. The initial terrifying moments of his long descent expanded to hours. The thews of his legs felt as though they were ripping to ribbons in the scarcely controlled glissade down the mountain. What seemed hours compressed to a moment as the basin of the cirque came up to meet him, forcing Jason relentlessly toward a dark crust of trees. At the last moment he whirled away, tracking northward, fiercely flailing with skis and poles.

The small grade slows him and Jason stops. He leans on his poles, stunned with relief, with the weakness of a great gratitude. He slips backward a bit, his legs trembly, exhausted.

Made it!

He looks up at it, thinking, *I made that fucking headwall!* Joyfully the words replay themselves, cleansing him of terror.

I'm alive on the backside of Jasper Mountain!

Looking at the scarcely glimmering height, he is thrilled. Shadow surrounds him but the headwall soars monolithic and crystal white.... Pure, he thinks.... Holy! The high top of the great curving wall, maybe 500 ft. in height, shows plumes of snow lifting like swirling veils off its mysterious rim. Listening he hears these winds conversing, speaking with the mountain, roaring. This is the fierce face of God. Never will you forget its awful aspect.

Its appearance is sublimely remote and disinterested but its impression upon him is personal. Digging in with his poles, Jason is filled with the thought of it... yet...vaguely aware that the great headwall thinks nothing at all of him. He is tiny—minute—beneath the vast purity of this mighty circular wall.

Where did you come from? Why didn't anyone tell me you were here?

But this immanent place will give him no answers. He feels the cold here as a burning and lets his gaze fall. Now he looks around. Shadow is deepening, light fading fast, seeping out of the great encircling snowy bowl.

He turns his back on it, facing the long dark arms of the woodland, set there as though a bar to his escape. Conifers, scattered nearby, seem to cower in this piercing wind. They are ancient, scrawny and bent. Jason glides down toward the dark ranks and finds the wall of conifers breaking. He enters into their shelter. Now he stops briefly to turn and glance backward at the great sudden source of his awe and predicament. He turns back, glides on.

Slowly, finding his way, he skis deeper into the wind-breaking arms of bent spruce. He finds deepening dimness and shoves his mask and goggles up under the hood of his parka in remedy. It seems an age since he handed those limp twenties to the tobacco chewing lift-shack man. The eerie wind roaring high above upon the headwall sounds. He shivers, moving slowly among the trees, the sweat of his turmoil chilling him. Shivering, shivering he seeks a way down.

Find a good logging trail... something white, smooth.... Then it wouldn't take long to ski down into Gottheim. There's bound to be a light from some chalet or other. Something will show when I get past this scrub. *God! it's cold!*

He stops among the close branches to take off a glove and feel inside his parka for something to eat. Before leaving the condo after lunch he slipped a few fruit rollups into his pockets. Now he rips at the wrapper with numbing fingers, fumbling; tears at the cellophane with his teeth. The dried fruit will sugar him slowly, restoring warmth and encouragement.

Night has fallen, his eyes acclimating. The temperature on the slope is dropping even as stars appear in branches above him. Chewing, he moves on, his skis turning through the narrow crooked ways. The boughs up here are heavy with smoothly sculpted snow forms. Some other time he would be fascinated but now he cares only for the twisting trail on which he finds himself. Maybe it's a trail the deer make in summer. Or maybe it's no trail. He must keep moving, moving, following gravity's lead. The roar of the headwall is muted now but still pursuing. Their thunder erupts at the tips of his skis as, startled, wild wings graze past. He slips; but snowy arms of spruce keep him upright. Wild himself, he hurries on.

After a bit, on second thoughts, the presence of the gamebird has reassured him. Jason admits to himself that being up here alone is stressing. If even Brandon were here now! The guy's not such a jerk, really. Just an intrusion. *Maybe he can't even help it.*

Knowledge that there are creatures on the mountain with him comforts, but in the dark he misses much: the three-footed track of the varying hare, the lacework of the deer mouse's threading tail under his long artificial feet. Coyote and bobcat tracks cross, telling the tale of animal interaction.

After a long struggle among the trees he finds.... The problem with this deer track...or whatever—it's not going anywhere! The trees are closer than ever. Crowding. He can no longer turn or even move much. It's hopeless!

Panicking, nearly entangled, he looks wildly round. Wait—that looks promising there on his left... an opening. Now he can descend.... But... after a hundred yards this game trail also disappears and he is left amazed again among the boles. His only comfort is that the trees are taller. A good sign, says half his thought. *But it's darker and there are too many and you are trapped like a rat*, says the other half.

The cold of night has seeped into him, sucking on his marrow. Already his feet are aflame with pain. *Your face is almost tire rubber. Touch it to make sure you have live skin.*

But too quickly he brings his gloved hand to his face, accidentally punching himself in the eye with a ski pole. Pain and fear leap up, throttling.

Jason stands very still.

It's happening. I'm here on a mountain in Maine. At night. In January. Am I going to die?

Grandmother-Wind and-Weather shrilled out to her grandson Jasper Mountain. *That ignorant arrogant child on your head!*

But strong Jasper answered, approving him.

Wind-and-Weather bent fiercely over the round white head of her grandson, replying, blowing the boy off the summit.

While the light from the little moon still gleamed off his head, Jasper said, *Contend!*

Then Grandmother-Wind and-Weather lifted great plumes on the mighty brow pouring cold fury upon Jasper. In winter, wind is wedded to mountains. She would compass surrounding mountains in her thick blankets. But their summits remained low before great Jasper. His is the one crowned in krumholz, his decked most in the glory of crystals, his the shape of perfection.

And he confirmed, saying, *Then he will acknowledge he knows not what keeps him alive.*

But Wind-and-Weather screamed over his summit, bringing down clouds with her out of the North. The night long she would contend with the mountain over the mortal. Vapors drift now past the glimmering face of stars.

Jasper Mountain is submerged in storm.

Wind beats upon the trees above Jason where at first he founders then, arising, flounders along its alien flanks. Overhead branches creak and crack. Here the trees are high and deep in old and new snow. So the skis are his allies. If he loses them now he will die on the mountain; sink in deep snow, struggle and wade then collapse from exhaustion and cold. Keep my wits, keep my skis, not go casting them off in a panic. Use hop-turns around trees and my skis will bring me down into Gottheim, at least to the highway, some house where I can call Mom.

He is grateful for the downslope of Jasper: The way in which he finds guidance simply in continuing down. But sometimes the downslope way is compromised, blocked; his progress routed by tangles, deceptive dips, ridges, sudden ravines. The storm engulfs him; the blindness and horrifyingly pure smell of snow. He fights the desire to curl up and sleep against the trunk of some tree, burrow himself into the snow.

The skis on his feet become alien appendages, his boots concrete castes he should molt and leave behind. Briefly, at moments, Jason feels himself still schussing the great headwall. Coming to himself once, squatting amid the flying leaves of the beech thicket and clinging to the slender twigs: These are the autumn leaves of some other life. A warm life on the far side of some distant planet. Jason clasps the frail stems of these trees with fingers unfeeling, struggling up and still—miraculously—locked to his skis. Crying in anguish he pulls through the thicket, helping himself along on their outstretched hands. His poles are gone—lost among the thicket through which he struggles, or lost in the fir wood he happened through some time before. Experience is shattered, marked not by time but by passage through stages of woodland—phases of forestation characterized by the hand of man, or of God. Height, density, blowdown, cutover.... Terrain makes all the difference. Once he traversed acres of open territory, what he hoped would be smooth skiing, only to be checked in his crossing by the treachery of hidden debris. Had he known that these snags were but the leavings of loggers, he might have been encouraged to search out a skidder trail, something plain to lead him out of the woods and down to the road. But ignorance, and storm-panic, prevent this; leaving Jason open to exposure, laying him bare to the torment of wind driven snow.

The young skier, gasping, keeps moving, moving when he might stop in some hollow beside upturned roots of a downed pine—willing his feet move on the hated skis. Only as one can they make it together downmountain into the recognizable land. A mythic land of safety, sanity, kindness and health. There was such a place once, when he was a kid. Jason feels sure he will never be that kid again. He will be blessed to arrive with arms, hands, legs, with a face.

The trees around him creak and clash, reporting like gunfire. Fiercely the weather of Jasper Mountain plucks at him, reaching its apex of fury. Now blind, unaware, the boy stumbles forward.

Grazing his forearm, something startles him, and he shies away. *What is it? Did I imagine it?*

But again the thing comes at him, now brushing his leg. Stopping, he feels for it, grasping feebly with his numb hand.

Here it is again. A dog?

The creature has come to him, halting his progress. Jason allows himself to be checked by this scarcely touching animal, and squats on his skis, feeling for its pointed face and large moist nose. Too gentle and silent for a dog, its face is slender and quieting. Can this be a deer?—but it's almost invisibly white.

The deer allows him to hold its warm neck in his arms, to sag some against it. It hardens its small body to stand against Jason's sagging weight.

This is death. *I'm gonna die.*

The deer has come for him out of that strange place of stories and dreams. *Is that where people go... when they die?* Dying would account for the creature's odd hue and behavior.

Is he leading me there?

Nerveless and weak, Jason cannot speak. Go... go on to the place you're bringing me. *I'm ready to go with you now.*

Aching and cold he trembles against the deer in the storm.

And the deer turns, Jason still leaning upon it but pulling himself up out of the snow. Floundering and wallowing, the deer leads on as Jason takes courage and, again, to his skis.

The creature leads him along the lip of a precipice unknown, on through the beating and keening of the storm. Here Jason finds thickets on patches of rocks cleansed by the wind. And, as they go, he becomes aware of the drop-off beside them and of naked treetops bristling in the flying dimness beyond. *Wouldn't death would have led me that way?*

Together they descend as the ledge lowers itself gently, merging into the forest floor below. Jason has glided past his helper but now returns to him over the snow. The skis set the boy above this wallowing creature but he finds himself stooping to stay with it, accepting what guidance it may give. Now, with relief, the boy feels the strong presence of sheltering rock above. Where once it would cast him to his death it now stands over him, protectively, a monstrous rock.

The deer stops. And Jason rests, leaning shoulder and side against the great rock. The deer stands near, its warm side against his shivery leg. Out of the wind now, Jason dozes off, drifting in vacancy. Soon he is traveling again through images in some terrifying dream. A noise, a limb falling perhaps, wakes him with a jerk. He comes to himself, finding his shoulder against the rock, the deer by his side.

As if its terrible fury and fire were slaking, a change is felt in the blast high above. As though the storm has had enough of him and begins passing away. The change is perceptible to Jason, who has lived in it almost from before its onset. He has been beaten, made to believe in death, but now begins believing in life again. Will he make it out of this dimness and thrashing? Will he yet come to tell her of this night? He pictures her lovely face full of rejoicing, relief.

But this is the backside of a January snow storm in the mountains of Maine and Jason is still lost in the woods. He looks down at the deer, at its pale back. Pale, as though the storm has seeped into it. Strange strange deer. *Where have you come from? Why hasn't anyone told me of you?* Gently his awe suffuses him with gratitude and peace.

As these thoughts occur to him Jason lifts his gaze and finds himself staring at something familiar. In a moment he recognizes it. A light. Through dim creaking woodland a tiny light shines. Fitfully. Jason looks away from it, hopeful. He looks back. It is. A light.

He says this aloud, but softly, to the deer. Yet the deer has already moved a little toward the light. Now it stops, as though pointing with its pale muzzle.

Did you mean me to see it?

Jason cannot bear to break the spell of his peace with skepticism. After all that has happened. ...To do so would be—*I'm grateful.* Maybe the deer *did* bring him here. But could it, really? He saved me from falling. What's so hard about him showing me a light?

He can scarcely command his legs but, with great effort, he turns his skis. The strength of the deer still seems hardy, sinewy. *Please, little deer take me to the light?*...

—

The great world beyond his control was filled, suffused, peopled with caring. He lay on an old couch in the bearded man's dim kitchen, heaped in quilts, hearing the quiet rustle of the fire in the stove, the comforting smell of wood smoke in his nostrils. He heard the stove door squeal shut but did not open his eyes.

Jason had not known that some people have gifts of caring for others: that it could be an art form like rock-and-roll or photography and requiring skill, precision, like that used in shooting moguls or carving through the turns of the slalom. They knew exactly what to do when they saw someone hurting, went through the necessary steps with agility, as though in a tender ballet. Coming in off the mountain he learned this; coming down from heights where he escaped being destroyed. Caring permeated creation... in the form of people just doing what they were supposed to do.

His shaking and shivering were abating, but his cheeks and nose seemed to be missing, sheared off by the wind. Yet, with broth and warmth penetrating him he might go home soon, even with this face-firing pain. The man said an ambulance would be coming. The man said he would be going to the hospital.

The man had believed him when he told of the deer, though at first Jason thought him pretending; just to be kind. The deer was gone when he opened the door and saw the boy collapsing there. Swift and sure the man's foot released Jason from the impossible lengths of his skis. The arms were strong in lifting him into the shadowy kitchen, the long hands tender in releasing numb feet from the bondage of their boots. His humor was quiet in telling gentle jokes on himself and on Jason: about the lack of service, the poor accommodations and nonexistent lift lines on this side of the mountain.

"The white deer... real?..." Jason murmured it more than once while the wind roamed under the eaves and roared on the mountain above. "A white deer?"

The man came near. "Yuht. Real as you or me. Been roaming Jaspa Mountain since he dropped fom his mother's womb last summer. We call 'em Sugarloaf cause he's so white. Pure white."

The man stopped then, thoughtfully fingering his dark beard. Light from the living room beyond threw a gleam on his white-blond hair. He went to the counter to get Jason cocoa. When he came back he said, "You could do something fah Sugarloaf."

"How?" His voice was a whisper.

"Don't tell."

"Don't tell he saved my life?"

"Lots'a people'd love t'bag that deer. ...If word got round. Caunt you see him stuffed and mounted in the lobby ovah theya at the resort?"

Jason lay silent.

Whether to give Jason space to think or on some errand, the man went into the next room. Maybe he was getting ready to go to work. It must be morning. The sun would be coming up. Jason sipped the cocoa, thinking about what the man said of the deer.

All he would ever want to think of for the rest of his life was the white deer. He wished he could be here with him now. He wanted to lay his hand on its bony head, feel its thin furred ears between his painful fingers. He wanted the deer to lead him through the rest of his life. His heart filled at the thought of the deer walking with him from class to class at school, the deer going down to the hockey rink for practice, the deer kneeling beside his desk in the bedroom while he studied chemistry.

—It would never work, never. Jason would leave the woods, leave Maine. Already the distant wail of the ambulance told him. The deer would stay here, and he would be gone to a bright place bustling with noise and people in white, caring for him. The little deer would remain quiet, anonymous, safe. Here. This house would be here, and the man... in the middle of the deer's range: this man, this kind man, regular blue-collar man. And all Jason could do was be in suburbia where he came from... but now looking after, always thinking of what he had seen. The deer will always be... and what had really happened. That was memory now, it couldn't change.

The man returned saying, "Theya almost heah. Y'folks'll be glad t'see you. Police called 'em."

Jason scarcely acknowledged these words. He was thinking... but now drifting off again. Had he been sleeping just now? Was there a storm... I dreamed?

The shadow of the man loomed over him still. Looking up, Jason whispered. "Was there a deer?"

"A white deah, Sugarloaf. But don't tell anaone. Keep that deah safe."

God's Creatures in Winter

James Fay, a developer at Jasper Mountain, sat across from Theodora Prescott in her snow-bright kitchen in the village. He was full of plans for Mason's Mills, already under construction in the wilds of the borderlands of Quaker and Gottheim; having financial backing from resort owner Harry Golding. James was looking forward to moving into his own home, being built in the development, come spring when the budding leaves would enhance its beauty. The old settlers' mill had flourished during the last century and its foundation stones, near his unfinished house, lent it a solidity and security which added to its appeal.

James had other plans as well, plans for himself and Theodora. He wanted to marry her this spring or early summer when the house was complete.

Theo's own home, in this historic residential heart of Gottheim showed her taste for the fine old things. James called regularly on his fiancé to set him straight about arcana for historic simulation. He admired her antique pot rack hanging above the butcher block from the pale stamped tin ceiling. Even its utensils were authentic, both iron and brass. Under one window stood a slate sink with splashguard of pink marble, flanked by sideboards of wormwood. The windows above were divided lights; snow cover without reflected soft light into the room. Theodora also contributed valuable guidance on his business attire, for instance, convincing him to import linen handkerchiefs to wear in his breast pocket.

James Fay was still smarting over Rhetta Bearce's polite but pointed attacks in editorial letters to *The Village Voter*. The old girl had accused him of lacking authenticity in his design for an extension of Gottheim's traditional village and, in part because of her, he continued a target of anyone angry over the plan. They accused him of tasteless architectural eclecticism, of backpedaling and reneging on his promise of authenticity. He needed Theo's help to avoid similar impugning of his recent project.

Mason's Mills was now the one he wanted to be remembered for. His greatest hope always lay in the latest effort.

Now, over midmorning coffee with her, he said, "Think of it, Theo. This is aimed especially at people who care most for family life. The life *we* like. The planning board, especially that notable but overly vocal Mrs. Bearce, will *have* to sail this through. No possible way they can find it objectionable. I followed every ordinance to the letter and on time!"

Theo sipped her coffee, daintily. "Well, it certainly helps that you were the one to dream up this concept in the first place." She beamed. She was always beaming at James and believing high things of him. Every night she thanked God for sending him. His love and presence in her life imparted stability that she had not dreamed of even six or eight months ago. Being loved was the most wonderful feeling in the world—and James the most wonderful person to bestow it. He had come, bringing God with him, and now she knew with certainty that God is love.

James smiled his shiny indulgent bespeckled smile. Cluster development had been pivotal in his relations with the townsfolk. Of course, Harry Golding had been the one to present it to them. The virulent resistance of these people to Fay's charm had surprised him. He was good with people from away. He could sell upscale strangers garages for elephants, being a master at mining images dear to the heart of yuppies. But it had taken a Golding to break through to Gottheim's leading citizens. They were every bit as tough as any old Mainer.

"The sweetest part," he said, "may have been my proposal to deed all the natural areas, horse paths, hiking and cross-country ski trails to the town. That way *they* can be responsible to the DEP. Now if only that misguided New Age hippie would leave me alone, Mason's Mills will be ready for the summer building spree." He frowned, remembering too late as he always did that Eloise Patadoe might be related to Theo. "She's not an old friend... or anything?" But—it might also be advantageous if she *is* related to Theo.

Theodora's eye had been caught by some movement in the bright yard outside. Vaguely distracted she turned back to him, laughing. "Goodness no, James! *She's* not from here. *She's* been in Gott'im less time than it takes to be born here!" Theodora was fond of putting it this way, indicating the premium placed on having ancestors who settled the town— or, at least, were around to contribute something in the previous century. Eloise Patadoe dated only since the back-to-the-land movement of the late '60s and '70s. But Theo knew that in colleges across the state the newer tradition was heralded as an active demographic phenomenon.

She pushed her chair back and went to the window. "That awful squirrel, James—at it again! I've tried everything to keep those gray squirrels away from the feeders!" She gave a disgusted wail and rapped sharply on the pane, but the huge rodent simply turned its fat backside and bushy tail to her, ignoring the sight of her threatening white knuckles. "I do *not* want those things eating the birds' food! Look at him! He's practically inhaling that seed!"

James helped himself to a sliver of the almond spice pastry which, along with coffee, scented the table. He wished she would stop going on about that creature. Her behavior bored and irritated him. Sometimes it made him consider forgoing these midmorning get-togethers. Why she tended to these obsessive fixations. ... She was a bit bonkers. Originally this trait had attracted him, but lately its charm eluded him. If only she would settle down and not let little things bother her. *Lay off, Theo*, he wanted to say. But he gave his response a soothing quality instead. "You want squirrels to make it through winter, too, don't you?"

"Well... yes. I guess I never thought of it that way. Thank you." Theo came back and sat across from Fay. She leaned over her coffee toward him. "James there's something... well, I'd like to confess something. You might... remember last fall... when I was, well, distracted about something?"

She paused and he nodded adding, "Yes, but you seemed to straighten out all right after your baptism...." He gave her a quizzical look.

She hurried on. "I-I've been somewhat concerned...—because you're a religious man." Her gaze slid away. "You might—you know... be offended. But James, you did say confession—and repentance—is what God wants."

James felt his pulse quicken. He looked at her fearing a sordid confession. Was she about to tell of former (and probably botched) affairs? Things had been going so well! She had made a beautiful confession of faith at the altar following that poignant baptism. And he was looking forward to a wedding solemnized in church and honeymoon bed that was as clean and fresh as—himself. James Fay had managed to keep his virginity despite temptation and hoped she had to. God knew it wasn't easy in such times! But it *was* possible—and completely desirable to him.

Although it was a cold January day in a drafty old house, he felt a faint sweat forming on his brow and above his upper lip. He kept the dread from his voice, feeling a reluctance he could not cover. "Yes, Theo. We are to confess.... If we must."

"Well...." She dropped her gaze. "The wages—" She swallowed and looked out the windows. The squirrel had gone but she didn't notice. "The wages—at Gottheim Chair—?" She missed seeing Fay's shoulders relax, his brow smooth out. "...For a long time, decades even, they weren't as high as maybe they should have been." The last was said all in a rush, and then she stopped and turned toward him, a part of her auburn hair falling across her eye.

Never had she appealed to him more. Tenderly James prompted her, leaning toward her to take up her hand. "Theo, I don't know what you're talking about but it can't be as bad as this."

"But it is." She allowed him to continue caressing the back of her hand. "For years there was a sort of... arrangement... to set mill wages—by the owners. Even... even Father and Gramps. They all agreed on exactly how much workers would make. And on workers being blackballed if they quit one place and... so forth. The sawmills paid highest and the smaller wood mills would keep a wage agreed on.... That was until the national minimum wage was instituted, I think. Then that was the minimum. That way," she went on as if he did not understand, "owners were assured of maximum profits and almost no competition for workers. You see how advantageous it was."

"But was it wrong, really? How was it immoral? Was there a law against it?" Gently he let go her hand.

"I never consulted my lawyer.... Just been— uncomfortable. Look at industrial wages in other parts of the country and what about rates and paper companies? Those mills started out just like the lumber and wood-turning mills."

"Yes, and look at the quality of the workplace in Gottheim Chair. No toxic chemicals to worry about, no unhealthy atmosphere like you find down the highway in Guildford. Theo, these workers of yours have had a job they could count on for most of their lives. Maybe that arrangement ensured this."

"But James, those wages have never been enough to support a family."

"Yes—the families here have had *two* breadwinners... and well before people were doing so in other parts. They've been out in front with equal pay for equal work. Don't people stay married here better than on the national average? They do all right, believe me, Theo. They do."

He had picked up both her hands again and bent his head to look encouragement into her downcast eyes. Such concern lifted her gaze and she smiled a tentative if vulnerable smile.

"James.... It's wonderful of you to be so understanding." She had expected a shock to his sense of fitness and conscience. Yet, even as she spoke, she felt unconvinced, maybe even a bit disturbed. Was James' lack of censure his charity shining through? His forgiveness for error seems full and complete. Can it be right to think it too easy? He says these things because of his love. Yes, she saw it now. She should be relieved.

She squeezed his hands. "I'm trying to make it up to them, really I am. Now they're wages are nearly as high as Bearces'!"

"But I'm sure it isn't necessary, Theo." (How *does* that tumbledown place stay in business?! Should not ask, however. Just keep my mitts off. Leave it alone.)

"No, James. I want to do what's right. If at all possible. Your faith and concern for what's right was—has encouraged me!" Her smile beamed out on him.

James smiled and returned the pressure of her hands.

Stamping snow from her secondhand L.L. Bean hunting boots, Eloise Patadoe steps into the office of *The Village Voter*. She strides up to the battered pumpkin pine counter, declaring, "Here's the ad for my wholesome delicious goats milk cheese!"

Seated at his desk, James Nutting looks up from under his green visor at her horsey face, saying dryly, "I don't eat goats milk cheese. It's not me you have to sell."

"I'm merely hinting at the content of the ad." She digs in her old leather zipper case, pulling out a typewritten sheet. "Also, I want you to consider this letter to the editor. Can I get your reaction right now?"

"Ms. Patadoe, does it occur to you that I might be busy working?" But he rolls back his squawking desk chair and comes to the counter.

"This *is* work." She says it boldly. Everything Eloise does is bold. She may go flat and weak inside at times, but nothing of that leaks into her expressions.

Her gaze wanders to the huge press in the back while Nutting reads. The monster sleeps, she says to herself. In an age trending electronic, the vintage machine shakes this turn-of-the-century building whenever an edition goes to press. When the building stops moving, Rozelle Wight, an attorney on the second floor, comes down to pick up a fresh copy of the week's paper.

Dear Editor,

I see we have our good times in store from Mr. Fay & Co. as they plan another big addition to this formally humble town. The Gottheim Theme Park and Brewing Co. is set to specialize in New England Family Fare and Landscaping. Mason's Mills, that once hidden gem of Gottheim town history, is to be excavated and prettified with clusters of imitation capes, gingerbread villas, sanctified saltboxes, and Georgian ticky-tacky. I was hoping to avoid being pressed into service as the Grinch who sabotaged the entertainment industry, but Mr. Fay's plans for my backyard, specifically my side yard, precipitate this. I refer to his attempt at establishing his point of egress (such would no doubt be his term for it) beside my hitherto secluded goat pasture and breeding area in the bordering township. (These properties abut).

I'd like to suggest that Mr. Fay take his clusters and arrange them in another point of egress—one located in a part of the human anatomy not generally associated with parks and amusements. He is not going to finish this project without a fight from the hippie element of the more remote, but vocal, town next-door. Sincerely, Eloise Patadoe, Quaker Plantation.

The letter provokes little more than a sheen in the brown eyes of Mr. Nutting's gaunt face. He looks up from the type script saying, "We can use all but the second from the last sentence."

"Poop! That was my best line. You should've seen the goats' reaction to it."

Nutting gives her his dry steady look.

"All right, all right, Mr. First Amendment." She shakes her blond ponytail, grins like a horse, and says, "Does that remark about cheese mean you won't except a brick in trade for the ad?"

Elda Simon had been in the barn since 3 a.m. nursing a wounded raccoon, a raven with a broken wing and an older fawn who had stepped into a trap. At daybreak, stooping with weariness and pain, she came into the kitchen through the back door bringing January cold and the smell of musk. The red kerchief on her head was askew, a pucker of worry between her brows. She did not notice her grandson Daniel sitting on the couch near the woodstove quietly feeding peanuts to a red squirrel.

After shutting the door on the emerging sun and snowlight, she heard the chattering of the critter shucking its peanut. Yet Elda was startled when she heard Daniel say, "How's things in the barn, Gra'mutha?" He never called her Grandma or, especially, Grammy as other Mainers would. *Grammy* just seemed too familiar to him, and though she was shy and sometimes awkward in conversation Daniel perceived her, rather, as withdrawn and stiff.

Elda straightened, her expression of worry smoothing itself out. Her voice, while not exactly light, was not unpleasant. "Thought you'd gone b'now, Daniel." He had come to stay for the week, as usual, but he should be gone on the school bus by now, headed for ninth grade homeroom at Hazel Newell High School.

"Teacher's conference's day today. No school. I can work in the barn. If y'waunt."

The frown returned. "Well... it's s'nice of you to offer."

She said it slowly, trying for a grandmother's courtesy. Elda was about to brush him off, dreading the obligation to crank up social coping mechanisms. Think of the awkwardness and trouble. A wild stumble through verbal minefields. Her natural mistrust; involuntary concerns over missteps in caring for the wild ones, doing of chores as they ought to be done. She lacked natural grace in giving directions tending to nitpick... whether internally or out loud. Her instructions would come out halting, confused, or sounding like an insult to her helper's intelligence. She might suddenly bark some idiotic command. But—aside from all this piddling aggravation there was a profound worry she wanted to conceal. Once— Lord such a short time ago!—she had got on fairly. Now she was failing, the barn getting away from her. Just how bad... she didn't even know. How well are the animals being cared for?—now that she could scarcely see to do the work as it should be done.

Her careful manners and nice if labored way of speaking told Daniel a deflection was coming. With a plea he cut off her rejection. "I can do it. I need something t'do." Not true. Daniel had plenty to do—too much in fact. But he could no longer let this weird troubled grandmother walk in and out of his presence without some form of personal contact. The mute sorrow of this situation troubled him. Even father was quiet now, more like Daniel than Daniel had suspected he could be. His father was more silent distracted remote. The boy recalled that even glorious Gloria Fay's neglect of his father's love had not so silenced him... as did this twilight of grandmother's. Besides, Daniel liked being in the barn with the animals. As the squirrel turned the peanut over and over, he looked at its hyper heaving sides and almost smiled.

"Got to eat," Elda declared. "Had any breakfast?" She turned to hang up her coat.

Handing the squirrel another peanut, Daniel shook his head. "Just got up."

"Okay, we can have it togetha. Waunt do toast?"

"Can I do the eggs?" There was only discomfort in watching her cook. He wanted to broach the subject, get past the awkwardness of letting her know that he knew. —What if talking only increased the awkwardness?

"Okay," conceded Elda, heading for the bread box. In a case like this she was a pushover. "Toast is mine." She thought, *If I can't talk—toast!*

Daniel washed his hands at the sink then went to the refrigerator and got out eggs. "Like 'em ovah easy, scrambled?"

"Whatever is easy." She got out bread, waiting for Daniel to finish seasoning the pan and start the eggs before starting toast. The smell of hot oil filled the kitchen. She went and got juice from the icebox, heard eggs crackling and sputtering the pan, and pushed down the toast.

Just for something to say Daniel dug into his own curiosity. "How'd you s'pose that Jason guy missed those big houses up theya that night?" Daniel had been with his mother and brothers last week when a teenager from away got lost all night on Jasper Mountain in a storm. He wished he had been here to see the survivor firsthand. He could have reported on it for *The Voter*. His first opportunity to break into print. He itched to get out of his gopher rut at the newspaper.

"Caunt say. Sugarloaf brought 'em down."

Daniel was skeptical. Balder had told him of the white deer's part in the rescue, leaving Daniel to ponder what it meant. Not that he disbelieved... exactly. "The guy never mentioned it to Libby," he said. The reporter at *The Voter* had gathered Jason's story from the ski patrol, from Balder, and from Jason before he left the hospital in Guildford for home in Massachusetts.

Elda made no answer. She had tried everything to keep Sugarloaf away from humans; away, even, from herself. Depriving herself of his company had been the hardest part—that, and the way it made her feel to shoo him away. She continued to pine for his dainty mother, Posey. Having to frighten him and miss getting to know the doe's offspring—. Sugarloaf would have replaced what the hunter took away. Sadness and purblindness where her companions now. But there was comfort in recalling the conversation she had overheard, while sitting in the front room, that dark early morning when the lost boy showed up at their door. She blessed Balder continually for inviting Jason to "keep that deer safe."

Daniel shoveled beneath the eggs, breaking one accidentally. He decided to scrambled them. Soon he was scooping them onto their plates. Elda added toast and they sat down to eat.

"Gran'mutha, ever seen that flag ovah tother side o'the valley... way up on a ledge. White flag?"

Taking a bite of toast, she nodded. "Robichaud's flag. Been theya years. Don't suppose it's the same flag all the time. They must change it. But I caunt 'memba a time it waunt theya.... Maybe when I was a girl. No, I think even then. Cuss that family waunt theya so long as others around.... people whose ancestors settled the place. French, y'know."

"So?"

"Used to be a big difference—not so much now. Lots of bigotry against the French. People used make jokes, I spect. Maybe you heard 'em." She shied her small smile at him.

Daniel reached for his juice. He could see her relaxing. "That have anathin t'do with the flag, you think?"

"I would." She stopped as though considering. "That flag... always made me feel...." She shook her head. "Something."

He waited for her response, wondering if she was really thinking of this for the first time. Maybe it was something people were just used to. Maybe they don't even see the flag anymore. Would he be like that one day? Would the flag just stop impressing him with its spirit of.... He said it aloud: "Victory? Defeat?"

"That's it. Victory."

"Like they came here from away, and it took 'em so long, struggling, but they made it."

So'll you, she thought. But she said, "I don't think—when they first put it up theya, they still had a way t'go. And, it's not like it's ovah yet. They're still working on it. Those ah Robbie Robichaud's boys cutting up on that stumpage up theya on Parsons Knoll above us, east. They got trailers on Robbie's land, so one of them prob'ly put it up on the ledge."

"We saw 'em cutting up theya last week, Cindabilla'n me." He didn't say Cindabilla had gone up there to smoke reefer, that he went with her to try talking her out of it. He was going to have to give up that girl. But how could he? It wasn't like she was just anybody.

He finished his eggs and toast. Grandmother had got up to take the kettle off the woodstove. He took the plates to the sink and went to the refrigerator for more orange juice. He sat at the table again and began idly brushing crumbs on the checkered oilcloth into a little pile. Grandmother had come back with her steaming cup. The smell of instant coffee perked them both up. He tried not to be obvious about it but he had been watching her since she came in the door. At the moment it appeared she was looking off in the direction of the coat rack, but he had the feeling that she watched him, carefully, on the sly of her vision. Balder had described macular degeneration to him.

"Gran'mutha," he began. "What is legally blind?" There. It was out in the open now.

She made an involuntary movement and was quiet again, looking quickly away. "Is that what Balda said?" She still had not got used to saying, "your father."

Daniel nodded, then wondered if she caught it, so he said, "Yes."

"Well for me it means seeing light and shapes. And having to pay attention. Details sometimes get away. A stump might be a rock'n vice versa. I look at you and see maybe a—something—your head, maybe no face."

Just talking she had given him a lot. And he understood a little better what she was up against. Daniel flattened the tiny pile of crumbs with his palm still damp from holding the juice glass. He scraped them up again with his thumbnail, saying, "There's a blank spot in the middle—most every where y'turn?"

"Yuht!" She came down quick on that affirmative, swung it straightahead like a sword.

There was silence in the room. Then to dispel it they spoke each at the same time. Together they stopped but each began again. Grinning she said, "You go first."

"I was just gont say... I could tell you what things look like... when we're in the barn. Like, if a deer's got something wrong with its eye —I could describe it."

Elda hesitated. Carefully, her instinct being to repulse this kind advance. Yet, hearing the earnest spirit of his voice and for the first time recognizing something of Balder's childhood speech, she delayed her parry. Some sacrifice was called for. Somehow, Daniel must have his caring acknowledged, not be treated as though he had just come in off the road. Why was everything so difficult? Lord all these nagging concerns. But he's not from away. He's from here, from her. How could she ever find anything genuine—if she did not take Daniel's offer seriously?

Hers was an inward sigh. She said, "Well... sounds like a good plan. That might help. Yes."

"Good. What was that you stotted telling me?"

"Which?"

"You stotted telling me?..."

"Oh. Most forgot! Theya's something we could do—maybe this spring." She had intended saying something *you* could do, but now Elda could maybe see herself working with Daniel—if the impulse did not wear itself away in regret when the weather changed.

"You saw those loons last year? They been having a hard time lately, what with more people coming, new houses'n all. Gott'im's busier, ponds is more crowded. Something's wrong with their eggs, too. They're not sturdy. Loons need help raising theya young. We could build floating nests for 'em." She waited for some hint of interest, turning the coffee cup around in her hands.

"Cool," he said. "How?"

"With narrow logs, little longer'n pulp logs, to make a square frame. Then we put screen on the bottom, fill it with dirt, leaves, weeds, twigs, stuff. Then anchor it in a cove'n leave some slack in the line in case of changing watah levels. Did you know they hardly walk on land? Caunt get away from predators except by deep diving."

He nodded. "Fatha told me theya bones are solid. Making 'em good divers. Maybe wintah vacation we could build one in the shed."

Elda could not catch the light of interest in his eyes, but speed and lift in his voice were unmistakable. She smiled and, for an instant, he saw her white wrinkly face glow transparently. She finished her coffee and stood. The kitchen was cooling a bit. Should put on more wood. Daniel had come out of his chair too and for a moment they moved as one toward the wood box.

Shyly smiling, she turned aside, letting him tend to the fire. "Be back in a minute'n we can go out to the barn." She scuffed into the next room and began climbing the stairs to the bathroom, too embarrassed to use the one off the kitchen.

But, an adjustment had been made in the relationship. Elda would continue in her little hesitancies, her stumblings; never quite getting the hang of dealing with Daniel... or anyone. Despite her self-consciousness she carried on, more or less attentive to others, even sometimes deeply enjoying their company. With her it was continually like a Maine winter evolving toward spring: stop and start, surge and sink. One day budding, the next wintry again. The spring will come someday. And summer, full of fruit. But not for Elda. *Not*, she thought.

She took the stairs slowly, wondering over Daniel. Where did this boy come from? How had this happen to them, Balder and her? It would not occur her that Daniel was the result of seed spilled passionately over the ready walls of the womb. She would not try to answer the question posed by her wonderment. No answer would be worthy enough, nor contain the whole story.

This was rare. A weeknight when both Rhetta and Lyman Bearce were home. Both occupants were descended from Gottheim area lumber barons, tough ambitious men who had come into Gottheim with axes, crosscut saws and portable mills; men who knew how to organize and put people to work. Rhetta and Lyman each exhibited the toughness and organization of this joint heritage. They were fearless, stubborn, aggressive in what interested them. And each could be belligerent or beneficent in pursuit of some goal. For them to be at cross purposes was something anyone in Gottheim would pay to see. Now that the kids were gone to America's corners, fierce displays of puffed feathers, of beaks and talons, might electrify the house for hours, even days. Hissing and snapping and separate beds were not uncommon when Bearces were in their frays.

On the north side of the house, pine woods sent near a bristling wedge. Lately, a pair of great horned owls cohabited there. Although sharing the territorial woods, the owls lived separate lives much of the year, but occasionally meeting in provoked attack. The female is notorious in Gottheim, having made the front page of the weekly with her predatory escapades of the previous spring when domestic animals and pets had come under her taloned onslaught. Asa Bartlett still had a scar on his temple to prove the formidable character of this owl. And Elda Simon had mended its wings twice—for assault by bullet and birdshot. But now it was mid-January, and the strange chemistry of creaturely sexuality had begun making inroads. At night the two Bearces, lying awake in separate rooms over some spat, could hear the gutturals of predators in love.

Week nights were busy nights for Bearces. Lyman had selectmen's meetings, the Knights of Pythias, Academy Board of Trustees, Rotary and Maine Timber Growers, and others all spread out over the course of a month. Sometimes he would attend the historical society or other meetings, if the speakers were addressing something in which he had a direct interest. Rhetta worked on a number of committees, besides the Planning Board. She was interested in Chamber of Commerce, the Birches Cemetery Association, legion auxiliary, the library, historic preservation, etc., many included meetings of a seasonal nature. An evening home together was rare, and the nature of these found times was seldom predictable. The pair could be as sociable and affectionate as a couple of old lions greeting one another after a dry season apart; or, as on this night, going at each other like mated great horns in July.

They were in the corner (master) bedroom which, in daylight in summer, overlooked on one side a long curve of the drive with its flowering rhododendron planted twenty-five years before by Rhetta's own hand. Outside tonight starlight and moonglow shown coldly on snow but, inside, Bearces were arguing and heedless of moon and snow. Rhetta stood tall and formidable in a silk wrapper, her hair half in curlers and face scrubbed of makeup. Eyes sparkling and jowls trembling, she had come out of the bath to continue "this discussion" as Lyman tried to sneak in and retrieve clean nightclothes. She faced him squarely across the great fourposter, telling him what she thought he owed the workers of the Bearce family's mills. As yet, no one in town understood why Theodora Prescott had raised the wages of her own furniture mill. As she spoke, Mrs. Bearce emphasized each point with a jab of her hair brush in his direction.

But white-bearded Bearce, almost as tall and somewhat portly, was not going to stand meekly under her know-so-much manner. There was no way he would agree to this. He stood coldly eyeing her, reflecting back her fire off his steely white front; as though he were a block of ice reflecting a blaze, unaffected by its heat. He let his partner sputter herself out, then said was cool precision, "Owe? Talk about owing.... Look what the town, hell, the whole region owes Bearce's. You know so much about heritage, New England heritage. What would it be without New England mills? 'N' waya would the mills be without a surer hand to set a solid economic strategy? We provided culture a'plenty, have these mills, fah the people of Gott'im. You, an arbiter of culture, ought to know this. Any money made on checking wage escalation has gone back into the community. You know it. I know it."

She switched tone and tactics on him, adopting his coldness. "Do I?" She would not let him appear the cool client, the reasonable one trying to undercut a hysterical opponent with calm logic. She swept the room with her hand. "Does the rest of the community live like this? Doesn't it occur to you that working people might be trusted to spend theya own earnings, and determine its use and benefit to the community?"

"Doaw. Does not!" He thrust his big hands into his pockets and leaned forward, hooting. "What would they do with it?—drink it away. They'd come to work worse'n they do now. Workmen's comp'd go up. Think of the time Octavius Peabody came in pissed'n got sliced up good'n propa? *We* end up paying fah that, Rhetta."

"Lyman Bearce, they're not all like that! You know it."

"Do I." This was a mockery of her choice response, and his eye upon her was cold.

Mrs. Bearce thought of all the hard-working mill wives she had known over the years; women who had come into the smaller wood-turning mills in order to eke out their husbands' wages. Some decades gone, while traveling elsewhere in the country, Rhetta found that blue-collar mothers did not work much outside the home, as traditionally they did in Maine. Now she wondered if the setting of wages occurred elsewhere in the state. Were workers who quit a mill elsewhere punished with the blackball? In any case, she could not well answer his accusations about local drunkenness. Alcoholism seemed endemic. The police log published in *The Voter* yielded proof every week of Lyman's accusations. There was so much abuse on these back roads. She bit her lip and dropped her gaze in the face of his challenge.

Her honesty quelled his distemper. The fragrance of victory almost brought a smile to Lyman's lips. Quiet came into the room, and he saw that the old girl was his.

Into the silence came the staccato *hoo-oo*ing of the great horned owl, muted by the pine woods and panes of glass. The female responded to the male's more distant, deeper and prolonged, call. The call spoke of cold and the dark, of thick pine boughs. Of January snow, of ice and sleet and moon. Of silver light on ponds. The calls echoed the fierce ardor of great owls. Those brutal birds were suited to the rigors of winter mating, laying and brooding. Fearless they were, building not their own nests but usurping the large nests of squirrels, raptors, even of the eagles themselves.

"Hear those owls?" asked Lyman Bearce in a low voice. He had stepped to the window, head cocked to receive the eerie cries. He reached to turn off the lamp by the bed. As a young man set over a logging crew in the deep woods, Bearce had seen such a pair. In response to her mate's song, and gift of a mouse, the large female had lowered herself urgently, leaning forward on the branch before the smaller male. Spreading her tail feathers, like a cooped fowl, in ardor she humiliated her dignity. To the young Bearce, it had appeared an act undignified to both partners: a joint bundle of feathers rhythmically humping, fulfilling the ecstatic urgency of instinct. Later had come the long cold nights of patient watchfulness, the sexual ardor of both replaced by the vigilance of brooding and nurture.

He said, "I read in a book once.... The author called them saturnine, savage...." He said this softly, as a tentative offering from Lyman to Rhetta.

"I'm not surprised." She said it low. "They seem—like that." She had been retreating to the bathroom to finish rolling her hair for the night, but something in Bearce's manner made her stop. She had long trained herself to stand and reach for any straight drop of Bearce's honey. It was rare enough, but—the old woodsman could still drop sweet when he wanted. Silently she moved around the fourposter and came to his side, listening to the owls. Their shoulders touched, his arm went around her broad hips. They might listen at the window awhile, they could end up listening from the big bed.

Hannah Sessions was Cindabilla's grandmother and she was slowly losing her mind. Like the mountains around her farm—slowly shedding grains of granite, eroding away in streams and creating sandbars along the shoreline of the pond—Hannah Sessions' mind was losing vital grains of thought. In this simple process of weathering, concepts sometimes came in pieces triggered by the spoken phrases of others. Words might elude her, faces appear and pass but their names just don't come.

Outside Hannah's decaying old cape, the young apple trees she planted three springs ago were being secretly girdled by mice. Mice passed one another on tiny trails beneath the snow, nuzzling furred sides with sensitive whiskers as if to say, *food's up ahead*. All but two of the little trees in the orchard would dry up and pass away this coming summer because Hannah forgot her precautions to prevent winter's rodents from nibbling strips of bark around the circumference of each stripling. Outer bark, succulent inner bark, including the precious living cambia, would all be eaten away. Round and round the mice were eating. Fattening beneath safe snow cover, while great storms came down over Jasper, roaring. All this circular dining would forever break the finely tuned communication between hidden nourishing roots and the slender canopy of its outer visible form.

Sometimes Daniel Twitchell actually worries: How do all the creatures make it through winter? Daniel himself is a somewhat unusual creature, a worried and helpful teenager. Or is that so unusual? He grew up in a household slowly rendered dysfunctional by alcohol. There is hope now that the situation has altered—just maybe.... Yet Daniel has not altered with it. He is still fraught with the urge to watch over situations, alert to cues of developing extremes. It's part of his attraction to Cindabilla, part of the reason his fellow teenage traveler is dear to him. Cindabilla lives with her grandmother and her Uncle Ferddy and his girlfriend, Babette. Sometimes Cindabilla's messed up mother stays with them in the sway-backed cape of the ruined farm.

At a far end of the property, in a nook between mountains, a bunch of beavers live in a bog. They have a great stout dam and a winter's lodge full of edible trees. There they spend the season in an upper chamber, munching away on popple. During their first summer as friends, Daniel and Cindabilla spent some time there watching the critters on the sly. This stealthy exercise taught them patience and how to stay awake in trees and avoid falling into the pool. The beavers worked incessantly, never stopping except to eat and sleep. Once Daniel and Cinda saw the dam break and the water drop. Immediately the huge rodents waded in and swam over to repair it. "Like little buck-toothed Mainers," whispered Daniel to her. She said, "They waddle'n flap like um, too."

Daniel forgets those summer evenings when worrying how creatures will make it through winter. He thinks instead of the short January afternoon spent in the woods with Elda Simon, sawing down cedars for deer. Watching the trees fall he thought that just chopping them down would be enough to help deer survive, but Grandmother, having lugged up a snow shovel, busied herself clearing a path to the deer yard several rods away. There the herd had trodden and fouled the yard and were ragged, sickly and thin. When he asked why the shovel, she replied, "Deah's so stupid, they starve without an easy way out the yard."

"Caunt they just look over here, see the cedar'n come get it?" Can they be so dumb as to starve with food only a hundred feet away!

But, shoveling, Elda just shook her head.

Sitting in the hayloft with Cindabilla, Daniel thinks of this. Uncle Ferddy's wolf hybrid, named Demon, lies at their feet. It's late afternoon and dark out. The dim barn beneath them is lit with a few pathetic hanging bulbs. Looking down they can see the breath of cows filling their stalls with vapor. Half wolf, half dog, Demon stares at the cattle, speculatively.

The two adolescents sit on bales of hay, glancing at Daniel's history notes and trying not to move around. You can ruin good hay by playing on it, roughhousing; but it hurts nothing to sit quietly leaning back against the bales, smelling the fragrance and warmth of summer in the bundles. Cindabilla has known forever that being careless with the bales can ruin fodder. Even so, to Daniel's disgust, she is lighting up more reefer. Calmly, he mentions again that this is a lame thing to do in a barn full of hay. She responds by calling him names beginning with the letter w and prefixed with the word worry: worry-wart, worry-wasp, worry-walrus, worry-wrapping—paper. The cleverness of this cracks her up.

She falls off the bales giggling, clutching the burning joint while cupping it protectively in her palm. The boy, in his leather jacket and stocking cap, grabs the notebook they were holding between them. Water sloshes out of the bucket by his foot, the bucket he made her bring up in case of fire. He notes to himself that the sweet-burning smell of the drug is like burning hay. Watching her pull straws from her ginger ponytail, he considers that the drug heightens her sense of humor. He has seen this level of idiocy before—in his own home in Phoenix.

It was a sight, the combination of reefer and alcohol at those parties Petey and Mother used to throw. Daniel cannot square the inconsistency of Cinda's marijuana use with her urge to break coffee-brandy bottles over Uncle Ferddy's drunken head. He'd like to drop her stash into the bucket. Everything they've been reading about land speculators of the previous century is hilarious to her, but when he asks what's funny she stops laughing, thinks a moment, says she can't remember, and starts laughing again.

Ferddy's wolf hybrid continues staring at the cattle below. Two are black calves, born last spring but still unsold, though now stolid and strong.

Also among the herd are two old cows that don't look particularly healthy to Daniel. He sees that Demon's gaze goes most often to them.

Demon is Uncle Ferddy's idea of a pet... bought last summer after Cindabilla accidentally shot him in the rear. No one could prove she shot him, but Uncle Ferddy knows. He enjoys the idea of Demon insuring that nothing like that ever happens again. For insurance of her own, Cindabilla has taken time and the skim of farm produce and slaughter—on the sly—to befriend Demon. Now it's a tossup whose "dog" it is.

Of course this demon dog makes Daniel uneasy. The boy likes the idea of *wolf*—wild, pack-living creatures living on the fringe of things. They are hunters, hierarchical, howlers, mysterious, untamed. He likes the idea of *dog*—people-specific, family friend, tame, semi-trained, rascally, lovable. Two good concepts, domestic and wild. Why try to splice them and throw it all out of balance? What makes him extra uneasy is an Uncle Ferddy owning one. The experiment with these natures has brought Demon willy-nilly into existence—nothing you can do about it now—but what you don't want is this "pet" in the hands of a man with no grip on the reality of warped instincts. It's more like vice versa, so don't go letting him own and operate one.

"Look at'im," whispers Cindabilla, seeing Demon so attentive. "Ferddy prides himself on 'em—drunken ol'Babette-beater. Thinks he can identify with him. No way! It don't do Demon justice!"

"Maybe he's *just* like him."

"No way. Is not."

"Is too."

"Is not."

Daniel stares at her sucking on the reefer.

She says, "Is not."

"Is."

"Snot!" The girl rolls away, giggling. Daniel grabs the notebook again.

He says, "Don't choo think Demon misses the pack?"

"Who'd you think we ah—Gram, Ferddy, Aunt Nellie, Babs'n me?"

"Who's the lead wolf, then?"

"It sure ain't Babette. Ferddy's reduced her to blubber. Once Gram was lead, but now it's me'n Uncle Drunkman."

"Which means Demon submits to neither. Wouldn't want a baby around him. How you keep chickens'n pigs I d'know."

"He did get over the fence once. Ate a Piglet."

Daniel is getting nowhere with his notes on land control in Maine. The focus in history this grading period is regional. For a while he shuts up, letting his eyes scan the page, leaving Cindabilla to her pot-induced giggling.

"Evah notice," he says at last. "Maine's map is different than other New England states? Look." He has flipped to his laminated map of the region in the back of the notebook. He shows her. "No roads up theya. No towns, anathin."

Her eyes tearing from the smoke, she squints at it in the bad light. "S'all woods up theya."

"But how'd it happen." Should he even bother trying to get her involved?

"Papah companies."

"'N' how'd *they* get that land?"

"Won it in the lottery."

"Mrs. Mason says it's a result of state legislators being land'n railroad owners in the last century. They made laws to suit, paid hardly any taxes."

"Like my answer betta."

"Guess what, you're partly right. Theya *was* a lottery fah land in Maine. Didn't work, though. Before the land grab the Massachusetts legislature tried everything to get rid of land."

"Now people'd *kill* fah some. Fact, somebody did, last year."

Daniel lets it pass as reefer imaginings. "What about Gram's land, though. She'd get rich selling to developers."

"Don't think Ferddy hadn't thought of it. Gram wouldn't hear of it."

There is silence. Cindabilla drops the last of her reefer roach, sizzling, into the bucket. She reaches out to tickle Demon's nose with a piece of straw. He sneezes and licks his chops. The girl giggles. "What was we saying?"

"About Gram not letting Ferddy sell off."

"Oh.... Time'll come, though, she caunt do anathin 'bout it. You said something about land grabbing?—he's one t'do it."

"What would happen t'you then?"

"Whad y'mean?" She is stroking Demon's coarse hair.

"Won't he kick you out—if Gram's not... quite there?"

Her hands stop stroking and she glances quizzically at Daniel. "Why would he do that?"

He looks at her wide soft eyes. Her dilated pupils. Cindabilla is stoned.

"He shrugs. "Ferddy don't exactly *like* you."

"What's that got do with it? He's my Uncle. Might kill me, but he'd never kick me out."

Right, thinks Daniel remembering the wolf pack. A wolf might dominate and chastise, but would it kick another wolf out of the pack? He has never studied wolves but, one day, he might get the chance.

Loki

When it came time to hear of it, Chrischana would decide that her intuitive procrastination had been a good thing: Petey Prince was never going to make it. He *would* come back and start pounding on her again: he would he would he would.

Petey Prince found his way back to alcohol in Gottheim, falling in with Ferdinand Sessions and Alvin Robichaud. Of late, when it came to socializing, the Robichaud twins were pretty much split up and gone their separate ways. What the hell, thought Alvin, it was January and you could only stay sober as long as the saw was in your hands. Or, according to Petey, while in the fucking paper mill. He thought he had a better excuse than whatever Ferddy's was (Ferddy didn't need one), or Alvin's. But then, he did not know about the tattered flag flying on the cold ledge above Robichaud's, or that Alvin could not get it out of his mind. Peter could not get his wife to come back, his counselor Hermann Gottesman was on his case to think about being useful to others and the God-awful paper mill was getting to him. Get out the violins, get out the sombreros.

Evidently he had forgotten that alcohol made him insane. That it made him hate her with pretended impunity.

I'm a changed man, he thought sentimentally. "You shouldn't be doing that," Peter said to Ferddy after the other slugged Babette on that blistering January night. Babette had run into the bathroom and locked the door.

"Shit," said Ferddy. "I'll bust you instead, flatlanda!"

The words they spoke resembled mere sounds, muddled and slurry like the sodden brains in their heads. Sitting at the kitchen table beneath a single glaring bulb, gentle Alvin looked on, slobber-eyed but pitying, as the brawl erupted in Hannah Sessions' kitchen. She came clumping down from upstairs to see what the matter was. Hannah had pretty much kept her nose out of her son's petulant brawls, but now that she was losing her mind she would come clumping down, her long gray hair wild and nightgown flapping... and she always misunderstood. Tonight she thought Ferddy was her long dead husband, Brazelia, horsing around with his brothers, Barbour and Absalom. Brazelia was deceased fifteen years, and Barbour and Absalom never came around anymore.

"Brazelia! You boys just watch the crock'ry, heah?" She croaked this and Petey turned to see what was talking. Ferddy cracked him a good one—a perfect sucker punch that sent them both sprawling. Together in a clatter of chairs they fell back against the porcelain sink, ripping its curtain and exposing the plumbing, a couple cans of scouring powder that had been used up a decade ago, and two cases of empties covered in dust. "Fucking asshole," Ferddy slurred, trying to pull himself up by the curtain, which tore the rest of the way. He hit his head against the box of empties, cursing. As Petey rolled away with his hand to his eye, Ferddy lay there, uttering unintelligible threats.

Sitting there still, Alvin thought he heard the word *Demon*, and decided it was time to go back to Emma. He slipped out the gable end door into the brutal wind, wondering if his pickup would start.

The gale was roaring through the valley, waking his slobber eyes. "Holy fucking funeral march!" He pulled the door of his truck closed after him, fumbling for the keys.

"Keys keys, fucking keys...." He said it under his out-pouring breath, searching one pocket after another. He felt the ignition with his finger, searched his pockets again. The wind blew a spray of snow from the field across the hood. Again he searched his pockets, mumbling. "Just lay down a minute," he said, resting his head on the seat. "Find the keys in a minute...."

The door of the Cape Cod house slammed, but Alvin never heard it.

Petey Prince left the sagging snow-caked house, hurrying to his own pickup parked behind Alvin's in the dooryard. For an instant he wondered why Alvin's truck was still here. Then, forgetting that Babette was holed up in there, he thought maybe the logger had gone to the can instead of slipping out the door as he had first supposed.

Well leave 'em to the madhouse, then, he thought. *Jeezus Crowbar!* Where'd this fucked up wind come from! He hurried to close the door and turn the key in the ignition, gunning the engine. For a minute he sat there, trying to clear his head, staring out at Jasper Mountain where it blocked the stars and showed itself faintly white. The wind had chilled and waked him. Now it buffeted, rattling the truck. Jeezus, I'm drunk. Got to go see what's his name, the big man in Jericho. Whad'll I do?—can't live with drinking, can't live without it. Why did that bitch leave me? Are you gonna start blaming her again? She did nothing but live right. God help me.... Lord Jesus, I'm fucked up again!

Peter threw the truck in reverse and turned the wheel, backing. At first he did not see the wolf-hybrid come bounding around the corner through blinding snow. Snarling and snapping, it charged the truck. Peter looked out the window at the pale working jaws. Demon leaped onto the hood, growling, challenging him through the glass. The screaming wind gusted, as the dog's claws scraped the hood and frosty glass. Peter put the pedal to the floor, flew a dozen yards and stomped the brakes. Demon kept going and hit the lane, but he scrambled up on the gritty ice. Peter turn the wheel and drove across the snowy yard and into the road. Off his shoulder he saw the demon dog, hurtling through the snow fields to intercept him. But the pickup was faster, leaving the wolf loping behind. Peter Prince drove off, with a glance in the rearview mirror. The black speck that was Demon moved behind in the shimmery snow-gusting night.

Cindabilla went to school in a daze, seeing little, hearing nothing. *Why couldn't it o'been Uncle Ferddy? Should'o'been a skier, at least, why?"*

At dinnertime, Daniel noticed her silence. The cafeteria hustle and clatter was a sea of sound in which they floated together isolated, as the lunch line snaked along. *What's the matter, Cindabilla?* He wanted to ask.

Then, finding conscious comfort in his attentive silence, at last she murmured, "Why'd it have t'be Alvin?" Her pale eyes turned toward him, questioning, before turning away again.

"Why? What happened?"

But she only stared past him, silent again.

After school he went as usual to *The Voter* office to start sweeping the floor. Mr. Nutting in his green visor stooped over the stone, setting type for the week's edition.

Daniel scanned the backward letters, reading the lead upside down. *An area logger was found frozen in his pickup truck, Monday. Hannah Sessions' teenage granddaughter discovered the body before school, outside her house. Alvin Robichaud was thought to have lost consciousness in his vehicle, and it is believed that alcohol played a role in the ....*

Today was Monday. Daniel looked away.

"Loki's beating one of his children." Small explosions of boiling pitch popped onto the hearthstone. Watching the fire crackle, Gloria Fay said it dreamily. She sighed.

102

"Who's Loki?" asked Theodora Prescott, Gloria's future sister-in-law. "And why would he beat his children?"

Staring into the fire, Gloria made no answer. Her irritated brother James answered for her. "Loki is one of her heathen gods." Lounging beside Theo, he pursed his lips and cocked his gaze toward the ceiling.

From a comfortable chair Gloria looked over at the flames reflected in his glasses. The niche in which they sat, above the Great Room, was glowing and shadowed by the play of firelight from the hearth. It was intimate space with its own small fireplace. She said tartly, "He's not my God. He, big brother, is the Norse counterpart of your Lucifer. I just happen to enjoy reading about the gods—Teutonic or otherwise. Is that so bad? I find it intellectually stimulating." Again she turned her eyes toward the living flames.

The nook, in which they relaxed after dinner so intimately, was dark. The diaphanous blaze across from them was set in the midst of weeping stonework. It gave the setting a somber medieval cast.

Idly pinpointing the source of James's irritation, Gloria became aware that she had been ignoring his fiancée again. "I'm sorry, Theo," she said. "What would you like to know about 'my' Loki?" She shot James another glance.

Theo understood that she lacked Gloria's approval and could never be admired by her. She felt, even while striving for the other's respect, that she was merely tolerated, the object of recollected kindness. Almost in her mid-thirties and a few years older than her betrothed, Theo had learned that she was never going to be the wise, poised, cool, undisturbed and dignified thing that she longed to be. She wished only that she did not care. If only she might stop trying to work herself into some elusive but desired form. She said, "Well, I just wondered why he would beat his children, but, if he's a devil, I guess that explains it."

Golden Gloria hid her impatience behind a smile. "It's part of the story of Loki the Mischievous. Whenever the fire crackled, old wives would say Loki was beating his children."

Theo smiled back, her prominent teeth and receding chin tucked beneath her bird-like nose. Dainty and refined in posture and bearing, she was dressed with taste and care. Theo often reminded James of fragile spring flowers. It helped that she worshiped him, made him feel admirable and wise.

"We can learn a lot from the tales of old gods and goddesses," argued Gloria. She was thinking of Balder the Radiant, who was destroyed by the treachery of Loki. In the tale, this active jealous malice became Loki's undoing, for the gods could never forgive Balder's loss. Gloria continued. "Loki married Glut, whose name meant glow. She gave birth to two children, Ember and Ash, who were regularly beaten by Loki. Apparently Loki was the god of fire who corrupted himself for the sake of his own glee."

"Oh. I remember you saying once that these stories originated in Iceland? That makes sense because Iceland is built on fire? They'd just about have to have gods who could come from a volcanic region. We've all heard about that trench in the Atlantic terminating there —or something— right?"

"Yes, but they didn't know about that then," said Gloria. "It was just to show the dual nature of fire: They made Loki and had him turn bad."

"Before Christianity came along and made more sense to them," breezed James. Dryly he said, "Then later people from a totally unrelated and secularized culture would throw Christianity over for that senseless stuff again."

But Gloria was too tired and dreamy from a day on the slopes to snap at his bait. Let the little hot air balloon float itself to the ceiling on its little superior hot airs. No need to look, she could see the self-satisfied smile her wiry blond brother would wear. He was *sooo* good at what he did: He merely pointed at a piece of prime property, said the word *condominium*, and (with a maximum of grief from the planning board) a condominium would appear. He huffed and he puffed and all their strictures fell down. The huffing and puffing made him the butt of jokes, but Gloria noticed that he frequently got what he wanted. Harry Golding thought he was a gem of a salesman because James could sell off those condos and ski hauses before they were piled together. He was good at evoking them for prospective buyers. She knew she was no match for his rhetoric or insistence, yet she kept her own counsel, answering him back. But generally not out loud.

Even so they were close as siblings, if not so friendly of late. Staying together at their parents' condo, each worked toward a firm financial foothold in Gottheim, with a certain amount of recognition thrown in. It cast a necessary zest into their lives. They were earnest, hard-working, talented, and believed or at least tried to believe that these other things were subordinate to what was truly valuable: a basic underlying decency. Their closeness clued James Fay that Gloria persisted in thoughts of the mechanic, someone named Balder, long after denying interest in him. But she denied it because she was getting nowhere and thought it best to give up and move on. Or try to move on.

Gloria stared into the fire and thought of Loki plotting to use the god Balder's blind brother against him. Why does her Balder insist on traditional values and children? She has answered him back several times but he remains intractable to the point of seeming not to care if she wrecks her life on inconsequential trysts with others. Maybe these thoughts are worthless, but he certainly needs no help from Loki in plotting against himself. Does he feel the pain he should be going through? Every time she saw him he seemed as cheerful and unperturbed as the time before.... With absolutely no sign that he knew she has been to other beds.... That she was in no way, shape, or form true to his impossible conception of love.

But it wasn't like they had a commitment... yet what *was* it like? They had feelings... feelings that would grow stale and dissipate over time... if left unattended. She wanted to prevent this with a living arrangement. One that would safeguard her status and career. She must be adamant, true to herself. How could she compromise by joining with the man who found her dreams fantastic and futile. The man talked of living in what he called the real world, but his "real" looked like fantasy to her. Having adjourned to The Coffee Story after bumping into one another in the store, Balder had proceeded to fill her ears with plans to make *Simons Ledge* yield what he described as its wild "commercial" bounty. Mushrooms, roots, berries! If that wasn't fantastic and futile, what was? With humor she reminded him of the highly efficient network in place all over the globe which saw to it that more people were being fed than ever before. He had chuckled and said it was better for its people to be made out of what grows in Gottheim because that's where they live. Fantastic! "The place is made of them and they should be made of it. People here would be better off not being made out of Mexico or South America." She had laughed of course, asking if he planned to do without coffee. At least he enjoyed her wit.

But her dreams of a consulting career in Gottheim and the prospect of a beautiful new home for herself—he thought these indulgent. He did not say so or accuse her in any way, but his wisecracks showed plainly enough what he thought of any plan connected with the ski company. Did he think people had no business exercising talent, know-how, or capital? The social and psychological professional agreed that work in the service sector is *not* unhealthy or degrading. Providing work in Gottheim, clean, nontoxic, non-industrial work, was not something to be ashamed of. Gloria sat by the fire, meditating this. A sputter of sparks from the hearth scarcely roused her.

Vaguely disappointed, James saw that his sister would not be provoked into engaging him in religious debate. That extra cup of coffee at dinner had primed him to expound, but it would be no fun if she continued to slouch there gazing mindlessly at the fire. Its yellow gaze reflected from the dark pupils of her eyes but her expression was in no way kindled by it. The antique owl andirons, standing tall before the flames, showed fire in their yellow gaze. He had always admired those owls for the glow passing through their glass eyes.

He sighed. *Well, Theodora, it's you then.* He turned to the lady who made him feel wise. "I saw a bumper sticker that cracked me up today. 'Keep Maine Green,' it said: 'Shoot a developer.'" He laughed his popcorn laugh, a sputter of little explosions like the popping of corn. "It was on a brand new four-wheel-drive pickup, as shiny as the day it came off a lot— even with all the snow, sand and salt we've had. Like the guy had something to complain about.... That's the kind of guy I'd like to convert to our clusters. It's such a great concept, the cluster.... You won't be sorry you invested, Dory."

"I never could be sorry, James." She brightened at his attention, eager to please and be pleased. He had not needed to ask if she was interested in supporting his project. But she had another reason for investing, as well, something of which he had no inkling. The mountain was the real future of Gottheim these days: The woods could not last forever, she thought. She had reasoned it all out—forgetting her laughter of only weeks before when someone mentioned the decline of the woods. Gottheim Chair's own decline was derided among area business people and attributed to her mismanagement. In her low moments she had to agree with them. Then she came upon the verses of scripture that led her to believe her ineptitude was predestined by the sins of her ancestors. In spite of her fear of other mill owners' possible retaliation, Theo had raised employee wages. She shrank whenever she saw Lyman Bearce... which wasn't all that often now that she had changed churches, but he always stared at her keenly and did not speak if they happened to meet.

"Know what I've been thinking lately, James?... That Jasper Mountain coming into my life this way might be the signal for me to go ahead... with something I've been planning... ever since...." She did not finish the thought aloud. James already knew about the sins, but he *loved* her. She could not quite bring herself to confide these things to Gloria. Gloria was a flaming liberal, always championing the little people... but this she would like.

James leaned toward her intently and there was an eager interest visible just behind his fire-bright glasses. He felt sure she was about to do more.

Triumphantly, she burst, "I want to give Gottheim Chair to its employees!"

His gaze drifted away. He had to consider and turned back to the fire. Gloria sat up suddenly in her upholstered chair. This was just *too much* instability. She stared at the back of Theo's head in disbelief. What in the wild world was this woman onto now? At once Theo's harebrained idiocies became swiftly charged with import unseen until now. Everything she had ever said or done now gathered to itself presentiment. James turned just a bit, sending his sister a flickering gaze, a slight frown of warning.

But Theo saw the signal. Although she had perceived movement she did not see Gloria's expression. Yet, it was not necessary to see her fiancé's sister. From the changing expression of James's face, from the change perceived in Gloria's posture, a change of attitude was betrayed. Theodora waited anxiously for James to compose himself. He always did. He was wonderful at covering any disturbance, at changing an awkward situation with loving assurance. Swiftly and surely he would put her at ease with but a few words of comfort. He could coax both himself and her into comfortable compromise on an instant's notice.

But the expression of comfort does not come. James looks away. He stands quietly and walks to the fireplace, staring down. If only she could see through his back into his face.

His sister comes forward in her chair, with a look of disbelief ripening to scorn. Fidgeting, impatient, she bores a look into James's backside. Why doesn't he speak? Gentle the situation?

But James is staring down at a crusty dark char of wood, its undersides glowing. The fire needs fresh wood. Even the tall owls' eyes have stopped glowing.

A stack of birch and pine nearby suggests itself. He stoops to gather three sticks. Theo begins twisting her hands together. Now she laces and unlaces her fingers.

"Theo," says Fay. He lays a log with curly bark on the live coals. Quickly its curls catch. Flames roll themselves around the wood, a firm sure hand of fire. "Theo, you shouldn't do that to the legacy left you by your father."

His back toward her, he lets the statement hang in the air.

Now softly, "Think of it, Theo. The beautiful chair factory, maker of fine shaker-style furniture, your great-grandfather started it. Remember that heritage, how those elegant chairs furnished the finest resorts in New England and upstate New York. You can still find those chairs in the old resorts in the Berkshires and the Adirondacks. He was an upright man, beginning with the best motives: to make beautiful furniture that would last, chairs to hand down to one's descendents. There is no way you can even know if he was involved in—that... other business. No way at all. How would he feel, knowing you gave away what he worked so hard to achieve?"

Mute, a pathetic dejected look sank into Theo's features. The slight sagging of age, just beginning in her face, was hung with the sadness he kindled in her.

"Look at that factory now, Theo... what it's become in Vernon's hands, your hands... in this last generation of Phineas Prescott's descent. You two cousins have let the place deteriorate to the point of collapse. Your series of... erroneous investments... that elaborate generating system you bought.... These things have contributed to the factory's decline. What your workers need, if you want to help them, is a steady and knowledgeable hand at the helm. You can't just throw the place to them—to the winds."

Gloria has sunk back, resuming her lax self possession. Momently she feels sorry for Theo. But her gaze rests dreamily again in the fire as she contemplates the renewed images of her thoughts.

Turning from the hearth to his fiancée with a tentative look, softly he says, "You understand what I'm saying?"

With sad eyes she looks at him, her chin sunk into her neck. She bows her auburn head meekly before him, tears glistening, slowly shaking her head. "Oh James...."

Now he came to her. "Dory." It was tenderly said. His hands reaching for hers, he kneels on one knee. "Dory, don't worry. It's the last thing I want. Please. We'll work it out. Now that I see how real your concern is. A conscientious concern for your workers. We'll work something out—you, Vernon and me." He lifted her woebegone chin with two fingers, tilting it upward and catching her eye in a pleading look.

Hopeful eyes turned up to his. Things *will* be okay. James will bring her through. He had not left her comfortless, shut out. He was bringing her back with his great understanding.

She sat back, looking over at dreamy-eyed Gloria. James' sister glanced back an abstracted smile. Theo turned toward the fire again. The room was warm, but she shivered. Already, outside the lodge, January's cold had put on a sudden warming trend. But James had placed two more sticks, of pine, on the fire. He stood back, looking with disgust at pitch stuck to his hands. Flames took hold of the logs. Orange fire leapt up playing over the wood, strong. Soon they would sputter and pop, a tiny fireworks exploding in sparky showers. Loki, beating his children.

James drove Theo back into Gottheim, waiting to see her safely into the house on tree-shadowed Swann Street. He kissed her on the threshold, holding her some moments. Again he kissed her, saying good night as she stepped inside. He turned and walked into the surprising evening air. January had softened. A thaw was on. Snow beneath his boots in the drive had turned to slush and rivulets ran into the street. He loosened the buttons of his overcoat then surprised himself by taking it off. Think of it! Wasn't it just a day or two ago that one of those loggers he hired froze in his truck? Shy man. Quiet. Good worker.

Fay stamped the slush, salt and sand from his boots, and climbed into his gleaming BMW. The street lamp shown onto the dash as he flipped through his keys. He started the car and rolled down Swann Street. He now had his doubts about the best way to handle Theo's—idea. James always tried to be particular and conscientious. She should not be encouraged to do such a thing to herself. Gottheim Chair should be made a viable company or else sold for scrap. It had an expensive generating system, and a prime location on the highway between the resort and village. This incident had confirmed that Theo needed him desperately. She was fragile and screwy and lovely and loving, and he was completely happy in her. This would be a good Christian marriage. Theo would be a kind submissive wife. The Scripture and common sense would prevail in their union, and Theo would be safe knowing that he would look out for her interests.

... Even so, he wasn't quite comfortable. You had to look out for the one you loved, but you also had to be careful of that element of self-interest. *Always seem to have a problem with that.* It's tricky, trying to come along in the world. But it can be done, carefully and without corruption. His personal income was growing (unlike his sister's—who seemed content to bestow her professional energies for very little compensation). His fiscal equality with Theo will quiet his conscience. Then they will be one in every way: Theo Prescott will be Theo Fay. The date will be set. They will arrive in the same place at the same time.

The slushy turnings of Gottheim brought Fay to the highway. He turned north, heading for the mountain resort and his parent's condo which he currently shared with his sister. His own home at Mason's Mills would be ready by late spring, summer. If only Gloria would find what James had found. He worried about her, suspecting that she was becoming promiscuous (although she would never use that term). James could not believe that what she did with her own body didn't matter. That is a disastrous supposition, he thought, its potential great for harm. But if that fact eludes her (by some fantastic notion that evil can't happen to her), then the sheer *ugliness* of bedhopping should deter her. She has such a sense of beauty, of elegance and charm—of the fitness of things.... Why can't she see its application in this? She would never confess to anything specific, of course, but when she says things like "It's just sex, Jimmy," what can he think? As though intimacy were something to be used and carelessly tossed aside. He himself was looking forward to sex with Theo, but it will be a sacrament—as well as fulfilling and fun. He had succeeded in repressing the gift of God, and now he planned to enjoy it. *And I don't think Gloria is really enjoying herself. She seems downright miserable to me.*

Gloria sits on the sofa staring at the night-blackened glass of the living room windows. The lamp on a corner table shines, reflecting her back to herself off the otherwise darkened panes. She has flicked off the television following a report on a hideous new social disease. *Incurable.* One that has been haunting the homosexual community—but now they say it can be heterosexually transmitted. This mere information has evoked sudden panic and she cannot rest her mind on a thing without feeling the fear of this report. Her intrauterine device can prevent pregnancy, not disease. Gloria clutches at the arm of the sofa, picturing submicroscopic bodies busily infiltrating her cell surfaces... reducing... even destroying their capacity to produce antibodies. A tingling sensation sends ticklings through her arms. She sits momently paralyzed. Suddenly Gloria jumps up, rubbing her arms, runs to close the drapery. Stop that! She tells herself. You're being hysterical!

An abstracted glance into the parking lot below shows the high beams of her brother's BMW cutting through the pink glow of parking lot lights. Yanking the cord she closes the drapes and scampers across the room to shut off the light. For a moment she stands, torn between a desire for mute safety in his company and the dread of exposure. Yet at the sound of his step outside the door she flees to her room, swiftly shutting the door. She does not turn on the light but sits tensely, taut as a night before storm.

The night softens into a mild subtropical mood. Daytime brings a ripening through the mountains as the next night approaches, threatening to turn summer out of the atmosphere and down onto the slopes. Summer settles to warm the stiff limbs and thin twigs of the trees toward incipient budding. Thickets, soaking up moisture from this thaw, begin reddening. In the morning people will marvel, coming out to greet the next disturbing phase of their lives. They will wonder over the electrical storms that passed well before dawn. They will even take an acrid whiff of the passing age.

Not long after Alvin Robichaud froze to death in his pickup (his chainsaw and protective gear in the back), the weather turned wicked freakish. So warm is the night that a few vehicles loaded with teenagers head out toward Quaker Town in search of a place to party before the weather hardens up again. This is no Gott'im January, that's sure. A thaw is usual, but this one is balmy enough to make summer hearts kick and call. Tonight just has to turn out awesome!

The international cross-border tire dump of Ceylon Segar will make an exceptional party place. Imagine the freedom of bouncing—bombed, bonkers—off the top of some pile of rubber. No punishment!

Daniel and Cindabilla are crushed into the backseat of Jenna York's powder blue '74 Plymouth Volaré. Jenna worked evenings washing dishes at the Pennywhistle Pub in order to buy this car. She found it in a rural used-car lot in Copenhagen and fell for its soft color and low feminine lines. It had dingy white bucket seats so she scrubbed that vinyl for hours trying and failing to bring back its marshmallow whiteness. She plans to write Heloise for tips.

Some kids have already begun partying, tilting back bottles of Budweiser in the back of Buster Boone's pickup ahead of them. They dash empties against rocks along the edges of the wooded road, reveling in the crash of broken glass, yelling.

The vehicles turn off their headlights as they slide into the exit at the far end of the tire dump. Ceylon Segar's office is in a secondhand trailer, at the opposite end, beside the shed housing an old combination backhoe/bucket loader next a huge pile of sand. Their plan is to stay away from that end of the dump in case Mr. Segar (pronounced Cigar) shows up unannounced. Jenna pulls up behind Buster's beat-up Ford truck. The vehicles vomit kids in all directions. With exaggeration they try to keep the noise down as the teenagers regroup, some of them scattering over one immense pile of tires.

"Mr. Nutting, there's no way to contain sound in a group of hormone saturated bodies. There was more energy there than the headsaw at Pale's sawlog mill. Think what a carload of that kind of energy could accomplish if it wasn't intent on partying. Visualize it helping at a natural disaster. Picture 'em filling sandbags beside the flooding Mississippi." Eloise Patadoe will say these things later, when she tries to help reconstruct the night's events for the editor, corroborating what Daniel Twitchell himself will finally have an opportunity to report.

Their eyes adjust to the dark on the drive out to the multi-million tire dump. The air the adolescents tumble into is fresh and mild. Dampness comes on wings as it lifts the hair of these children of Gott'im. Their vehicles are parked in a puddled lane between two mountainous piles. Tires are scattered about on patches of rotten ice and in muddy puddles. The puddles throw back dim reflected light from a few tall lampposts. The atmosphere is so saturated that it too seems to give back the light. The tire mounds rise around the kids in massive smelly walls, some draped in melting snow. The dripping and dampness is over everything. These huge piles remind Daniel of the great wood-chip and pulp piles at Adirondack Paper where his father works. Except there the smell is of butchered wood overlaid with the toxic stench of pulp digesters.

The party split into three, more or less distinct, groups; with a quiet couple or two drifting away from the more social center. The groups drape themselves across lower tiers of one monstrous pile. Three conversations are brewing, three elements in the variegated dialogue abroad in the last decades of the 20th century since the first advent of Christ.

Weasel Whitman's group sits highest atop the pile, alternately smoking pot and downing Budweiser, searching for the best buzz; taking loose sometimes headlong leaps onto the bald castoffs of a gluttonous and spendthrift society. Tonight Weasel's group jokes loudly about dumb Frenchmen and, from time to time, calling out mockery on the second group below. This bunch sits a bit isolated on a lower tier, talking philosophically and pronouncing on the fate of the world: quieter and not quite solemnly led by Simon Perkins and John Brown. Daniel and Cindabilla are in the third group which stays more or less on the puddled ground talking of many things. The conversation ranges a wide and desultory course, including substance abuse, the size of the tire dump, the latest gossip, records, the new compact disks and VCRs, TV shows, *Flashdance*.

At some point the conversations of these three groups will converge and an angel of the air (now lying in a large mud puddle) will lift itself and hover in Snotty Cob's lurid face, grinning like hell. Eloise Patadoe will show up then, casting her unique brand of weirdness into the gathering of this strange January night.

Cindabilla opens her blue denim pouch to take out, with a flourish, her long-stemmed clay pipe. She packs it loosely with home-cured marijuana leaves from her stash. The pungent smell of burning grass mingles with the moist air and stink of vulcanized rubber. Some of the kids stare at the pipe in amazement. "Found this in the dump next the old cellah hole in the woods back o'the farm... when I was little. Really had'd dig, they picked ovah that dump s'much. Come direct from China... when it... fell through a crevice on tother side o'the world." She grins. "Worked its way down through earth'n come up tother side till it reached the ol'settlers' dump. Frost upheaves"

"You're full of it," says Daniel. "It was brought d'Portland by a sailing master and sold to a potato farmer."

"My version's betta. You want upgrade yours a li'l just take a puff." She points the stem of the pipe in his direction.

"No thanks. Don't need no head full o'dope to heighten my memory loss."

Jenna breaks in. "Daniel's right, Cindabilly. Weed expands your mind, and then, being too big fah your head, it drifts out your ear holes'n floats into the air." She points to the misty low skies. "Look. I can see your leaking mind drifting up theya now."

Involuntarily Cindabilla looks up, her eyes wide. She drops her gaze, glaring at the other girl. "*Shut* fuckin'up, Jenna!"

"But Cinda it happened to m'Uncle Benny when I was in seventh grade'n now look at'em! He's over to 'Gusty till his paranoia goes down." She says it all with a level face.

The other grimaces then grins back at them, turning her back to scramble up the pile.

Daniel looks admiration at the dark-haired Jenna, her mouth firm, attractive eyes full of humor. Suddenly he decides that her tactics are cruel and he follows Cindabilla up the pile until they are ten feet above the kids on the ground. Jenna takes a pull on her bottle of Bud and smiles up at them.

"My brains might be leaking," quips Cindabilla "but that stuff'll *pickle* your brains! Uncle Benny, Uncle Ferddy—what's the difference? Ain't neither what we gont be, right?" She rolls her eyes.

Jenna screeched. "No way! That slob-eyed brute! I'll never be that bad." Her tone is solid with confidence. "The way he goes bout it's all wrong. I just get t'the place waya I feel nice'n happy, then stop. Stop right theya. But not them." She throws her hand in the direction of Weasel Whitman's group. "Drunks like that keep going till they fall down. Look at them!"

They looked to see Weasel up there, tottering. Down he tumbles, like a bag of disjointed bones. He lies in a heap, one arm and one leg partly submerged in a mud puddle. Rolling over with a groan, he pushes himself back up, heedless of ridicule shouting, laughing, filling the air. The remaining boys up top follow with copycat tumbles. Then they all climb up the pile to their sixpacks again. They upend cans, wobble about, and start the process all over again.

Weasel wears an innocent blithered face. To Farty, Burpy and Snotty—his target audience—he yells out, "What's smotter'n a French kid in Headstart?"

No one is bothering to answer. Burpy is entertaining himself with the pastime that earned him his nickname. Farty upends his can. Snotty just grins and waits for Weasel to provide the answer.

"Two Frenchmen in med school!"

His friends laugh, sleepy-eyed, shaking their heads and having heard this one time too many. Snotty grins, waiting to hear another.

"What's scarier'n a grammy's ghost?"

Farty, Burpy and Snotty just grin.

"A naked dumb French grandmother's ghost!"

"No no," objects Farty. "A dumb French grammy ghost dressed t'look like Stephen King's grammy."

"What's cold'n harder'n skier's snot?" Weasel yells, looking around to make sure of his audience. He's got the attention of everyone, including the group to one side pronouncing on the fates of the world. Jigging on his tire, Weasel says, "A Frenchman taking a nap in his pickup—at 20 below—while his keys sit on the dashboard."

Silence. A movement of the skies draws off their attention. All look toward a faint flashing in the southwest. Remotely thunder sounds. Farty and Burpy decide to laugh. They laugh so hard... they roll into Weasel, taking him down with them. Snotty just grins and clambers down to where John Brown and Simon Perkins sit shaking their heads. The philosophers begin buzzing over Weasel's tasteless joke.

Nearer the ground, Cindabilla says, "His brain's so pickled he clean f'got his father married a Frenchwoman. We all got French in our families some waya. Weaz, you shithead, your own mother's French!"

Weasel is sprawled on the ground in a puddle, his eyes closed. It looks like he has stopped breathing. But he moans and turns onto his stomach, the side of his face all muddy and wet.

"In't dead yet, anaway," says Cindabilla, sucking on the narrow stem of her pipe. A little above, Daniel and Jenna watch its contents glow.

"Somebody ought do something bout these tires, says Jenna's boyfriend, Almon Ouellette. He's a gangling basketball player, and not generally known for environmental concern. He has been casting an astonished gaze across the piles ever since Jenna pulled her Volaré into the fantastic setting. Under the influence of Cindabilla's pot it feels like something out of the movies, some sort of science fiction or horror show.

Simon Perkins calls out from the little group above: "You know who's gont have do something bout it, don't choo? Us, that's who. Those friggin'yuppie baby boomers is making messes like this all over the planet—expecting *us* t'clean up after 'em!"

Cindabilla laughed her squeaky laugh. "Ceylon Cigar—a fuckin'baby boomer?"

Someone says, "What's a yuppie?"

"S'a inside out hippie give birth to a puppy."

Something comes around the base of the tire mountain, turning all eyes. The party freezes, staring at Eloise Patadoe with her horsey face and awkward walk. She is wearing a tie-dyed T-shirt and denim overalls.

"Well don't stop on my account. It's just me, an errant baby boomer... but you can treat me as a figment of your imagination, if you want."

Her sudden appearance, coupled with the faintly charged atmosphere, suits the fantastic frame of mind that has taken possession of them. Almon Ouellette stares at her like she is the Holy Mother come down to bid them good night.

She says, "Glad to see others are concerned to keep an eye out for Jasper Mary's treasure ground. Indian treasure *is* buried around here somewhere isn't it?"

"Shit," slurs Weasel from his puddle. "There's no treasure in this mud."

"Evidently," says Eloise, eyeing him pointedly.

Tentatively, a couple kids laugh. She is after all an adult. Sort of. And they *are* trespassing. Was the reminder about the treasure sarcasm?

Then, as if to emphasize her statement about him, Weasel retches. He wallows to his knees, vomiting.

Everyone groans. Jenna moves away.

Crossing the puddled lane, Eloise keeps walking, rounding the corner between monstrous piles and passing out of sight. They stare into the dim direction where she has vanished. "Was that f'real?" whispers Almon Ouellette.

"Real as the six fingers on the ends o'your hands," retorts Cindabilla. "Anybody else got puke?"

Laughter erupts through the group, breaking the spell.

Their former vigor dissipated, still Farty and Burpy recommence wobbling on tires. The party's interlude with Eloise has started the night in a new direction. Softly, a sort of depression settles. The couples who initially wandered away now drift back. Nothing much is said until Buster Boone notices that the gas cap on his beat-up pickup is missing. He circulates, asking who took it, but no one seems to know. A flash lights the distance, and a tiny rumble of thunder is heard. At last someone says, "What's that smell?" They all start sniffing the air. "It's ozone," says one. "Storm's coming."

Another says, "That's not ozone... it's..." (*sniff*) ... "rubber burning."

"Rubber burning?! You shittin'me!" exclaims Cindabilla.

"Tires is burning!" Yells Daniel.

But they stop where they stand, listening, as a distant bleating approaches, followed by the pounding of quick feet. Snotty rounds a corner of the great pile. "Help!" He cries. "Tires is burning! Whad'm I gont do?!"

Galvanized, the kids come to him, leaping across scattered tires, splashing through puddles and slipping on patches of ice. As Snotty turns, they follow him around the mountainous pile. Across the lane, ahead, an intermittent glow of fire shows through heavy black smoke billowing down toward them. Cascading, it mingles with the saturated air. The black breath of burning rubber and flakes of ash fill the lane, as panicky teenagers hurry toward the fire—then scatter back from the snapping, hissing and popping of the blaze.

John Brown, whose father owns an excavating business in Gottheim, scrambles off toward the opposite end of the dump were Ceylon Segar has his office and shed. Seeing his plan, Jenna York runs after, calling him as she heads to her car. The others stand back, talking at once or staring wild-eyed over their shoulders, everyone wondering what to do. As Jenna catches up, John Brown jumps into her car and they speed off. "Waya they going?" Someone wonders, and Daniel answers, "Prob'ly gone to call the fire department."

Everyone talking excitedly, the kids head back to the pickup. Someone says, "Snotty, what the hell'd you do?"

But weak and white Snotty merely blinks. He stammered, "S-simon said it was up t'us t'do something bout those tires. I done something!" He flings his arms up across his eyes. "The wrong thing!" Trembling, blubbering, he leans against the grill of Buster's pickup.

"Shit, Snotty," says Cinda, tempted to put her arm around him. But Snotty's name is apt, and she can't quite bring herself to do it.

"Whad Snotty do now?" It's a sleepy slurred voice. They look over to see Weasel still in the mud but now lolling against the tire pile.

"Nothing! Just set twelve million tires on fire."

"That what I smell?"

"Doaw. Just marijuana burning. Go back t'sleep."

Daniel steps away, listening for the distant wail of fire engines. The others grow silent as well, leaning toward the direction of Gottheim, hoping for the faint whoop of the volunteer call. But Weasel is saying, " We betta get in that pickup'n get.... Big trouble heah...." He continues lolling there, still unable to move.

But the sound...hooking the group's attention...is the sound of an engine approaching from the far end of the dump. Then through the dimness and murk a dark shape looms out, roaring. Its bucket high and full, the loader lumbers toward them. A cheer goes up. John Brown is coming with a load of sand, Segar's makeshift provision for such an emergency. Snotty lifts his ragged head, snuffling, wiping snot. He follows the hollering stampede toward the fire.

Waste is a terrible thing to mind.

Daniel Twitchell reported the evening's events to James Nutting as accurately as some veteran reporting an incident witnessed in war-torn Lebanon. Eloise Patadoe came in to tell what she had seen, for, after smelling the fire upon entering her goat pasture, she returned in time to watch John Brown manhandle burning tires with the backhoe and bucket loader. He had succeeded in isolating and smothering the fire that snotty had started with gasoline soaked rags from Buster Bean's pickup truck. No one left the scene until certain that the fire was out. By then a storm had blown in with its reassuring load of fitful rain. The teenagers crammed themselves back into the vehicles and departed for Gottheim. Eloise stayed behind long enough to satisfy herself that the fire was well and truly history.

Two days later, booted and bundled, the editor of *The Village Voter* stood on the dismal summit of Jasper Mountain with Julius Golding and his niece, Amanda. Having taken aerial shots from there for the paper, Nutting held the camera in his gloved hands. The scene, both above and below the summit, was like a living Hendrich canvas inspired by Norse mythology; as though an old storyteller of early Icelandic epic poetry had breathed upon the mountainous white landscape of Gottheim to create the mythic picture surrounding them. Fantastic black billows churned up out of the low place that had once been primeval woodland, since vanished along with its aboriginal personification. Ceylon Segar's own treasure, of steel belts and rubber, and oil from under the earth was on fire down there. Though they were hard at it, nothing could be done by the good people of Gottheim to stop that fire.

Tires. Tires made somewhere in the Midwest, down South and elsewhere in the world; tires driven on the nation-wide network of highways and streets until they were worthless: These tires poured particles and ash and smoke down on the village. These tires, aflame, were busy making their own weather.

James Nutting had spent most of the past 48 hours trying to unravel the story of how it happened. That the story had come to him was no surprise. He had been reporting and editorializing the ins and outs of this DEP sanctioned tire dump ever since Ceylon Segar opened it with no discernible plan for recycling the tires. Nutting thought now that the only question had been when. When would this story of disaster be written?

The three on a mountaintop were aware of the changing shape and drift of the fire cloud. According to weather and wind direction, it would change. Today the billowing black went up, gathering in an anvil-shape, trailing and falling upon the wind. The white landscape of the surrounding fair Meguntics contrasted sharply with this apocalyptic fall of cloud and ash. For the moment, the slopes and vicinity of Jasper were spared the indignities of this baptism of filth. But shortly, as Julius Golding was now thinking, the winds would swivel and return to lay the burden of this burning upon the white dome where he now stood. James Nutting said something to him and he turned, noting Amanda standing a little apart and gazing raptly off into the dark cloud. But, helpless, Golding would attend to Nutting instead. He would submit to the newsman's questions. He had a certain amount of respect for the village editor's background. Hadn't he been a journalist in Montréal—or was it Toronto?

Nutting raised his voice to repeat himself. "From I've managed to piece together, contrary to gossip and early reports, the fire was not set by kids. A witness, that goatherd in Quaker, came around last night and said she had seen the kids after the original fire was set by one of them. She watched them extinguish it, she says." Nutting looked squarely at the resort owner. "She also told me she saw lightning go down into the dump— several times—from the upper window of her goat barn. The dump itself was out of sight beyond the puckerbrush. But it was quite a display, according to her. She didn't think much beyond that until she woke in the morning to—this." His eyes swept the scene. "Now she's convinced those strokes brought on the disaster. According to the state fire marshal's office, ignition was scattered, not localized. One of my employees was there that night, a trustworthy young man. He says the first fire was started by a loose cannon but was dead out when they left. The three accounts agree. I'm just not prepared to blame the children—although at the moment the authorities seem to. They were very stupid: drinking, driving, trespassing."

He hesitated. "In print I will not be calling this a freak accident. That interpretation is sure to be put forth if the children are cleared. This state, powerful people in the state, have known about this accident-waiting-to-happen.... Allowances might be made if these tires had been used on Maine roads by our residents." Nutting continued looking at Golding's eagle-like face, the wind blowing stray wisps of dark hair from his hood. His voice fell a bit, beneath the wind. "Maybe we've all been less than good stewards."

He had spoken in earnest, trying to be heard above the breeze, but he said these things with immense sadness. Golding thought the voice of the editor made audible the look in Amanda's great eyes. He watched his niece as Nutting continued, "So here we are, Golding. Our readers are going to want to hear from you and your brother. What will this mean to Jasper Mountain? To the Town of Gottheim?" The pages of his little notebook rustled in the wind. Golding was an impeccable man and, to the recurring surprise of the editor who had interviewed him before, a somewhat diffident man. Yet at times Nutting judged him arrogant.

The resort owner lifted his gaze from Amanda. "I'll give you something, of course, but you may want to ask Amanda some questions. You may want to ask her entire class. They've all been working on the tire problem—at least until now."

Once more he looked out toward the great cloud of ash and smoke. "We've heard from those with condos or timeshares who have family members with respiratory problems. They'll stay away. We have our well-wishers who are taking a wait-and-see attitude. Some people are excited by this disaster, waiting for the inevitable wind shift like a pack of hyenas: people with no financial or emotional stake here. As for the town, you'll have to ask them, but it doesn't look good for our plans to extend the commercial center. I can hear our investors trying to tiptoe away. As for the jobs, we'll have to wait and see. We'll have our losses, no doubt, and must deal with them as best we can. I hope it won't last long."

He scribbled some, then Nutting said, "You still have other resorts, more recently acquired, some deals still pending. How will this affect that? Will you be able to fold your tents and quietly make your way west?" There was a dry challenge in his question.

Golding suppressed a grimace, his eyes still on the smoke churning, lifting across the valley. He made a brusque retort. "It's not that easy." He was not where he wanted to be at this moment. He would have preferred the solitude of the office, calls outgoing on business. What could he do? When he got down from this apocalyptic summit the Portland reporters would be waiting to aim their cameras at his face. He tried softening his answer. "I just don't know yet, Nutting. I've got business associates to talk with."

The editor rephrased the question, but Golding remained intractable. Nutting looked down at Amanda, who moved near her uncle to slip her hand in his. Her features were soft, framed with strands of escaping hair. "What do *you* think, young lady?" He left the question open for any type of answer she might feel led to give. She was part of the generation on which these things... were already falling.

Amanda hesitated, at last replying in her small voice, "I don't know."

"Are you worried?" He asked it gently.

"Yes."

"Shall I come to your class?"

"Ask my teacher please." She was not comfortable with the way the editor spoke to Uncle Julie.

"And who is your teacher?"

"Mrs. Carter."

He wrote it in his notebook. "Thank you." He closed the pad.

He turned to take one long look. *The scene is set.* It will stay this way a while. He greatly hoped that something could be done and he would spend his days trying to find out what, but his doubts were entrenched. He had discovered, when he began reporting on Ceylon Segar's dump, that no officials were working on contingencies.

They Suffer in Gottheim

On the first day of February, Chrischana finds herself crunching up Blackwell Mountain, toward the top of a knoll once owned by generations of Twitchells, now in her hands again—thanks to Balder. She has borrowed the man's snowshoes for the trek, helps herself along with old ski poles, and follows the long-tailed track laid by her youngest, Nathan, son of Peter Prince. Fueled by a burst of child's energy, Nathan has gone ahead on his pair of Balder's childhood snowshoes. At times she sees the track here, or spies his tousled head behind a stump. Or she might see an eye peeping at her around a beech or birch. He likes to pretend he's a hobbit, accustomed to vanishing when big folk are near.

They are on their way to see what winter has done to their camper, and to check on the equipment for sapping. When the weather changes they will commence making maple syrup. Today the air is crisp and bracing, full of winter's freshness and appeal. All is covered in cool, clear snow. The sheen of it comes through naked trees on the hillside both above and below. Here and there she has a view of Mount Howe with its white bristling slope across the valley. The smell in her nostrils is refreshing, so clean in contrast to the nasty air of late.

Her thoughts are full as she climbs the rise on the winding snowy road. The lower parts of the hill have been easy enough even for Nathan, a snow machine having been through to break the trail. But here and there she can see a dismal black underlayer, laid by Ceylon Segar's spewing tire fire. Successive layers of filth have been poured out on Gottheim and surrounding areas. But there is no mind for it, such as she has daily in the village. Her thoughts now are on other things, things she has some control over. Tire fires are the domain of others involved in its problems and resolution. She may think again of the fire, near the end of her climb, when woodland and Mount Howe no longer stand between her and views of that great plume, shedding its dark load in the distance. The descendant of pioneers thinks now of her syrup-making venture.

She pictures herself toward the middle or end of the month, possibly the beginning of the next, clanking along distributing galvanized buckets to outlying trees; lugging coils of tubing, snowshoeing from tree to tree; tapping, laying lines along the hillside to funnel all the incipient sweetness. Sweetness looking and tasting and feeling like water, going straight down into the holding tank and evaporator where, by means of fire, it thickens to rich consistency, heavy with godly taste. She can see sweet vapor ascend and drift away. She's picturing syrup bottled and beribboned in the exhibition hall at the Fairgrounds next summer's end in neighboring Blisville. She will walk into the white-washed barn—a barn brim full with home-crafted goodness from neighboring farmsteads and townlots—the place where people still delight to see what their hands can do. Tables and shelves and walls full of fancy quilts, needlework, hand-knits; everything imaginable pickled, canned, bottled—home-brew and mincemeat, forty kinds of vegetables, home baked pies and candies, saltwater taffy and fudge. And among that outlay, golden and glowing, a mason jar, quart jar of Twitchell Farm maple syrup. The jarful will remind everyone of Gottheim's first paying industry, and of a time when people eked out their livings by boiling down sap—something that the tree itself thinks of each year.

Chrischana pictures the bustling white barn at Blisville Fair: a shrine, the jeweled fastness of the exhibition hall, top to bottom with brightly colored things in glass. The thought makes her winter weary soul sweet to think of it, refreshing her own little hall of thought. Coming up to the camper in winter, getting away from dishwashing in the restaurant or cleaning others' houses; getting out of the apartment—someone else's property, which she shares with her three sons; getting out like this reminds her of how much she has. What if camp is entangled in town regulation, or locked away up here in winter? What if it is made of tin and 6 x 10? *Up here I'm free awhile.*

She is about to round the corner leading onto Buck Hill Road. Straight ahead the track branches, reaching toward the top of Blackwell and cleaving woodland, then clearcut, toward a wooded crown. Somewhere up there, curving out of sight, the white path leads to the sky. Nathan's long-tailed track starts up that way, but veering abruptly into a thicket of hemlock on the right. Chrischana stops to take a breath and look again at the high snowy trail. The noise of her crunching snowshoes goes still, as silence comes.

The sky up here is holy blue, not a trace of boiling filth from the poor little town next-door. Sky up ahead holds its promising mystery, a majesty and power in its occasional cloud. *But no home to me,* she thinks.

Just an old Mainer, me, needing homely comforts... the woodstove, funky sauna, snugness in weathertight walls.

Still... the sky.... *It makes you think.* She leans on the ski poles, still catching her breath at this crossroads in the puckies. She is tired after all, climbing the hill. Sometimes... nature, family, industry... aren't enough. You want trusty arms, deep rest.

She thinks of Balder—and then thrusts the thoughts away. Life has *gone on.* And on and on. Balder belongs to Gloria, heart and head, and I'm.... just about to reach out to Peter. Again. (Reluctant as she feels.)

She has always had a strong sense of the fitness of things, a feeling for what is appropriate and interlocking. There is an orderliness to life, a pattern. When she can find and accept it. Often she does. *The right pattern comes before what I think or feel.* Thoughts and feelings change; impermanent. Thinking and feeling come best in the pattern. I do best there.

Tears well in her eyes. Didn't I learn it in the Hard School of Rejecting Balder? Rejecting the wise pattern once... you go forward in it when you find it again. You don't go groping back, rummaging bitterly through memory, dreaming of things no longer there.

Chrischana turns, starting along the Buck Hill Road, away from the low summit of blue and white. But now to her ears comes a disappointed squeak.

Nathan pokes his head from the thicket to see her disappear into mixed woodland along the track. "Ain't cha gonna look for hobbits?!" He hates the thought that she would even pretend to leave him behind. Scudding along he comes up behind her, worried, wishing to grab hold of her coat but the snowshoes prevent him.

She wades on, wrapped in her thought, but aware of his quick clumsy steps behind. She knows these thickets, the woods sloping upward on their right, downward on the left. The snow cover makes crosses of white on the dark furry fingers of conifers among the naked popple and beech on either hand. Above her runs the ribbon of blue, for the trees are young, immature. You see through the part in their ranks.... That's what's so irksome about Gloria. A woman who does not know how to engage life. She's still a girl—at twenty-four? Five? She seems bent on throwing away one of the best human beings ever to pick up a wrench. "Doesn't see the consequences—like me back when."

"Huh?" The voice squeaks behind her.

"I just walk in that office o'hers! That'd get her attention. I could tell her what's what."

"Why?"

Doaw. *Caunt just manhandle life's stubborn customers.* I'd've stood no one man-handling me. Day dreaming. Got no business meddling there. Got to be clearheaded, fair. But that girl's got problems. Life's got be glamorous, exciting. Timid, partway, self-involved. Everything carefully controlled, Gloria-controlled. Thinks it's either/or. Either Gloria controls the course of life or Balder will. No one controls life. We only collaborate with it. Who could make her see it?

"Not me." She smiles. I can't even stop myself thinking how other people should live.

I can collaborate. I can go back to Peter. Not tonight. Not tomorrow.... Next day? (Have t'see bout that!) But not for Peter's sake... nor even the boys'... or even because it fits the pattern. No. Because it will engage me. It's *my* life. The rough and tumble, give and take.

Yes, they all knew those sweet days, in the beginning. Maybe if we try... he is trying after that botch-up. Showing something, at least. That he had... he has parted with the idea that he has the *right*... should be able to manhandle, dominate. He *knows* now it in't right. Bless that Hermann Gottesman! Got to acknowledge with some act. One that will lock together all the pieces: Nathan, Benaiah, Daniel, Peter, herself. Peter. He'll have family again, a committed lover for his reward. It... wasn't easy for him either.... When will it happen? How?

Nathan has been surprisingly quiet trudging beside her. No whining, no complaints. Climb's not easy for a kid. She turns, looking down on the small pointed face. "Keeping up okay, Frodo?"

He smiles up on her.

The road takes a turn, coming clean of mixed thickets. It starts up the last leg through tall hardwoods. This last track goes through sinking powder. The machine trail has departed and they are on their own, working harder. Nathan needs help... but at last they come out on the hilltop below the clearcut summit. They look out on the valley opening below.

Beyond Mt. Howe the smoke of burning goes up. Black, and contrasting like an evil vision in the snowy hill-land, it pours into the sky, sifting out its filthy burden. Just outside Gottheim, there is burning. How long will it affect their lives? Even on a day like today, when she desires to think of her own industry and engagement, Chrischana would embrace all Gottheim. Thinking with gratitude of being here in Maine, she embraces the whole worried community. All are engaged with making do—either overseeing community concerns or small family tasks. In the city she knew almost no one and could scarcely care. Now, standing here, gazing out on that smoke, she recovers the memory of an ancestor. A young man wounded and treed on Puzzle Mountain with an agitated bear roaming and restive below.

"Kilt by bear." The boy had written on his handkerchief with his own blood. A band of neighbors, with torches and trumpets, went into the woods looking for him. They found him after dark, alive, still clinging to the tree.

Sitting in The Coffee Story, cup in hand, Gloria waits for Chloe and Eveladore: a pre-meeting meeting with coffee and conversation, a fun way to start on that emergency campaign for the beleaguered Chamber of Commerce. The Coffee Story is a good little place, full of framed artwork on white walls and the smell of freshly roasted coffee beans. In the rear of the wide open Italianate house stands an antique brass roasting machine. Gloria sits musing in the fragrance of the morning's roast. The conversation she had with brother Jimmy over breakfast plays again through her mind: She will have to... to rethink her take on Theo. Only out of courtesy, or a sense of discretion, has Gloria kept her patience with the other intact. Theo lives in her on very scary dreamtime. The things she comes up with can scarcely resemble reality sometimes. There's been no substance to her, just a wild career from point to point, zigzagging like a token in a pinball machine; certainly lacking even the control of Pacman. But—at last—here's something to make you stop and think: Real reason. Theo has grasped an important truth—in her latest spectacle.

Over his eggs benedict James again spoke of trying to keep Theo on track. "She's been slipping back into that restiveness she was troubled with—before that wild announcement about giving away Gott'im Chair. I thought she was all straightened out, but now—"

"—What *is* her problem? James, you *know* sarcasm and irony aren't my way, but Theo manages to push my boundaries." She could not conceal her annoyance from him. Lately, he doesn't seem to mind irritation where Theo's concerned.

"Just some idea that she owes it to them. Thinks they've been exploited—in the past. Of course, I disagree. Completely." He emphasized the last point with a tap of the side of his hand on the tabletop: "These people had jobs (*tap*), make a living (*tap*); something that would not have happened without these mills and the owners looking out for them. Somehow she's lost perspective. But she doesn't talk about it anymore. Not since I let her know what I thought. —But, disturbed all over again. Let's see if we can keep her thinking straight."

"What does she mean, exploited?"

"Oh, just some notion that her father was involved in some sort of plan to fix wages. Long time ago." He gestured dismissively.

"You mean—conspiracy theories? She has those?"

He stopped to look at her. "Theo's not crazy, Glory."

"But what does she base it on?" Gloria stopped eating her granola and yogurt and set down her spoon.

"Things she overheard as a child. Apparently they met occasionally to reaffirm their agreement, an old-time blackballing and wage setting thing. It's ancient history now. She even says maybe the meetings stopped years ago. Boy, is she afraid of Lyman Bearce on the subject. She walks out of her way to avoid him."

"James Fay, those kinds of backroom agreements are despicable! Don't treat this so lightly." She leaned over the table suddenly, hissing at him.

"*Backroom*! Gloria, for someone so big on the taint of labels, you should know better. We just disagree. I could debate it with you but you'll only see it as cloak-and-dagger and smoking guns. I've got more important things on my mind." It was time to short-circuit this time wasting: "Have you forgotten about Ceylon Segar's bombing of our project in the Village?— or what's happening to Mason's Mills? Of the soot hill this place is becoming? Eat up—if you can. I've got a strategy session later this morning and have to prepare. If there is such a thing." His gaze gripped hers through his glasses. "This is ruination, Gloria. Forget archaic practices that no longer apply. What do you think will become of it all? All our hard work, the plans? Please don't talk to me about those workers. Half of'em are dead! We've got living workers to think of, the young people in this town who make a living off this resort. I'm afraid to look out the window this morning!"

They looked reflexively toward the great windows across the room. The once pristine view of ski slopes was now filthy with ash.

Gloria looked back at him, dropping her gaze. Plainly he was scared. She herself was not so upset over the fire. Fear had not hit her like that. His face made her want to shrink for guilt. And to comfort him. But how? All her words on the subject seemed too little. Her talk would seem glib, but she could not help the remoteness she felt. The magnitude and intractability of the situation numbed her. She had an odd urge to suggest he pray. But Gloria kept quiet. After her own standoff with faith it would be just more words. And, with the way things were between them lately, he might even think she was mocking him. At last she said, "I'm sorry James." She pushed her half-empty bowl of granola away. Maybe that would convince him of her sympathy.

Eloise and Sherla Simon come over with coffee to sit at a neighboring table. The Coffee Story is filling up but, absorbed in her thoughts, Gloria scarcely notices. The two talkers at the next table are on break from running errands, come in to enjoy a spot of gossip and commiserate over the disaster. The conversation started after a chance meeting in the grocers'.

"So... it was the devil that started the fire in the tire dump... you say." Sherla jogs Eloise into continuing. The former has a nice round face and twin dark braids, a certain comfortable fullness stuffed into her jeans and blue flannel shirt. Her barn-mucking coat, faintly redolent, is draped over the back of the dainty soda fountain-type chair. The paper cup warms her pudgy hands and she possesses the happiness one might think of while looking at apples hanging from full boughs. At home she bakes bread of coarse grains for her family; also makes and sells white butter with a raised design.

"Eloise, you were born off-the-wall." It's a compliment, a complaint. "Where do you come up with these things?"

"Shouldn't conjure up those images about birth and walls," says Eloise. "Mama wouldn't like it."

Sherla spills tendrils of laughter. "You were the one who told the town it was lightning. Now you think the devil is lightning? Or the devil controls lightning, maybe."

"The devil *wishes* he controlled lightning. And as everyone knows (smiles) he fell like lightning from heaven."

"He?" Sherla arches an eyebrow, smiling.

"The-devil-wishes-he-or-she-controlled-lightning." Eloise rolls her eyes, the glasses on her nose reflecting rectangles of light from the windows. "Let us assess the devil's sex. Like with the wish to control lightning, the devil wishes the devil had a sex, wishes it *could* have sex (otherwise we would not see the devil trying so hard for it in our all-out culture)."

"So how did the devil start the fire? By rubbing two sticks together up there in the clouds?"

"The devil is not a Native American." It's a dry retort. "Maybe at one time, but not today. Today the devil is a three-piece suit and carries a briefcase. Yesterday he wore a conquistador's metal bonnet, bloomers and tights."

"So you saw him sneaking around the tire dump with a blow torch in his briefcase, and, deciding no one would believe you, said it was lightning."

Eloise gives a mischievous grin, shakes her dirty-blond ponytail and says, "It *wasn't* lightning that started the fire. The tires started the fire. Lightning hits all over the globe, continually—something like 100 times a second. The lightning belonged there. The tires did not. Someone in a suit and tie—coulda been a woman!—decided useless tires belong in little Quaker township, Maine. Several someones in suits and ties. Yes, I'm bigoted, but not that bad. The identifying feature of the devil is not clothes or vocation or sex but a foolish reliance on one's own machinations. I mean, night and day, there's no end to the vulcanization of rubber, and endless glut of tire manufacturing. Where are we supposed to put it all?"

"The Ayatollah is right, then? Corporate America—we *are* the Great Satan?"

"Maybe it takes one to know one.... What could be more devilish then fanaticism? Look at peer pressure. What's more Puritan than kids pressuring each other to do drugs, smoke, or perform some dangerous feat? The undoers of repression can snake the most devastating oppression throughout society. Ever see *Twelfth Night*? Sir Toby is as correct as Malvolio, and probably a lot more potent and hurtful. Repression is the 20th-century sin that psychiatry tried to bludgeon us with."

"Oh come on. If it takes one to know one, what does that make you?"

"Well, I do keep goats." She smiles toothily.

The other sits back, thoughtfully chewing her muffin. At last she says, "Who's the devil around Gott'im?" Lowering her voice she leans forward. "No, don't tell me: remember that time we worked in Copenhagen, turning out brush handles?" She hisses. "They turned off the heat during second shift because the bosses and office workers went home."

Is it the hissing or mention of millwork that wakes Gloria from her reverie? How long the two women have been sitting here talking she does not know, but she recognizes Eloise by her reputation and the fact that she is a foe of James on the Mason Mills project.

"They really get away with it," Eloise is saying. The other answers, "People still work all night in this terrible cold.... Minimum-wage and chilblains—in this day'n age!"

Gloria glances at her, looks away. Boldly she eavesdrops on their talk under pretense of staring out the window.

Says Eloise, "You think we have it tough, you should hear the old-timers talk. Sometimes they worked twelve, fifteen hours and got paid for ten. Their sandwiches froze. No coffee breaks. And some of these mills are still owned and operated by the same people—or their descendants."

"At least now, people can get compensated if injured on-the-job."

"If they can keep workers compensation going. Politics is trying to overturn it every day from too many abuses, they say, but what's the incentive for policing conditions without it? Do you ever see OSHA going into these little places?"

Agreeing and congratulating themselves on their insight, the two women stand, pick up their cups and napkins and head for the door as Gloria looks after.

"Hah!" Eveledore yelps, spying her while coming in with the cold behind the departing hippies. The girl has a killer overbite and her great grin is like a shiny wall coming at Gloria. "Thought I was gonna be late!" Manner breezy and broad, Eveledore with pixieish haircut above the wide sexy smile; her features bright as brass with the power of her confidence: She's got unstoppable personality and knows how to keep you right up there with her, even in the midst of disaster. Vel is ready for the long haul, up for this adventure of Gott'im's volcano, or "apocalypse" as she refers to it... being not so glib as to use the term holocaust. Yet many agree that the scope, smell and sound of the thing suggests a biblical idiom. "I want to stay and watch the unfolding," she said yesterday. "Think of the stresses it will put on the townspeople. We are in the right place to study the impact of catastrophe." Her interest in the social aspect of Ceylon Segar's aborted attempt to earn an industrial living off the land of his ancestors signifies with her association in the International Institute of Coordinated Experiments.

"Right up IICE's alley," Gloria had observed agreeably. IICE meets informally only in summer but, as with her own situation, some members with second homes in Gottheim have an emotional stake in the community. Skiing has always been a bonus.

The third member of their party, the intense, dark, pensive and angular Chloe, comes in behind Eveledore. Together the two step up to the counter for coffee and croissants, returning to Gloria's table with the fresh scent of coffee and pastry, the rustling of napkins.

Eveledore is saying, "We don't hear complaints about snow from the locals anymore. It's all about ash. The sky is snowing ash and flakes of unburnt tire. Complaint is a sort of mitigator for the helpless."

Chloe's response, between bites, is somewhat dry. "In the same way that disaster mitigates our focus sessions?" She looks directly at Vel. "You forgot to tip the counter folks."

"I didn't forget. You tip too much and it evens things out. Too much breeds unrealistic expectations and spoilage."

Chloe picks up her cup, sits silently, but her dark eyes do not turn away. Eveledore, with clear green gaze, just smiles at her. She shrugs her coat onto the back of the chair. "Have either of you heard about Gwendolyn Bella—institutionalized by her sister two weeks ago?"

Gloria grimaces. "I knew it! The sessions last summer were too much for a... a fragile psyche like hers."

"I agree," says Chloe. "She had this genuine sweet air, very refreshing. Why would they want to change that? It was a mistake—trying to instill assertive values and attitude in someone like her."

"It was what she wanted," counters Vel. "She was sick of being the weak one. In any encounter. She *wanted* to be more aggressive."

Chloe shakes her head. "Would she, though? Maybe she was just being true to what she is—by caving to the influences in that session. The whole program was geared to consciousness-raising... and it became an irresistible atmosphere for someone like her. After all, she happened into the sessions as a diversion—advertised in *The Voter*. ...She was just another tourist or summer—"

" So you're saying—" interrupts the other.

But Chloe's look is piercing: "That atmosphere overwhelmed her, crushed her! That episode in her last session should have told you something."

"Sometimes an episode is necessary if you want a breakthrough." She puts pearly fingertips up to loosen her tie. The room is warm and Eveledore is insistent, giving no ground on this.

"Don't you mean break*down*?" Gloria has been sitting with an empty face but now she speaks. Recalling Bella's hysteria makes her unhappy. The heat of her feeling rushes out in flippant irony. "Like if you want to make an omelet, you have to break some eggs."

"Couldn't've put it better," says the other with a touch of hauteur.

Gloria's answering silence is neither hostile nor friendly. She looks thoughtfully at the bold young woman across from her.

Chloe has finished with Eveledore on the subject. She blots her lips with a napkin. "Looks like we got an omelet in Gott'im. And what are we going to do about it besides take notes? Will we just poke and probe or is there some action we can take to alleviate the pain? Do we know what civic leaders are doing; or Augusta?"

"To find the answers to these and other burning questions, let us adjourn, copies of *The Village Voter* in hand, to our own fact-finding meeting." It is smartly said, Eveledore swirling the last of the coffee in the bottom of her cup. "Let's hope that sourpot Nutting sends someone to report on it. Better destroy the croissants and go." She puts the last bite into her wide mouth and stands, picks up her suit coat and turns toward the door, leaving the table littered. With a wave of her hand, she turns back to cut Chloe off. "Don't say it, Chlo. It's what you stuffed that tip jar for, deah." She smiles her killer smile and breezes out the door.

The moon is up but its light, fitfully fringed with pine, is alternately blocked by ashfall. Ansell Robichaud is climbing the ledge among the thick trees: a difficult climb through ice and snow, grabbing at branches and scrabbling up icy rock. He has no crampons or ice-climbing equipment like that worn by those who climb for sport. He wears steel-toed boots—good protection if a limb should fall, but in February they freeze the feet fast. Shivering with cold when he first came out, his limbs warm as he climbs.

Nothing would prevent him from climbing this ledge tonight, nothing prevent his communing with Alvin. Or, to put it in his own terms, Ansell is thinking: *Gont climb the ledge'n put up the flag.* It's something he has to do, what this piece of time is for. He has to put up the flag tonight.

Trees around him are mighty with age. White Pine here is girthy and tall, its once smooth youthful bark now crusted in thick ridges of age. On the side of this cliff they catch the light. So, if hazardous, climbing is not impossible. Yet Ansell has to make sure of his flag tree. Hell! If he climbs the wrong one now.

For the trees and the night he cannot see it coming over the mountain behind him—ash from the tire fire falling on the breeze. He smells it, feels it fitfully sifting across the bridge of his nose. He winks it loose from his eye. Ash *plinks* on the sleeves of his nylon jacket.

The new replacement flag, dark, is neatly coiled and wrapped around his neck, tied under his arms. He feels it bunched around his shoulders and under his armpits, the breeze tugging at its edges. The first thing will be to get the old ragged, sun-bleached flag off the limb. It was supposed to be Alvin's turn to change the flag. Now it's up to Ansell.

Searching among the high dark boughs he remembers the first time they made the climb as kids: serious, intent on getting that flag up. It was what a Robichaud could do in life, get that flag up. Since they could remember the flag has flown: tiny, white, high in the pines. As kids they talked of it, the twins, and of how one day they'd be the ones to put up the flag. Great Uncle Pierre Auguste, who spoke only French, told them one day they would. What a feat it turned out to be for them! Even tonight Ansell recalls the way his little heart thumped among his ribs as they climbed. It was the first time he noticed he had a heart. Breaths came in gasps, his legs trembling, feet scarcely touching each limb. Hand-over-hand, together they ascended, neither speaking. Never, since, has the intensity of the experience been duplicated. Never until now. Because Alvin was found outside Sessions' in his truck. Now life is intense again, but Ansell no longer craves intensity. He wants only to see Alvin alive. The thrill of life can go to hell.

High up there in the halfmoon light he catches a glimpse of gray. Pinkish gray moving among feathered shadows. And off aways the stars are snared, though every once in awhile their lights are snuffed. From the ash and burning tires, he guesses. Ansell sets his hand to the branch to get a leg up.

Because his feet are so heavy with years, the branch feels sure in his instep. The wind has knocked out the snow. He grips each branch hand-over-hand, smelling pitch. Through leather work gloves he feels the coldness and strength of each limb.

Slowly the logger ascends, sometimes climbing, sometimes clinging. Clinging he feels a stuporous life in the great tree. Even in winter evergreen manages to live in its secret layer of life. Ansell is jealous of it, thinking of Alvin, but then he relents for his realization that the tree's life takes nothing away which his brother might've used. It breathes with its own kind of life and they have always made a living from wood. There's nothing here on which to blame Alvin's death. He must look elsewhere for that.

Starlight and moonlight are spreading now, the tree's great branches parting. He leaves the closeness of needles, emerging into falling soot and pinkish night. He thinks the soot is proper to this night: The sky should be raining such sorrow. But in daylight he wishes it would go—for Emma's sake, for Mother's. The children. Let the dreariness of the ash fall off them onto him, remain in his own heart good'n proper.

High in the branches now, the tree swaying, Ansell sways with it. He's near. Where'd the flag get to? He leans out, one hand holding the branch above. There. The flag swishes, fluttering listlessly among furry boughs. Now it flaps high in a sudden gust.

Ansell climbs. Now, slowly, he hauls himself out; slowly, lying along its length, clutching the branch. The replacement flag, specially dyed by Alvin's wife Emma, lifts at its edges, still wrapped around him. They always used the white sheet, but now Ansell and Emma agree: black. "Don't think it'll show up much fom down heah," she said. Ansell only nodded his head but he thought the flag's meaning was different now. It stood not for triumph for the town to see but as a memorial, unspoken, for Alvin. That was all Ansell wanted to see. Black was the color of his grief.

The bough sways and Ansell with it. The whole treetop sways. The heavens sway, bending back and forth. The halfmoon and stars go up and down. Soot comes poring over him in a swift gust. Ansell squeezes his eyes then blinks. The earth is far, a long way down. There is Pale's sawmill spread out in the valley, glowing pinkish dark. Now that he is out in the open, the buzz-and-growl of the saws and separators comes up to him from that distance. His family's house below shows like a toy across from it, lights in its windows. The slope blocks his view of the two trailers, one for each twin, tucked beneath the ledge. Again the vapor lights and sound of the sawmill draw his gaze. The mill is one of many belonging to a family in Portland. Uncle Anseller worked there. Once. ...Didn't sober up properly before coming in one morning. Fell into a trimmer blade. Sliced into his lung, his breath and blood seeming to pour out of him. That was how he told the tale. "Thought I was all done. Wadn't though. Kep'right on living but not the same."

Swaying high on the pine above the valley, Ansell hears those words again. Swaying in the cold and needles, lit by moon and stars, blown about in smoke and ash. Clutching the limb, his dark flag flapping, wind-whipped, unfurling; the swift scent of pine pitch pierces him. He hears the words: Kept right on living, but not the same.

Winter and night in Jericho, and the conversation was desultory in Hermann Gottesman's *Kids Cafe*. Some teens were bent to their homework at a battered oak table with massive legs. Others played ping-pong while a few watched, swallowing sodas, snapping gum, jibing. There was an old pool table in the big room, and the gentle knocking of balls was heard from time to time. Hermann had a stereo playing a stack of scratchy platters that teenagers hadn't listen to for twenty years. Few listened to Elvis and Buddy anymore. The kids complained about this music to him. They wanted heavy metal or Prince, John Cougar, and The Gloved One. Hermann was deaf to it all.

He sat on the sagging couch, one massive hand seemingly always in a great bowl of freshly popped corn. Hermann was like a minor mountain, great in the knees, a mass of flesh, topped with dark curly receded hair in a tail, and beard. Peter Prince sat nearby in a dirty old wing chair. Though the popcorn on the table between them was tempting with its hot fresh smell, Peter never ventured a hand toward it. He drank coffee instead—as though his life depended on it. Considering what had happened to Alvin, he thought maybe it did. But if coffee were rescuing him from the temptations of alcohol, it made sleep harder to come by. And he was on southern schedule.

Peter Prince was friendly, compactly built, and green eyed through unruly brown hair. One eye was still bruised from Ferddy's suckerpunch.

Sometimes he was desperate with hankering for Chrischana. If only he could straighten up, quit listing like an old shed.... Was there *any* chance they'd be back together? No. No chances, only desperation. Desperation from now on. Sometimes Peter Prince believed in God and Jesus. Frequently he did not.

He watched the teenagers playing table tennis, shooting stick. He liked looking at the girls with their French braids, crimped bangs and straight-leg jeans. Girls didn't look like that when he was a teenager. They wore bellbottoms and ironed their hair or let it billow out like Brillo pads. But the boys in Hermann's Cafe reminded him of himself at that age, except for the jeans. They talked big, snuck outside to smoke, drink, get high. Hermann wouldn't let them back in when they did this.

Tonight was a school night so the kids began to drift out in twos and threes at about ten o'clock. By 10:30 it was quiet, the pinging and clinking of balls gone with the teenagers. The tobacco haze, which the big man permitted, was thinning out. Hermann had replenished the popcorn twice. He was drinking orange juice by the half gallon, pouring it over ice cubes in a tall plastic cup. Peter had made a fresh pot of coffee. It was time to get down to business.

"Know what that fire they got up there reminds me of?" Prince was asking. "Know that opening scene in the *Blues Brothers*?"

Hermann shook his head. "Never saw the movie."

"Aerial shots showing the God awful murk and smoke of some industrial section, East Chicago, I think. Stacks, fires, foundries, just pouring this filth into the air. Like the Flats in Cleveland where I grew up. Pollution so thick y'could swim through it. Honest-to-God. Half expected t'see a frogman with flippers'n mask bubbling his way through it. 'N'there were glowing spots in the darkness—like looking down into hell through a blow-hole. That tire fire makes me think the whole planet's turning into one big crematorium. No wonder they talk about a greenhouse effect."

"What you're describing reminds me of something more horrific." Hermann responds as though from a distance, sadly. "...Although... people are probably on to something with that term. We may live to find out how bad the warming trend can get, especially since we do nothing but fund studies. Science can frequently find things out but knowledge rarely moves anyone. Warnings are out there, we do know enough now to push for legislation but policymakers don't move until the agonizing pictures start rolling in. Take *Uncle Tom's Cabin*—not that I could get through Stowe's novel but, back then, it was able to emote truth people couldn't help but see. Feel. An imaginative depiction can kindle action but a dearth of images or strong books... that's why slavery continued, why Jews kept being gassed and burned. People could not grasp—really believe in the death camps until they saw pictures. They weren't moved until it was too late. The two wars—Civil and World War II were precipitated by agendas not specifically aimed at the evils of slavery and anti-Semitism but, if man's intention differed from God's, in the end they collaborated."

"That's another thing, Hermann. This question of free will we talked about... and how God won't prove his existence because that would violate free will... meaning we'd have no choice but to believe in that case. There's free will and yet—my question: Is this really free will? Why give us free will if the end result is we must capitulate?"

"That's good, Prince. Maybe it's just God liking a good story. Would you want to read a story where everything moved along just as you thought it should? What would keep you reading in that case? (Leaving out the question of omniscience.) But he would like it to be worth his while. If you believe that's God in chains, red with the lash, gassed. In your throttling hands."

Knocking a pack of Viceroys against his forefinger, the other dislodged a cigarette, smiling, thinking of God's reading material. "Think he's that simpleminded, though?" He snapped his lighter shut and looked around for an ashtray. He glanced up at the ceiling. "Just kidding."

Peter Prince blew smoke into the air, but sensing a lack of savor in his flippancy, he said, "I'm not superstitious, Hermann, but I swear d'God that tire fire gives me the creeps. Hadda see it up close—just once. Never again. The stench! Melting'n heat... besides the richest looking smoke you ever saw. No end to it either. Looks like it'll keep burning till it burns its way to hell. Make a good pathway for demons to climb out on. They're probably putting up signs down there now: 'This way to Gott'im,' or, 'Five more miles t'Gott'im.' My kids live there, y'know."

Hermann looked right at him. "Haven't your kids already seen the devil?"

Peter dropped his gaze. *He's really going to work.* Prince was silent, then quietly he said, "So you keep reminding me."

"Is it something you should forget?"

"Here we go with the probing questions. No. I don't think I should forget it." But his face hardened. "You know, if it weren't for— everything—I'd tell you to go fuck yourself."

"You just told me anyway."

Peter snapped, "You know what Hermann, you tenacious irreligious Jew? I'm never gonna get rid of this anger. Not in a hundred million light-years. According to this, I'm *never* gonna have Chrischana. Not to hold again. I'll never be fit to live with. One more smack on'er and I'm out!

"I'm out anyway." It was a mutter.

He went quiet again then said, very low, "Shoulda taken a bite outta Sessions' dog. I should have got out of the truck'n let the fucking thing tear me apart."

"This is doing any good, Prince?"

"What *will* do me any good?"

Hermann Gottesman drank his orange juice. In silence he let the question—a very good question—say itself again. He filled the tall cup once more. "I'll ask something designed to get you remembering the answer to that. But first tell me what all these things we've been talking about have in common?"

Prince stood, ceramic cup in hand though his coffee had cooled. He walked between two littered game tables, set the cup down and picked up a pool cue. Deftly he dropped the seven solid into a side pocket. He set down the stick, picked up the cup and walked around again, thoughtfully, resigned to these questions. "Let's see. Slavery, the Holocaust, smoke from thirty million tires, global warming—anything else?" At the bookcases he turned and came back toward the couch where Hermann sat like a mountain.

"Battering."

With a sidelong dip of his tousled head, Prince acknowledged the word. "Battering." He sat down, took another swallow of coffee and said, "Domination. They are all about domination."

"People dominate because?" Hermann was urging the answer toward greater precision.

Peter looked at him, then away. "Because they are powerless." He turned his back, shoulders slumping. "Because sometimes they can't control even themselves. Especially themselves. Can't accept what they are, what they've been given. Because they despise the weakness they live in... or see in others." He continued with his back toward the big man, slouching against the grubby wing chair.

Gently the other said, "What's despicable about weakness? About weakness or humility? Or harmlessness?"

Peter sighed. A long grief-struck sigh. He sat up a little, saying, "Nothing. I guess. There's nothing wrong with certain kinds of weakness. I mean, I like Nathan and he's weak—harmless. His being young'n innocent kind of appeals to me. It makes me sorry that someone stronger could come along and harm him. Someone tricky or mean.... Someone who might treat him the way I treated Chrischana.

"For years she came back to me after I hurt her." He looked seriously at Hermann n. "I used to wonder how the Jews could allow themselves to be herded away like that. But it never occurred to me to wonder how people could herd'em away. That's what I should've been wondering. But when I think of it—maybe I do know. It was like with Chrischana. She was the kind of person who could not believe that someone would really *want* to hurt someone else."

Hermann sat silent, intently. Prince was coming to it now, and speaking as though these things were written in some high calm airy place. Gottesman listened carefully, feeling as though the two of them were up there together.

"Goodness was so strong in her that she couldn't believe in that evil. She thought I would change or get the message or something. It took a long time and a lot of pain for her to be convinced of what I was. Am. And then she left." He leaned forward. "Hermann, there's hope. She *might* come back. Not because I'm worth it, but because she's good."

He stopped and leaned back, looking at the ceiling tiles.... "But there's still the problem of how to change. Where's help for that?" And he fell into quiet thinking. Hermann too was silent.

Then Peter Prince said, "Never mind, Hermann. I remember."

Hermann smiled. Not that rare a thing. He could smile over small happiness, instances of thought, pieces of conversation. But he did not smile without reason. Now he smiled again at Peter. "I eat a lot, Prince."

"Yeah, Hermann. I noticed." Then, in a mischievous play on probing questions and also because he was curious, he said, "Why'd you suppose that is?"

"It may be because I have a faint but entrenched memory of being hungry. It's always here."

"You, Hermann ? When were you ever hungry?"

"Long ago. I was very young." His mouth continued to smile but there was a fragrance of sadness in his eyes. "My father tried escaping by taking us to Romania. To Hungary. It didn't work. At Birkenau I was hungry."

Quakertown was so called by second-generation Gott'imites. The little group of people who settled the wild town next-door never actually used that appellation themselves. Shortly after Jasper Mary ceased roaming the byways and tributaries of the Arossagunticook, the strange little sect came, purchasing land from absentee grantees or their heirs. They made stranger worship in the woods beyond Gottheim and the mountain. Although the predecessor to *The Village Voter* was still a generation or two away, many Gottheimites were well read, exchanging books, periodicals and outdated newspapers from Portland and Boston, so they knew about Quakers and Shakers. Since it was known that dancing was part of the newcomers' ritual, the name Quaker seemed apt enough to townsfolk. For these strangers' name was unknown to them.

According to Dr. Kimball, the 19th-century Gottheim historian, the people who settled Quaker were virgins, their men and women celebrating celibacy. Describing their form of worship at secondhand he wrote of its slow beginning, measured and sedate, consisting of a kind of locomotive dancing and oral devotion. As though nothing in particular were going on. Men on the right, women to the left, they faced each other in groups. A rhythm and rhyme where soon perceived, a pattern of increasing complexity. Like a boiler burbling, it built to a particular and a peculiar pressure. With increasing speed came a release from caution, a casting off of the former pattern. Worshipers whirled and wailed unto the Lord, spinning off singly in ecstasy of devotion. As though each were now coupled with the Lord alone. The fully energized locomotive—of Dr. Kimball 's metaphor—had jumped the tracks, as though to head out of the mountains on a mission of its own.

The townsfolk of Gottheim longed to accuse the Quakerites of being no earthly good, but the industry of the sect precluded this. It seemed there was nothing these people could not accomplish. Each member was *master*, no less, of half a dozen trades, and could perform to satisfaction any other necessary job. Tailoring, metalwork, woodworking, invention, husbandry, all manner of needlework cookery beekeeping herb-doctoring and more: all done with artistry and perfection. In a little more than a dozen years, the tiny community had a prosperous commercial seed business and were disseminating a multitude of northern fruit and vegetables throughout the known world. They had a brisk export of blueberry blossom honey and maple syrup.

This shaking quaking sect of Believers in Christ's Second Coming had their peculiar secrets, one of which concerned a Sacred Stone. The Stone was boldly inscribed and stood in what Gottheimites whispered was an unholy hollow. Shadowed by hemlocks and ringed about by woodland, this setting suggested the rumor that these odd people actually worshiped that piece of rock. Rumors flew about this Stone. People said it was solid quartz. Others said imported marble, some said it was rubbed red with the blood of chickens or deer. No one actually believed about the blood of course (except children, who listened big-eyed to everything). "What was written on the Stone?" The children would ask. And certain fathers and mothers would reprove them for listening to outlandish tales. But others, as eager of voice as the children, would close their eyes and darkly intone: "The God, who has caused His Word to dwell here, destroy who shall put forth their hand to alter or destroy this house of God." Still others declared it said no such thing but only, "THE WORD OF THE LORD"; adding, "But folks oughtn't to set up worshipful objects anaway. Ain't propa."

The history of rumor recorded by Dr. Kimball states that the sect's members broke the Stone apart and buried its pieces in secret diverse places in an apparent attempt to stop the communitywide misunderstanding of the Stone's purpose. But no one actually knows what became of the so-called sacred Stone.... If there was one to begin with.

Few in Gottheim even remember that sect now, though it comes up at the Historical Society from time to time. Making her home in Quaker, and curious as she is, Eloise Patadoe has read Doc Kimball's history of it. Asa Bartlett and the faithful of the aforementioned society know the various peculiar histories of the little township. But, of late, Quaker is just a logged over sparsely occupied tire storage area, with a remote outback leading to vast wilderness—lakey, mountainous, filled with game. The whirling religious have long since departed. Celibacy carries its own peculiar and unspectacular form of extinction. The neighboring community of Gottheim is the poorer for it; just as they suffer from the departure of Jasper Mary and her clan. They would suffer if the hippies and back-to-the-landers in Quaker disappeared. But, largely, Gottheimites remain ignorant of this. Prosperous townsfolk feel reverent for remembering the Yankee pioneers and benevolent for, at last, allowing the French their place.

Another culturally important resident of Quaker, the most ancient, pervasive and enduring, is nonhuman. Regardless of natives or colonials or the republic, insect and animal populations have settled and moved at will here since the wasting of glaciers. Their pathways to food and water were secure and inalienable until the human invasion. Humans have paved the trails over with logs, gravel, asphalt and concrete. Humans have intersected and paralleled animal trails, but the innocent and ignorant continue to travel woodland, water and field by the only pathways they know, maintaining their ancient routes surprisingly well; the mothers of various species teaching the next generation, faithful to the point of slaughter.

A week passed since the tire dump began what Peter Prince called its continuing descent into hell. Then the numerous rodent population of Ceylon Segar's burning rubber and oil mountains began entering the village and the resort on the other side of the mountain. At night, as people slept in their snow and cinder covered houses, or dreamed in their condos, rats that had harbored in Quaker tires came looking for refuge and food. Some few old people, and some mothers, were awakened in darkness by the persistent gnawing of rodent incisors. They gnawed cellar bulkheads or on floor plates to gain entrance. They gnawed at convenient cracks in restaurants and trendy shops. Upon entering the grocers on Front Street, they gnawed their way into what seemed like rat heaven. Morning came and people awoke in quiet households where sleek guests had discreetly hidden themselves away for a cozy winter's day nap. Outdoors a few keen observers spotted what looked like giant mice trails inscribed in the sooty snow cover. The rats were so numerous in their role of hidden guests that household pets emulated a passage from Harriet Beecher Stowe and "gazed on the rats with respectful curiosity and ran no imprudent risks."

Elda, Balder, and Daniel have taken on the crusade for creatures. Balder is on nights at the paper mill so in daylight they come into the wood surrounding the fulminating dump to look for suffering or disoriented birds and animals. Through swiftly changing cloud of smoke and soot, sometimes laden with snow, they poke and prod the dirty cover of woodland, of puckerbrush, of former clearcuts. They venture into high woods where the saw has not been in decades. Working together or apart the little family gathers the sickly or fraidy-eyed creatures, bringing them home to *Simons Ledge* in cages in the back of Balder's pickup. The barn, into which the man had planned to bring a team of draft horses to help on his proposed farmstead, is now full of wild animals, mostly small. Daniel and his brothers busy themselves helping the legally blind Elda clean fur and feathers. They feed and otherwise help restore heart-breath-strength to the wounded population of wilderness surrounding Ceylon Segar's dump.

Today Balder is alone, wandering the southeast quadrant off the dump, searching the underbrush for frightened creatures that may have been left behind. The smoke and cinders come over him in waves when he reaches the high point of some knoll. There he looks out on the rapid upsurge of darkness trimmed low in flame and surrounded by a dense living atmosphere. Popping, cracking, and blowing. The filthy mass moves and breathes, heaving its breastful of fire in upwhirling, writhing flame. At intervals a blaze bursts up in dirty drafts, forming an undulant glowing face. It invokes that vision of fire, projecting across the low heavens and earth, in the red days when he was a warrior in the forest surrounding some unofficial enemy's hometown. That such a fiery face could come near Gottheim, spit and rain on the quiet streets of his familiar village, makes unspeakable sadness in him. When he looks on the downturned faces of neighbors, friends, acquaintances walking the dim streets, the wounds of Vietnam awake. When they look up to speak to one another conversation is of difficulties breathing or disruption of lives, the sorrow and darkness upon the white New England face of Gottheim. One or two have died of exacerbated respiratory disease on account of this.

But the punishment of this fire has reminded Gott'imites of tender relations too much neglected. Of love too seldom surfacing in healthier air. Seeing Asa Bartlett overtown, Balder would think, Why'd I never see the faithful way he has of going twice a week to wind the town clock? Year in, year out, no vacation, no honeymoon since—before I was born? Winding it evah week, twice a week, while I was lost in Vietnam.

Now, while he looks out on the great smoke of burning, the rumbling and blowing of its devouring fills his ears. Then some other sound, tiny and thin, comes up, its faint mewing waking him from his reverie. An animal is crying somewhere. Intermittently, the call comes a bit more distinctly now. From below the knoll behind him comes the sound of his name. Thinly, fine, the voice sends on the winter breeze. Turning, he looks down through tall trunks at the tiny figure in blue, toiling up toward him.

Who is wading through deep snow, following his snowshoe tracks, calling his name?

The joy of recognition and desire rushes into him whole. Gloria! And Gloria's voice. Here comes the creature he sought for, in soot, in ice and snow. Climbing toward him, growing in perspective, she rejoices him more than he can say. His great wish is for her to climb up this knoll, telling him that she comes to return his love. With the smoke of Gottheim's spoiling rising behind, the remedy for his aching heart is to see her face... come grave, smiling, saying, "I will. I will return your love."

But, for the moment, Balder will stay. Stay quietly waiting as she struggles up to him... so obviously ill-shod for the venture. Even now the disappointment of her rejection burns into him... deeply... as would her love. If only it would come.

Her day a dreary mix of snowfall and ash, she drove the back roads of Gottheim, disconsolate. Crusted in ice and ash, the wipers screeched back and forth across the messy glass. Gloria's hands clenched at the wheel as she hit an icy patch sidelong. A tiny yelp escaped her lips, but the car righted itself as she turned the wheel into the slide. Everywhere fell a dense mingling of snow and smoke, making visible the sadness and her inward distress. All that heady limitless opportunity for her talents, which she had so enjoyed in Gottheim—convulsing away, upward, into a sky of billowing filth.

How did it happen? How could something so far on the edge of her consciousness as a pile of old tires become invested with such power? Could a few bolts of lightning really transform this beautiful happy place into the media's next disaster? For weeks it is burning, never ceasing. They say this fire may take years to extinguish. Oh why hadn't she done more for Ceylon Segar!

Her field of reality had turned on end, spinning her plans away. At first unreal and almost peripheral to her, the fire had assumed absolute authority over everything. Jimmy was even talking as though they must leave. As though Gottheim and its dreams could just be thrown away. A nuisance he must extricate himself from at great cost and aggravation. He wants to salvage the future by moving west or north to one of Goldings' emerging acquisitions.

Can't *some*thing be done with the fire? Isn't there *any*thing, some contingency, some government bureau, disaster coping mechanism... but God knows they are trying them all.

Her mind sank lower, thoughts thickening and quickening toward chaos. Incipient until this mess came along, depression forced its inroads, pushing down on her: a heavy hand, mighty and enervating. Powerful panic swept through, carrying off her wits. Terrorized, she must stop the car before a loss of control bore her away.

"Are you with us?" It was a whisper, expecting no answer. Again she spoke it low, and again; parked there beside banks of snow. Curious comfort came merely in saying it, draining off some of the desperation. Gloria's religious upbringing had made this turning toward comfort familiar to her with its quiet associations of childhood. Again she asked this question aloud, maintaining the same low intensity. Driving slowly, saying the question, she became aware of the grace in these sounds. She was leaning softly into the wholeness of these whisperings. Nothing now but this faintest whisper of words.

The mereness of it balanced her. She felt it supporting her, lending its sure arm. Her own arm resting lightly on the wheel, she sighed. Having come to what seemed the extreme end of her wits all she found there was this question.

I wish I had sense enough to remember it. Had sense enough not to be upset over this fire. I... I'd like a lot of good things I don't have.

Tall and dark in this dismal fall, a wall of conifer curved just ahead from where she stopped. There she saw the pickup, its fenders mended, patches of spotty dull primer. Balder's pickup. *Let not your heart be troubled*, she thought.

She thought of this man with the white-blond hair and contrasting stern black beard—comforting. ... His Norwegian blue eyes that flickered with humor and irony, his sure voice sounding the pattern of the happiest old Mainer. His arms were what she longed for in dreams and out. Balder Simon. He loved her.

In spite of confusion and suffering—or, she thought, because of it?—she saw this. Gone are doubts and resentments that plagued her. Balder Simon loved her. No matter what. No amount of distrust would stop his love. Gloria pulled the red car up behind the pickup and got out.

Stepping carefully in the ice and grime, she walked past it. Looking up the roadway and off into the woodland she wondered which way to go. The road had been plowed, maybe early this morning, but new soot and snow had been laid since, covering the dirty plowbank lining the curve. There she saw the tailed track of snowshoes, climbing over the row. It led off into dark woods on an old discontinued twitch trail.

Snowfall wet her cheeks and lashes. Her breath came in clouds, mingling with the acrid smell of ash in her nostrils. She looked at the dark speckles on the arm of her down filled jacket, the match of her blue ski pants. Her stylish boots of Moroccan leather were wet, pelted with it. She looked again at the trail. *Should not wear such boots through deep snow.*

She longed for Balder. If only his track doesn't take me far. She thought she could do it... if the way were not long. It was February but not bitter: A fool would tackle a track like this under harsher conditions. She nibbled at her lip, chiding herself. You'd do it in a moment on skis. Still, she equivocated. Don't go too far. Not onto an uncertain terrain. The boots are just wrong.

Gloria clambered over the plowbank, following Balder's track. It was work wading through the snow. Layered in crusts of soot and frozen rain, the snow did not bear her weight well. Many steps were taken on top of the cover but often she fell through. Sometimes she floundered, wallowing. And with each awkward step, frustration mounted. But she had come into the walled woodland and was now committed. To lay here wallowing or turn back would disappoint the momentum of her quest. And of her longing love.

At first the way wound through high evergreens later yielding to hardwoods. Now she saw the trail mounting toward a steep knoll. Through naked trunks and snowy limbs above she saw the black cloud of burning rubbish, billowing, and edged in a fitful glow. She ceased from her struggling to gaze on it fascinated, but again dismay clouded her. Then she saw the red- and black-checked back of Balder in his mackinaw, tiny and high, backed by the flame wreathed in billows. From the distance she heard the fire's speech, screeching, rumbling and cracking. Erupting often with power.

Balder! She wanted to call but the name would not come. "Balder." She whispered it holding it under her breath.

Evoked by the surging mythic cloud, the Norse god of beauty, of purity and light, came lightening to mind. Frigga's son, slain at Loki's urging, by Hodur the blind. Balder the god, slain with mere mistletoe, a parasite. Everything in great creation, save this parasite, had taken an oath not to harm this gladsome son of Odin, lord of all gods. The great fire swelling behind, she thought of the god Balder's funeral pyre. The body of the god was set to burn aboard ship but, so laden with precious things was it, only a giantess could send it down the ways.

The awful spell and horrific stench of this place now mingled with that of the myth and, kindled by the mighty sight, she struggled on, up the steep knoll, calling to Balder as she went. He seemed not to hear.

The rumbling of the fire increased as she clambered up, its speaking in flames and burning swelled. Its roaring cast a reverie of awe upon her, and still she cried his name.

She saw his steps exaggerated by the snowshoes, and slowly he turned. Balder looked down through tall trunks, his stance above her one of waiting. Oh why doesn't he call out to me, answer? A darkening loss of confidence checks her. But she wallows on, slipping and sinking, wading through deep snow.

At last he called out to her, using her name. "Gloria! Atta girl! Come up heah d'me, Gloria. You're making it fine!"

He opened his arms and she came to him.

Oh couldn't you comfort me better. Why didn't you come down to me, she wanted to say. But now she was in his arms, weeping.

The man held her, feeling her slenderness against him. He felt her soft gold hair with his hand, gently smoothing it. Her hat had come off and he found her hair soft as rabbit's fur. "What's a matter, Glory? Anyone hurt? Anyone lost?"

"No, Balder." She said it against his rough mackinaw. "Just me. I'm hurt and I'm lost."

He hugged her to him, gently, strong and sexual, still smoothing her hair. She looked up at him, whispering. "I'm happy to be here, comforted by you."

He had to duck his head to catch it, listening thoughtfully. Again he hugged her, felt her deep sigh. "'N' I'm happy t'comfort." For a long moment they stayed so, together. Then he pulled back, looking down on her, eyes grave. But he smiled. "Think we could do this f'evah?"

Together in the embrace, they turned a bit, making smoke and tumult the background to the grace of this moment. The dismal drizzling had ceased and the wind increased, fanning the fire in Quakertown. It held her gaze and he saw it reflected in her eyes. Troubled, entranced, she said,

"What's going to happen? Will we be all right? Will the mountain go under?"

"Doubt it. Caunt possibly, not in this age. The resort might have t'go, though."

Her voice became excited, pitched. "But the skiers, the investors, the jobs!... the local economy of Gott'im! The pawithin. I... if only I'd worked harder with Mr. Segar!... we're ruined!"

"The pain." He said it gravely. "The whole place suffers." He shook his head. Gott'im'll go on... unda the cloud."

She understood him and wailed. "The resort! The investors, the project in Gott'im.... Balder!"

"Don't mean a thing, Glory."

She pulled back, looking at his fire bright eyes. Incredulous, she shook her head slowly. "Don't you care? The ones that *could* backed out. And Jimmy's responsible. There are debts to Savings and Loans in Massachusetts, in New York."

But Balder said, "Ask carefully. What kind of harm will it do to his spirit t'be troubled this way?" He shook his head. "I caunt lie t'you, Glory. The loss o'the projects don't mean a thing. The hurt'n your eyes means something. The *pain* of folks who lost money.... That means something. The other could safely be in the fire. Should I lie'n say it ain't so?"

"But it's my *life*." She pulled back, but would not loose herself from the embrace.

"No it's not, Glory. It's just something to do."

"You've no right to say that...." But, she wondered. *Let not your heart be troubled.* She leaned against the rough of his woolen jacket and said it low: "My life *is* mine. Isn't its meaning mine to decide?..." She stopped a moment, thinking. Again she pulled back, looking up. Seeing the irony in his eyes she recalled the conversation they shared once in which he had seemed to doubt her expressions of love.

"Oh Balder. I do! I *do* love you. Why won't you believe me? Can you see? Can't you see how I love you?"

He loosened his arm, letting her fall back more, but holding her still. He said, "Yuht. I do... as far as you're able.... Glory, I know the watchers in town've beat you bout the ears for what you tried to do f'this place. I'd be honest to say I don't always care much for the ways you had in mind to help'n encourage us. But I never doubted you cared—care now. You care as much about Gott'im as any soul here. Thank you f'that."

It was salving. She smiled some, eased. Gloria rested her arms upon his, and their legs adhered, cold thighs pressed together. The fire, visible through the woodland below, was forgotten in the kindling of this moment. Sexuality pervaded their embrace, tender and aching-sweet. They stood together like a sheaf of wheat, sensuous and bound, supported by its own rich golden weight.

"Balder," (she sweetly asked) "how is it that your love is better than mine? You don't give up your dreams... yet you expect me to give up mine."

Again he smiled that maddening smile. "We both care about this place. Maybe it's the difference in the way they're expressed." The irony of his expression deepened but his arm tightened about her. Her ski suit rustled against him, sexy and sweet. Like the rustling of sun-drying green leaves, ripening toward a full warmth. He said, "Evah heard the story—how the man'n woman fell fom grace? She fell fom ambition; he from desire o'her. They had a simple life, live together, enjoy all fruits but one...." He shook his head. "Wadn't enough fah her."

She smiled up at him, kindly. "Okay. True!—it's *not* enough. But... —let's look at this desire thing."

He grinned. "Wait a minute. Story's got lots'o points to it but another is, two heads to the family. Like Siamese twins—two heads, one body. No agreement but lots'o misery."

"But why's it the man's choice? To be only misery for one, then?" It was not even a halfhearted challenge. She was completely happy here with Balder on this knoll among tall trunks, the fires of hell just off their shoulders.

He grinned more. "I'd'know. May because ambition is inferior to this kind o'desire." He jigged her in his arms, grinning. Balder's sex came alive. God! He was happy with her! Gloria felt it through her suit and grew happier, too. A melting moved among her limbs, sweet tendrils twisting into every part. She was breathless, rustling wheat.

"But if that's so, why won't your desire let you fall—as Adam's did. Yours must not be as strong." Barely she spoke it, smiling. All this sweet teasing—too much to bear. How could he stand it—oh!

"Ah," he said and let her go. Their embrace was broken, they came apart. Beyond, the smoke and fire surged, rumbling. It boomed and roared. They turned toward its fresh speaking, hand in hand. Together they watched and were lit by it.

"I'll tell you, Glory." He said it as they came away down the hill. She was in his arms and disappointed once again. Carrying her, his snowshoes sank deep beneath their combined weight.

"Adam's dead. He didn't love enough. Should'o been willing t'walk through fires solely fah the sight of her."

He looked down on her gravely there in his arms. She was a sweet person, good, very good. But she did not love him. Yet.

Going downhill with Balder on his alien feet is not as awkward as she supposed. She is happy in this present moment, nestled in his embrace. Comfortable as a child in his father's arms, except for the top of her head itching against his scratchy short beard. Sign of his fatherhood, she remembers. This is how he cares, as protective and sure as a father. Could I love him like that? No. I can't mother anyone. Too careless; with my heart like a little stone. She sighs. Let this go on. Carry me home, Balder....

But at the base of the hill the man stops, his gaze on a twitching thicket. Something's astir in the hemlock seedlings edging the twitch trail. He sets her down, reaches into the dingy snow needles and comes out—like a magician—with a very lean patchy white hare. It squirms and beats with impossibly large feet. Then quickly it subsides, as though exhausted.

"Oh, Balder... so helpless. Is it in shock?"

"Don't look too chippa. Li'l snowshoe rabbit."

Opening his mackinaw he sets it inside, buttoning it snugly but not enough to smother. She smiles at its pink rabbity nose poking out, twitching.

"C'mere," he says hoisting her up again. "Take y'both to mother at *Simons Ledge*."

Through dingy snow and woods they go, the varying hare a little lump, scarcely felt between them.

"So small," she says. "A snowshoe, you said?"

He nods, scratching her temple with his beard. "They change color, spring'n fall, depending on the light. Brown to white'n back again. So they call 'em varying."

But Gloria has stopped listening. She thinks of Balder's mother, Balder's house. No, she cannot go there, not to *Simons Ledge*. That rambling old place, last century's farmstead. The barn full of wild animals and other people's children. Happiness will not go that far. It ends when this traipse in his arms is over. She will get into her little red Caprice, not his patched pickup. Return to the resort warmed and, in some measure, healed by his embrace. She will dream of this many nights and stay out of other men's beds. The *loneliness of other men's beds* is how she thinks of it now. Balder's nurturing, chaste embrace inspires her with better desire. She is more secure and, at night when she drifts off she will sometimes feel him there with her, loving and strong. But her dreams will try to work themselves into some semblance of her preferred reality... and that's when they will stop. Dreams of him stop when she tries to borrow his form for her purposes. For Gloria cannot picture herself in *Simons Ledge* and she cannot picture him anywhere else.

He is carrying her from the woods and she is busy with these thoughts. Tears come silently, roll down her cheeks.

He sees them fall, knowing she will not come. There is sorrow in the silence of those tears. But he does not kiss them away. He does not dare kiss the tears away.

The Village in Twilight

Weeks passed as changes became apparent in the village. At first skiers from Massachusetts poured in to see the spectacle, but poor conditions ensured that these visits would not repeat. Skiers stayed away and investment stopped, reversed, vacated the area. Ground would remain unbroken, new building stopped in mid-construction leaving their standing white skeletons. Back at the mountain, streaked and strewn like dreary tenements across Jasper's dingy knees, condominiums were abandoned. Dispirited, many of their owners tried to sell. Others held out hope of recouping, maybe next year. The tires will all be consumed some day, won't they? Going to the initial spectacular display, business scarcely dipped in the village. Restaurants, clubs, bed-and-breakfast establishments were all busy, domestics, cooks, waitpersons, clerks kept their jobs as news of the show spread before the inevitable slowdown. The locals, depressed by the intermittent atmosphere of darkness felt the call of their ancestral blood to make do. The old, asthmatic and ill, the young with developing lungs continued to suffer: on bad days they stayed indoors. Eight fire departments from surrounding towns moved several lots of tires which had been strewn in the woods to a new dump site in Copenhagen, one proposed by another would-be magnate. Loggers were employed to cut a buffer in the woods surrounding the fire. Experts from away came to study and suggest ways of extinguishing the hapless fulminations. Augusta appealed to federal agencies for help. But it was new, this aberrant variety of industrial terrorism; new from what went before, and answers would be slow in coming.

One bright spot in the gloom was the revival of Decatur's Diner. Secretly sentimental and reluctant, Lyman Bearce had not secured the buyer for his plum spot. He resurrected the grubby silver and maroon dining car, an authentic piece of history from the old Atlantic and St. Lawrence Railway. He had it hauled out of storage, set on a new foundation, slightly altered. A new kitchen was added to suit. Nancy's Neatniks in the village came in to clean and paint the diner's tin ceiling, strip the wax off its linoleum countertops, table and floor. Grease everywhere, thick with the dirt of decades, was washed away. Bearce even had some of the plastic booths recovered in vinyl. Of course he didn't smile, but Lyman Bearce was pleased that the diner was back and better than before. Since he had made some money on the deal in that failed ski apparel boutique proposal, things were sweeter than ever because the Goldings were taking hits. That fire was no doubt a terrible price to pay for things to be sorted back into their proper order, but it *was* entertaining to contemplate what would become of them.

The first day of the diner's reopening people came in early. Some were tentative and hushed, looking around. They sat themselves down before Melvinia, Chrischana, and one other new waitperson, all crisply attired in new aprons and perky little hats. Melvinia, ear rings tinkling, submitted to the hat because she did not want to discourage Decatur's niece, who came up from Mass to run the place. Gildy is young, a business graduate missing the friendliness of her hometown. The anonymous cubicle in the giant insurance company in Boston was getting to her in a way she had not foreseen. Despite his declining constitution, Decatur himself was quietly happy, content to sit on the stool next nearest the kitchen window, sipping cocoa and reminiscing with anyone who happened to plunk down beside him.

The Goldings of Jasper Mountain moved to Québec, leaving staff behind to run "the freak show," as Eloise Potadoe dubbed it. Even James Fay, once considered a top associate, was left behind. As Harry Golding put it, "I have every confidence that you, with your golden touch and gifted entrepreneurial sense, will soon sort out the various ventures in Gottheim. And there will be ample opportunity, before long, for us to work closely together again. Keep in touch."

Lyman Bearce and Jeffy Decatur are having breakfast side-by-side on their stools in Decatur's Diner. Chewing contemplatively, Decatur looks through the opening beside the coffee urn to see Gildy's capped but frizzy gold-red head and determined shoulders, where she stands at the grill carefully turning eggs and flipping pancakes. Happily inhaling the fragrance of homefries and spattering bacon, Decatur washes down his fluffy eggs and toast with a swig of Melvinia's coffee. "Y'see," he says to white-bearded Bearce, "having that MBA is nothing but a help t'her in running this business. Wouldn't be surprised if she does it even betta'n I did."

Jasper Mary does not say what Lyman Bearce thinks of that. He just grunts, eating his plate full of sausage and eggs over medium.

In a corner by a front window sits brick-redheaded Asa across from his wife Olive, a largish brunette; he with his plate full of eggs over easy, she with a stack of blueberry pancakes. Gildy has gone overboard with the blueberries, making the flapjacks darker and slightly unappetizing, but Olive is forgiving. She piles excess berries to one side of her plate with her fork in hopes that Chrischana will scrape and load it into the dishwasher before Gildy can see it.

Shaking his head, the fastidious Asa says, "I'd tell her about it, f'I was you. She ought see'em so's to learn." He looks over as Willie Kimball sits down in what was once Asa's regular stool in the elbow of the counter. Asa has given it up for the occasional breakfast out with his wife. The faintest look of regret surfaces briefly in his face.

Olive shakes her head. "Don't do to discourage hah, Asa."

"She ought learn it right."

Olive shakes her head vigorously. Her fingernails flash ice blue, waving her fork.

That was another thing. Asa wishes she would go back to the smashing red she wore when he courted her. He looks out the window, a bit dejected. Outside Abner Chapman walks along in his camouflage fatigues, head down, eyes on the puddled ground. To Asa he seems the embodiment of gloom, the gloom of a dark Gott'im morning. When's somebody gont do something fah that boy? For the first time, a bit of grace slips into the older man's thoughts concerning Abner... where once he had judged the other self pitying. Does the boy still wander some tortured and unceasing scene of fire and blood there in that steamy faraway Mekong Delta, or waya evah it was?

Willie Kimball has stood to move to the opposite end of the diner as Robbie Robichaud comes in the door. Asa pops his head up to shoot a wave at the logging contractor. Robbie gives a reverse nod without his customary bounce and smile. He sits down on Asa's stool across from the booth, within easy speaking distance. Nothing much is said, however. In his continuing grief over Alvin's death, Robbie is sober, inconsolable, lacking the alertness to sense his melancholy influence on those around him. He lives in a constant smear of gray. The weather of Gottheim perfectly suits his mourning, however. He continues working, bringing truckloads of pulp and saw logs out of the grim woodland, day by day. His nephew, Hiram, now works in the woods with Ansell, but it is a slog all the way. Ansell had always been a quiet worker, and now, bereft of his twin, is just no use in telling Hi what and what not to do. He gives the boy directions but if it doesn't take the first time that's the end of it as far as Ansell is concerned. Robbie has been loading pulp logs nowhere near the uniform 4 ft. length. They are either too long or too short. And a Robichaud teenager ought t've been born knowing how to lay a pine down. Robbie has seen Hiram notching his trees: It's a wonder he hasn't killed himself.

The steamy, hot-oil-biscuit-bacon-coffee atmosphere of the diner suddenly gives place to a more concentrated, a foul now-familiar, odor: the smell of burning tires comes among the regulars in bodily form. Ceylon Segar scuffs up to the stool that Lyman Bearce vacated moments before.

The spell of his rumination broken by the stench, Decatur starts back, a look of amazement spread over his bald bespeckled face. But for the fragrant clinking of flatware, diner life stops. Everyone stares at the grimy dishevelment that is Ceylon Segar.

In his first appearance in public since the disaster.

In a booth by the window behind him, Simeon Sanborn is thinking hard. For weeks he has been mourning the awful atmosphere permeating the village... but just yesterday he got a piece of good news. It siphoned off some of the impotence that has been gnawing at him since Goldings' resorts sent the price of property out of sight. Simeon has four children, all young adults, none of whom have been able to afford a loan for a place of their own. They were like sad-eyed Robichauds—trailers on their lot. Even the cost of an apartment in an old house in the village was heading beyond reach: Landlords could get more renting to weekend skiers over the course of a single season than they got renting to local people year round. Robbie's twins had dealt with the problem by setting trailers on the home place, but there was no option for Simeon's kids, his place being in the village on Livery Street. Everyone understood that development pushed Gott'im property into the realm of impossible. Until now. Yesterday Simeon's eldest gave him the news: A loan and house have finally come together. Gerta is going to own her own home. And it has just occurred to Simeon Sanborn that the smelly article, sitting right in front of him, is the reason why. A slow smile coming, Simeon stares at Ceylon's filthy backside a moment or two more. Looking around, he sees something akin to his own feeling emerge on the faces around him.

Once... twice... three times, Simeon claps his hands together. He keeps it up, deliberately, a few more claps echoing—one on his right, the other at the far end of the diner where Elvy and Ernest Sessions sit with their three little kids. They are having cereal together, a rare treat before its off to the dowel mill for Mother and Father, day care and school for the kids.

Clap clap clap clap. A chorus begins. Someone is banging a sugar dispenser to the rhythm of this slow applause. Salt and pepper shakers in hand, flatware bouncing adding a tinkling echo. Everyone in Decatur's is clapping or pounding the table. (Everyone but the contractor Evan Bean. He thinks ruefully of the boys he's had to lay off.)

Now Decatur is standing beside Ceylon Segar, pouring him a cup of coffee. Grinning, Gildy has abandoned the grill in the kitchen, to take the old fart's order herself.

Down in the elbow of the counter, Robbie Robichaud is smiling with his eyes for the first time since Alvin froze to death in his pickup six weeks ago. Across from him, Asa looks with resignation at Olive. Their fledgling bed-and-breakfast may not survive the ashes of this fire, but Olive is smiling, thinking of her children and grandchildren. She runs a blue fingernail along Asa's freckled hand. He sighs, saying, "Still got m'job, anaway. Mill's not hurt ana by burning tires." Olive nods her brown head, smiling faintly.

Ceylon Segar's smile is nine miles wide on his grizzled face. He looks around smugly, it suddenly occurring to him that he just might be bigger in Gott'im then either of the Goldings. For a few moments it is worth it to lose all that money in escrow and have his property attached for defraying of fire fighting and cleanup. And Gildy has just informed him that breakfast is on the house.

While he eats, talk in the diner heats up. Now that Lyman Bearce has gone back to one of his mills, it focuses on how gleeful he must be since Julius and Harry Golding have vacated town for whiter pastures. The sour

The sour apples over Bearces' handprints being all over Gott'im were shelved temporarily in favor of picking over the Goldings while they prospered here. The townsfolk have grown tired of this: of telling back and forth all the Goldings' peccadillos, describing in exaggerated and often erroneous satirical detail how they treat their children, employees, associates and spouses. Now they are free once again to concentrate on the latest piece of dirt picked up in the laundromat or grocery aisle concerning their own local homegrown and related elite. Eloise Patadoe, transplanted West Virginia artist and goat queen, calls it bloodsport.

The door opens and in comes Nellie Sessions, the frizz-headed aunt of Cindabilla. She is an amateur archaeologist who works in the local dowell mill at the outlet of the village pond, along with Asa and other locals. With *The Village Voter* under her arm, she looks around and sees the jubilee set lose by the stinking presence of Ceylon Segar. She is thinking, *Not a soul here's read this week's Bellyache.* Walking straight to the left end of the diner, she unfurls the rag, flashing the headline before Elvy and Ernest's surprised eyes. "LOCAL DOWEL MAKERS AND NAME SOLD TO CHICAGO COMPANY: Mill building and equipment to go at auction." Ernest whistles softly, reading the first paragraph, saying, "Says heah 58 families gont feel this. That's us, El."

"Chicago?! What's Chicago got do with it?"

—

"The King and all his company sat on their horses, marveling, perceiving that the power of Saruman was overthrown; but how they could not guess. And now they turned their eyes towards the archway and the ruined gates. There they saw close beside them a great rubbleheap; and suddenly they were aware of two small figures lying on it at their ease, grey-clad, hardly to be seen among the stones. There were bottles and bowls and platters laid beside them, as if they had just eaten well, and now rested from their labour." (*The Two Towers*, 207)

The three sat together in the cramped second-floor furnished apartment of a Victorian Gothic house on Kimball Street. Paperback in hand, Daniel sat reading aloud between his brothers on the scratchy woolen couch. His hair sticking every which way, Nathan leaned into Daniel's side like the disciple John leaning on Jesus' bosom at the Last Supper. The smaller boy's eyes looked unblinking upon the page; yet he saw, not the curlicues of the words printed there, but images conjured by Tolkien. Beside the two, sitting against the arm of the couch with the soles of his feet pressed against Daniel's leg, Benaiah stared at the book in his big brother's hand. He too saw the ruins of Isengard and the hobbits lounging here, peaceably smoking their pipes.

At the table across from the three boys sat Chrischana and Peter, also listening to Daniel read aloud from *The Two Towers*. It had been Chrischana's idea, late last year, to begin reading the trilogy aloud. Shortly before Thanksgiving, together they had tested the waters, discovering that Nathan was now old enough to receive the great story of the One Ring. Benaiah had encountered *The Hobbit* in school, and Daniel had long since devoured the three volumes concerned with the last war of the Third Age. Lately they had discovered that reading it aloud made Peter's visits a little easier, every family member being engaged by those events leading to the advent of Men's rule in Middle-earth. The three boys were quietly happy to see their parents harmlessly together again if only for occasional evening visits when neither had to work. They were reassured seeing Peter drink coffee. Mother having on her good blouse and mascara also made them hopeful. Now and then she would bustle about the tiny efficiency kitchen, fixing him a meal. Life in these moments was merely what it should be, yet to them it was keenly lived... as though a living good story.

"'You do not know your danger, Theoden,' interrupted Gandalf. 'These hobbits will sit on the edge of ruin and discuss the pleasures of the table, or the small doings of their fathers, grandfathers, and great-grandfathers, and remoter cousins to the ninth degree, if you encourage them with undue patience.'" (208)

But as the words came off his tongue, Daniel was dreaming up images of his own. While absorbed in the story before him, he yet kept in some part of his imagination an idea that came to him time and again. Daniel wanted somehow to reenter as though for the first time the subcreated world of Middle-earth, on a creative impetus of his own. For months he had hoped to start his own series of hobbit adventures, even making several attempts in notebooks when he could snatch time. But something always interrupted to ruin his momentum. Half-finished adventures were the result. With Benaiah digging his toenails into his calf, Daniel sighed but kept reading.

Across the room, Peter Prince heard little of the tale. He sat looking at Chrischana, hoping she would notice. If she would only give him her gaze. He wanted to look straight into her solemn Native eyes, drink from that well of patience and kindness. He longed to take her large and generous sexuality in his deft mechanic's fingers. He wanted her to want him again.

Then suddenly, as though rewarding his hope, she did turn her gaze. Slowly she smiled, letting him look into her eyes. She was coming to him now, full of attention... something he had not seen for a very long time. Her dimpled hand was fastened to her coffee cup but she opened her fingers, pushing the cup aside. Now her hand lay open on the table before him. Again she smiled that slow smile.

Slowly Peter Prince reached out for the brown fingers, covering them with his palm. Her flesh was warm and strong against it. Gently he held the hand, gently smiled. Her eyes warmed toward a faint suggestiveness. Then slowly she turned her gaze away.

Her face was turned toward the boys on the couch but she held Peter's hand across the table. It was not that he would never hurt her again. He might. *Probably would.* But now she had knowledge about him crucial to her security. This and only this made her secure: Peter had understanding. He still had the power to hurt her but understood now that he had no right. So together they sat at the table, leaning like bookends toward one another. When one or another of the boys looked up, he saw his parents clasping hands, leaning on their elbows and silently sipping coffee.

God was in the household with them. Everyone thought so whether consciously or not, and no one said anything.

Elda Simon holds a guided belief that she lives in eternity. She tries to live all her time each day. Knowing something of the metabolism of insects and animals, she thinks time is as elastic as need be for whatever creature inhabiting it. She gets a kick out of the fact that humans lumber and slur in comparison with damselflies. On the other hand, houseflies as a species have a long history and humans have not yet begun to live. The generations of flies out distance our own like the swift edge of the universe fleeing beyond remnants of light left in the dust of the original cosmos. Sometimes she wonders: Will the universe curve back to meet itself falling toward its own core?

Here is Elda's (and all our) descent into decay. The substance of her form mutates, deteriorating. For lack of seeing the fresh scribblings of ravens' wings where they have washed themselves in snowcover, she sorrows. Crossing on snowshoes she looks down on her hand in some patch of snowlight among the hardwoods but, where the blue-veined thin white parchment of her fingers should be, she sees darkness. The wiggling of her fingers hardly registers until she waves her hand into the peripheral light of her eyes. She has heard of the darkening of Gottheim and by it her darkness has deepened. Her nostrils smell burning, her hands help the animals harmed by it. She knows what the twilight of gods entails.

The world would think of her story (and ours) as ending in sorrow. But Elda thinks she knows something, dimly, about this bewildering house of life. To her, coming down mountain on Everett's ancient snowshoes, the fire is like macular degeneration. Because of this disease she stumbles over snags, watches for fallen trees out the corners of her eyes. Trying to stay with the twitch trails she largely succeeds. The snow is awful cold on her legs when she falls, joints ache, the pain dipping even to the core within her skeleton. On her side in the snow she wallows helplessly like a beached whale. Elda stops moving. She rests. Snow begins melting against her cheek.

Balder has described it for her, telling the fire as glimpsed in the distance, snagging the gaze, becoming a hole in the vision. Everything surrounding it becomes peripheral. Only marginally present, the village, the mountains, the river or intervale farms. But, if you look directly at the village, little and lighted and hopeful, the damage becomes peripheral.

Better, by loosing the bonds of fixation, you can scan the scene to take in all.

Lying here in the snow, Elda thinks Balder has experienced the three ways of seeing. As a child growing in Gottheim he lived like the second. From Vietnam he found a hole so black he thought he would never see light again. He went sightless a while... until he discovered Love sitting there in the darkness with him.

Elda remembers her little sisters—still rascally and sweet in memory—crossing into the darkness. And Everett also crossed over the dark river. She is crossing now, a too lengthy crossing. They married when she knew little, consciously, of love. All she knew of life—well it wasn't much. Just some intuitive stuff about animals. Knew nothing of Everett or mothering!... By time he died... she was looking for him everywhere. She saw his box lowered and covered in earth. Earth, earth he knew and worked intimately. When her sisters died she sought them; later she sought him more. Seeking and seeking... until he turned up in her half-wakeful, half-dreaming, sleep. He was attached to her and she to him. With the snow melting under her, she remembers: They were attached at the ear, her ribs to his upper rib, her cheek in his so close they were one. He was a limb of her being, and she of his. But of course in waking life he was gone, leaving only the ache of phantom pain.

Oddest things drop into your mind! The taste of semen, sour like frog eggs—or was it dragonfly foam?

A tiny gravelly sound escapes Elda, laughing at herself lying here. Ooo—her body is saturated with pain. *Well, your arthritis is worse, you nut, 'cause your lying in the snow!*

But she makes no move to extricate herself from this wallow.

Just some intuitive stuff about the critters.... God just must enjoy half-making His creatures. He gives us a body and environment, interests... some abilities... and leaves out the important stuff. Then, when He thinks you can handle the inability to handle things, he sticks them in on the sly: commitments, children, chores, blindness. You can't handle it, any of it, but it's too late. Look at sheep. So stupid he uses them as a metaphor for people. Now you've got no choice but to handle things, trying to make it all work.

"If only I'd see Sugarloaf." She says it aloud. She has never even had a good look at him. Always too busy scaring him off... and now with this black hole—can't even find a cup of coffee directly!—oh why'd they go'n shoot Posey? *Never* get used to that killing. God could come and explain it to her and still she wouldn't get it.... But... again... she can't quite believe in death, either. Everything dies, yes, but Posey is around somewhere. Little sisters'n Everett. "Just too blind d'see'em!" Everybody, *blind blind blind!*

Elda squirms around and blunders up, dusting off snow. She continues on until coming to an old deadfall. Leaning there, she hoists snowshoe feet over the prone trunk. Why not sit another spell?

People ought to have kids. World needs more kids, not less. What's wrong is theya's too many old people. Don't die off as fast as we used to. Refrigeration, sanitation, modern medicine, technology, keep us alive too long. What do we want to live for when kids are grown anaway? So don't I know Balder has Daniel, Glory'n all. He's safe now. Don't need me. I'm ready to go, huh, Sugarloaf. Her old fingers stroke his ear while the little deer nudges her.

Sugarloaf!

Her old face pushes into a grin. She has no idea when she first began stroking the pilar side of the white deer. Somehow he stole to her as she sat there on the deadfall. Her hands feel his knobby head. Soon he will be a button buck. She faces front, tilting her head, and can see his pink features on the edge of sight. Posey's fawn.

There is no thought of chasing him off. And Elda is very glad. Relieved. *Glad glad glad!*

Here they are, leaning together in the House of Life. Simple and soaking up the grace that was urged, patiently waiting for them to unite.

Decidedly, James Fay is not curious about Balder, knowing this mechanic inside out. It has been months since she spoke of him, now suddenly Gloria is talking about the blue-collar like he's Olympian or something. James Fay sighed when she insisted on the meeting. Just no success in wishing the millwright away. No success in a lot of his wishing away. He is surfacing in their lives again with a vengeance. At least he will be able to report back something to Dad.

He never met the man, but Balder read all the episodes and escapades of James Fay in *The Village Voter*. Today they will meet... if the man shows. In spite of himself, Balder is curious. Fay. The Golding go-getter who, until recently, ate whole tracks of Gott'im for dinner. For reasons of her own, Gloria is now big on this meeting. Balder takes it as a good sign. Once she was big on their *not* meeting.

Sitting at the bottom of Buck Hill, Balder is waiting to take them up to the sugaring-off party. He has just come back downhill on Artie Osgood's snow machine, having borrowed the sled to take them all up. A toboggan in tow, and Chrischana, Peter and the boys already on the hill where the evaporator steams its sweetness into the cool air: She's got the firebox stoked with ashwood, sap has been running for a week, snow falling every night. The woods are dense and dingy with it. Like the mill down in Guildford, the tire fire makes its own atmosphere. It can be clear as an icicle out in Luz, but hereabouts it will snow. Sometimes you have to turn on headlights to drive through. Luckily, for the sugaring-off today, the sun shines.

Mother's up there, too. Sometimes she sorrows him with those pathetic timid eyes of hers. He has read up on macular degeneration and talked to the doctor about her symptoms. Apparently nothing's to be done except the vitamins, but he has been urged to bring her for an exam to check the eyes for other signs of ill health. Sitting here on the snowmobile, he thinks maybe he bout has her to the point of consenting. Or maybe it's Daniel who's bringing her around. Balder grins. No way Mother'd say no to Daniel. Hey, they might even get her to take an entire physical exam.

But, standing now and shaking his head, he reconsiders it: Doaw. Don't do t'get carried away. Anyway, maybe he should consider carefully her hopes and dreams about dying. She *will* die someday. Betta get used to it. Again he grins. All get used to death—or die trying.

Theodora's custom-painted powder blue Saab 900 shoots down the plowed road toward him. It zips past, slides to a stop and begins backing toward him on the opposite side of the road.

"Balder!" Theo calls out, happily waving.

Balder is surprised to see her driving instead of Fay. She pulls over onto the shoulder across from him, turning off the ignition. Three people step from the car into the grimy road. The sun is shining on them, a strengthening sun shedding a larger light as the earth trails slowly back from its apogee along the ecliptic: This northland will lean again toward its own star.

Balder grins at Theodora. Gloria gets out behind, but his eyes now are all for the homely yet dainty Theo. In nature she has not changed. He feels sure she is still the same fragile person she was born to be. Like some ghost who isn't quite sure of its own reality. Even so *something* is different. Something.... she has done one right thing in giving Gott'im Chair Company to its employees. But why she did it, he has no idea. Unlike others in Gott'im, he does not think of this as just another of her harebrained stunts. To the village elite it is a nutsy act, in a long list of Theodora nuttiness. Balder would have liked to see James Fay get the news: His grin widens. *Probably did it first, told him after.*

Gloria hurries up to him, shining in the sun. Softly, lightly, she kisses his mustache. "Balder Simon, this is my brother, Jimmy Fay." She steps back.

The two men reach, shake hands. Balder grins his greeting, the short bespeckled Fay nodding. (As though their locally cultural positions and characters were reversed: Balder being from away and Fay with East Anglian ancestors living here nine generations.)

Balder says, "So..." and there is a slight awkward pause. "So, who's first? Here's the sled, anaone fah snowshoes?" All are dressed for a trek in the woods, ski pants and boots for the snow, nylon jackets for the sun. "Sugar's just waitin'fah us up theya. How'bout it, Fay. Snowshoes or sled? Theo, you remember how the machine works."

"Let James do it, show him how, Balder."

Gloria exclaims brightly. "I'm for the shoes!"

Balder shows the other man how to start the machine, give it gas, how to stop. The developer is not what he expected. Fay is not eager, forthcoming, or much of a personality... monosyllabic, taciturn. His sister stands looking on, unhappy, anxious.

Theo knows where the old Twitchell Farm once stood. The nearly deserted hilltop has been a favorite berrying spot, party destination, picnic and trek place for off-roading. She asks only about the last turn and location of the evaporator. In a moment they are off in a whining two-stroke cloud.

Standing alone with Gloria, Balder says, "He's glad d'be heah!" It's cheerfully said. "Why'd he come? Have to threaten him much?"

The unhappy look stays about her eyes but she returns his grin. "Said I'd marry you tomorrow if he didn't come."

She looks off up the trail. "No, I don't know why he came. Don't know why I insisted, either." She shakes her head, still looking the other way. "Guess I'm just... groping."

He takes her hand, begins examining her fingers. Lightly caresses them.

"Groping is not such a bad thing. Sometimes it's betta'n charging ahead. Most times. What's bad about being unsure? Shows a li'l humility."

Her look is dubious. "Humility's good—I know.... But it can be... painful. Why do we value it in others... but mostly never consider it? What's its real purpose, y'suppose?"

He does not respond right off, just stands gently regarding her. He says, "What a good girl—fah wantin'to know."

Gloria's smile is wistful as she says, "Maybe that would've been demeaning to me—once. Your little compliment there. Now I feel like you've given me a small piece of amethyst, of jasper or something. Thanks, Balder."

He moves closer, holding her. They lean together and Balder holds her to him, lovingly.

The God's Cycle is set in the early mid-1980s

Guide to Characters

Asa Bartlett. Amateur historian, Congo Church clock-winder, millworker, married to Olive Lovejoy Bartlett.
Olive Lovejoy Bartlett. Caregiver, family woman, dowser, operates bed-and-breakfast, married to Asa Bartlett.
Lyman Bearce. Lumber baron, selectman, married to Rhetta Bearce.
Rhetta Bearce. Committee woman, married to Lyman Bearce.
Babette Buck. Dowel millworker, Ferddy Sessions' girlfriend.

Jeffy Decatur. Diner business owner-cook, bird hunter.

Gloria Fay. Graduate student, IICE facilitator, sister to James Fay, Balder Simon's love.
James Fay. Ski resort real estate salesman, brother of Gloria Fay, engaged to Theodora Prescott.

Harry Golding. Ski resort owner, maternal uncle of Amanda.
Julius Golding. Ski resort owner, maternal uncle of Amanda.
Amanda. Niece to the Goldings.

Jasper Mary. Historical and legendary healer, storyteller.

Israel Kimball. Town recluse, former academy headmaster, scholar.

Jim Nutting. The weekly *Village Voter* editor.

Eloise Potadoe. Artist, goatherd, homesteader.
Theodora Prescott. Mill owner, IICE participant, engaged to James Fay.
Peter Prince. Mechanic, common-law spouse of Chrischana Twitchell, father of Nathan, Benaiah, Daniel.

Robbie Robichaud. Logging contractor, father to Alvin and Ansell.
Alvin and Ansell Robichaud. Loggers, twins.

Celon Segar (pronounced Cigar by the locals). Tire dump owner.
Cindabilla Sessions. Niece to Ferddy Sessions, girlfriend of Daniel Twitchell.

Ferddy (Ferdinand) Sessions. Town worker, Cindabilla's maternal uncle, boyfriend of Babette Buck.

Hannah Sessions. Farmer, domestic worker, mother of Ferdinand Sessions, grandmother of Cindabilla, sister-in-law of Nellie Sessions.

Melvinia Sessions. Diner server, domestic worker, distantly related to other Sessions.

Nellie Sessions. Dowelmill-worker, artifact collector, aunt to Cindabilla.

Balder Simon. Vietnam veteran, millwright, son of Elda, father of Daniel Twitchell, lover of Gloria Fay and Chrischana Twitchell.

Elda Simon. Animal rehabilitator, mother of Balder Simon.

Benaiah Twitchell. Adolescent son of Chrischana Twitchell and Peter Prince.

Chrischana Twitchell. Dishwasher, homesteader, common-law spouse of Peter Prince, mother of Daniel, Benaiah, Nathan.

Daniel Twitchell. Teenage son of Chrischana Twitchell and Balder Simon, friend of Cindabilla Sessions.

Nathan Twitchell. Youngest son of Chrischana Twitchell and Peter Prince.

Like this? Try the rest of the CYCLE.

THE GOD'S CYCLE

www.ingramcontent.com/pod-product-compliance
Lightning Source LLC
Chambersburg PA
CBHW021016180626
46814CB00003B/1315